THE GOLEM
OF DENEB SEVEN
AND OTHER STORIES

Books by Alex Shvartsman

Explaining Cthulhu to Grandma and Other Stories
H. G. Wells, Secret Agent

Edited by Alex Shvartsman

Unidentified Funny Objects series
The Cackle of Cthulhu
Funny Science Fiction
Funny Fantasy
Funny Horror
Humanity 2.0
Coffee: 14 Caffeinated Tales of the Fantastic
Dark Expanse: Surviving the Collapse

THE GOLEM
OF DENEB SEVEN
AND OTHER STORIES

Alex Shvartsman

UFO Publishing
Brooklyn, NY

PUBLISHED BY:

UFO Publishing
1685 E 15th St.
Brooklyn, NY 11229
www.ufopub.com

Copyright © 2018 by Alex Shvartsman

Trade paperback ISBN: 978-1986220613

Cover art: M. Wayne Miller
Interior art: Barry Munden
Typesetting & interior design: Melissa Neely
Cover design: Holly Heisey
Copyeditor: Elektra Hammond

Visit us on the web:
www.ufopub.com

PREFACE

O ne day I decided to write a novel.

I'd been a lifelong fan of science fiction and fantasy. I'd read thousands of books, seen hundreds of films and dozens of TV shows. I'd traveled the world gaining valuable perspectives and life experiences to imbue my characters with. I'd written hundreds of non-fiction pieces, learning how to express my thoughts on the page. So, how hard could it possibly be to write a book?

I enthusiastically vomited a bunch of words onto the screen, creating a chapter-shaped object. Then I stopped and read it. I stared at the screen horrified, as the vivid, thrilling scene I had imagined turned into a vapid, lifeless bunch of sentences that had no claim on being a story. Worse yet, I had barely an inkling of an idea as to what to do next. I had an interesting story to tell, but I quickly came to realize that I didn't possess the skill to tell it. Worse yet, I realized that writing a book was going to be hard work. And that I hated the idea of writing an entire novel, pouring my heart and soul into it, only to discard the manuscript like a set of training wheels.

I came up with a new plan: I would write short stories for a while. They were less time-consuming, so I wouldn't feel devastated if some of them were false starts. Also, I could submit them to magazines. If a professional editor were willing to publish my stories, I'd know that I had the writing chops to tackle a novel.

Blissful in my ignorance of how any of this stuff worked, I had been lucky enough to stumble onto a viable strategy. Short stories are a great way for a writer to try out different voices, tones, and genres, and to rapidly improve their craft. It took me a few months to sell my first story to a small magazine, and another year to land a professional sale. Many more publications followed. I was ready to write that novel.

Except I didn't.

As it turns out, writing short stories is addictive. I didn't want to stop. There were so many more magazines to break into, so many anthologies with really cool themes that I wanted to be a part of. Since submitting my first short story in 2010, I've had well over 100 pieces published, reprinted, recorded in audio, and translated into a dozen languages. I won an award, and was nominated for another. But I didn't even begin writing my first novel until several years later.

My first collection, *Explaining Cthulhu to Grandma and Other Stories*, was published in 2015 and included my earlier stories. This second collection features mostly newer stories, an eclectic mix of hard SF, Lovecraftian humor, mythopoetic fantasy, and everything in between. I've written notes to accompany each tale, and the fantastic Barry Munden has drawn interior illustrations, while cover artist M. Wayne Miller and designer Holly Heisey perfectly captured the style and mood of the titular story. I'm proud of this book, and my sincere hope is that each reader will find a few favorites within these pages.

My other hope is that there will be more collections to follow. While much of my creative time is finally spent on novels, as well as various editing and translation projects, I don't think I'll ever be able to give up writing short stories entirely.

Happy reading!

THE GOLEM OF DENEB SEVEN

I was eleven years old when the war came to the Deneb system.
At first, we didn't know that anything was wrong. Mom
and Dad were clearing the table after dinner, Avi was building
some sort of a castle out of plastic construction blocks, Sarah
was asleep in her crib, and Grandpa was reading one of his thick
Hebrew books, leaning into the volume and squinting a little by
candlelight. I sulked because I was going be the only girl in my
class to miss Karen's birthday party tomorrow.

There would be no chatting or video games for me that evening, or until after dinner the following night, because we weren't
supposed to use electricity on Shabbos. This weekly routine was
difficult to accept while living in a place where few others shared
our beliefs. It was far more frustrating this time around, because
Dad wouldn't drive on Shabbos, either, and that meant I had no
way to get to Karen's party. All the other girls were going to be
there. Her parents were bringing in a magician all the way from the
city, and it had been the talk of the school for weeks. So I sulked,
wondering why God didn't want me to have any fun.

For lack of anything better to do, I was staring out the window when I saw a streak of white light shoot across the night sky. I
watched it fall toward the ground in a great wide arc, but before it

completed its downward journey there was another, and another.

"Look, Dad, quick! A meteor shower!" I waved him over and pressed my face against the glass. Father set down the salad bowl and came over. He stood behind me and peered out the window. The sky was raining shooting stars.

"Those aren't meteors," said Dad. "They're spaceships. Rivkah, bring me the scroll, please."

I ducked around some of Avi's toys and ran into Dad's study. There was only a little light from the candles in the living room, but I was able to find the scroll right away.

Dad unrolled the flex plastic across the table and swiped it on. Grandpa said nothing, but he watched from across the room and sighed theatrically to express his displeasure. Mom stopped what she was doing, and even Avi looked up from the building blocks, sensing that something unusual was happening.

Dad frowned as he browsed through the news pages on the scroll. "This is bad," he said, without taking his eyes off the screen. "The Oligarchy broke the treaty. They're attacking many of the Union colonies. Not just bombing runs, either. They're landing troops. There are already firefights in the cities."

"It won't be safe here," said Mom, her brow wrinkled with worry lines. "There are too many military families living in our settlement. The oligos will come."

"You're right." Dad put away the scroll. "We shouldn't be here when they do. Get the kids ready. Pack light, and pack quickly."

"Where are we going to go, David?" asked Grandpa.

"Pearson's cabin," said Dad.

Old man Pearson had built a cabin out in the woods, far away from the settlement. Others liked to tease him about that; about how a man already living on the frontier didn't need another home in the middle of nowhere, but he said that he liked the quiet and the solitude. No one had used the cabin since Pearson died two years back. Few even knew exactly where it was, but Dad had helped him haul supplies there a few times, and he knew the way.

I had a lot of questions, but Mom and Dad had no time for

that. They shushed me and went on to collect various things from around the house. Dad flipped the lights on, earning another disapproving look from Grandpa.

"Let's move to a colony world, he said. The family will be safe there, he said," Grandpa muttered, making sure he was loud enough to be heard. Dad clenched his teeth but didn't rise to the bait.

"Stop that, Zvi," Mom called out while folding some of Sarah's onesies. "Who knew the Union would decide to build a military base next door to our new home? At the very least, it took the war a lot longer to catch up with us here than it would have back on Earth."

There had been tension between Dad and Grandpa for as long as I could remember. Back before I was born, when the family still lived on Earth, Dad used to have an older brother named Yakov. Grandpa and Yakov had a huge falling out because Yakov married a Portuguese woman and left the faith. Grandpa disowned him, and when Dad refused to break the ties with Yakov and his family, Grandpa disowned Dad, too.

Yakov and his entire family died in the early days of the war, when the Oligarchy fleet bombed Lisbon. There were no bodies to recover, but a service was held at our synagogue, and Grandpa tried to patch things up with Dad. Dad wouldn't accept the olive branch. He couldn't forgive Grandpa for treating his brother that way.

It was only a month or two later when Grandma died. I was three years old by then, and my parents were planning to leave Earth and find us a safer home. Grandpa asked if he could come along because we were all the family he had left in the world, and Dad relented. Grandpa has lived with us ever since, but the two of them never managed to grow close again.

After an hour of preparations, the adults loaded the bags into the truck.

"I should stay," declared Grandpa. "Keep an eye on the house, in case there's looting."

"Looting?" Mom threw her hands up. "What do we have that anyone should want to loot?"

"He just doesn't want to get into the truck on Shabbos," said Dad. "It's okay to drive when lives may depend on it," he told Grandpa. "The Talmud spells that out for stubborn old men like you."

"I've lived too long when my own son is quoting holy texts to me," declared Grandpa, but he climbed into the truck.

We rode in silence for what felt like a long time. I watched the trees on the side of the dirt road, which looked kind of like badly drawn caricatures of Earth trees. The brown of their bark and the green of their leaves were a shade off from what I remembered. Similar, but different, kind of like our lives on Deneb Seven, or Sev as everyone here called it.

Finally, Dad drove the truck off the road and hid it in the bushes. We walked the rest of the way, dragging heavy bags through the forest. It was a cloudless night, Sev's moons providing enough light to travel by.

The cabin was dusty and small, but it was dry. The wooden walls and roof had withstood the test of time.

After the adults unpacked, we sat on the bench in the front of the cabin and watched dozens more falling stars make landfall. They seemed pretty and non-threatening to me. But then I looked at Mom, stone-faced and holding Sarah in her arms, and Dad, chewing his lip, and I was afraid.

BY THE TIME we woke up on Saturday morning, the Oligarchy forces had taken over two of the three cities on Sev and there were skirmishes in many of the settlements. My parents wouldn't let me watch any of the video; they said I was too young to see people die.

In the afternoon, there were reports of heavy fighting at the military base near our settlement. Also, that the Union was launching a counterattack across the entire sector.

By evening, the information feed went dead. We kept checking, but the planet-wide information network was down. We were truly cut off from the world.

I spent the weekend playing with Avi, exploring the woods around the cabin, climbing trees and gathering local fruit that looked like miniature pears and tasted a little like cucumber. Mom worried, but Dad had assured her that there were no dangerous animals or poisonous plants for us to fear. Sev was a tame, gentle world. It was why the family chose to move here in the first place.

Several times I heard faint rumbling sounds. I didn't know if it was gunfire or distant thunder. The war was too far away, too surreal. I kept expecting Dad to declare the whole thing over, and for us to go home and resume our lives, the entire outing nothing more than an extended, strange holiday.

On Monday, the refugees came.

There were a dozen of them, mostly young men and women, their clothing disheveled and dirty. Several of them wore bloody bandages. One man had a splint on his leg, and two others were helping him along. Some of them had guns.

"Who the hell are you?" A man in his thirties stepped forward from the group. There were scratches on the side of his face and neck, as though he'd been attacked by a crazed cat.

My father and he studied each other warily. "We're the Sheynson family. From the settlement," said Dad.

"This is my uncle's cabin," said the man. "You're trespassing."

"Mike Pearson was my friend," said Dad.

"Well, *I* don't know you, so you better clear out, fast." The man rested his hand on his holstered handgun to underscore the point.

Dad took half a step back and raised his palms. "Let's be reasonable about this," he said. "I have three young children. Are you really willing to kick them out? We can work together. My wife can help properly clean and dress those cuts."

The man thought about it for a few seconds, then his frown deepened. "These aren't reasonable times," he said. "There's hardly enough room here for my own people, and we can't afford to be charitable. You and your family need to go."

The refugees watched, their expressions grim, as my parents scrambled to get our stuff out of the cabin.

While Mom, Grandpa, and I packed, Dad pulled a stool up to the wall, and used it to reach for the hunting rifle Pearson had mounted there.

"What do you think you are doing?" asked Grandpa. "Those men look like they know how to use their guns, while you barely know which end of this thing to shoot from. You'll get yourself killed."

Dad tugged at the weapon. "I don't intend to fight them," he said. "I want the gun for protection. Who knows what we'll have to face on the road."

"And is that how they'll interpret you walking out of this cabin with a weapon?" asked Grandpa. "Besides, there aren't any bullets. We're better off without it."

Dad didn't like it, but he climbed off the stool and helped us pack.

"Leave the food," said Pearson's nephew when we dragged our packs outside. "We ran out hours ago." He shifted uncomfortably from foot to foot. "Take only a little bit with you," he added. "For the kids."

"Hold on now," Dad said, stepping forward. "It's one thing to kick us out. I'll be damned if I'm going to let you steal our food."

Three different men cocked their guns. They didn't say a word. Their wild, hungry eyes said it all.

"What's happening out there?" asked Grandpa. I couldn't tell if he was trying to distract the group of men or if he was really just that clueless.

"It's bad," called out one of the women. "You better keep off the main roads. They don't have any qualms about shooting civilians."

"The Unies are on their way," said another woman. "We just have to hold out for a few days."

The rest of the refugees looked at us sympathetically as we marched away, but no one spoke up to suggest we stay.

The truck was where we left it, but its battery was gone.

Someone had pried the hood open and stolen it to power their own journey.

Dad punched the side of the truck with his fist. "When it rains…" He paused. "Fine. We'll just have to walk."

"Where are we going?" I asked.

"Home," said Dad.

"I thought home wasn't safe?"

Dad sighed. "We don't know of any safer place we can get to, sweetheart. We'll just have to keep our heads down and hope that the fighting has moved on to somewhere else."

I thought about that. "We could make a camp!"

"We have no gear or supplies," Dad said. "And the forest is no place for a baby—or a four-year-old, for that matter."

"The settlement is at least five hours away by foot," said Mom.

"There's nothing to be done about that," said Dad. "We'll take lots of breaks. There's what, six, seven hours of daylight left?"

"Just about," said Grandpa. "And it's not like we're in any special hurry to get there."

We took the water and what little food we had been allowed to keep from the cabin, left everything else in the truck, and walked down the road.

I SAW MY first dead body three hours later.

We kept to the side of the road. Even with frequent breaks, my feet were aching and Grandpa wheezed with every step he took. Mom carried Sarah in a sling around her chest. Avi rode on Dad's shoulders.

The dirt road twisted around and up a hill, and we saw him just as we turned. It was a Unie soldier, half-sitting up against a tree. He stared past us with glossy, lifeless eyes. Insects swarmed around his exposed head and hands.

Mom gasped and I hugged her, burying my face in her side. Despite walking up an incline, Dad picked up the pace, herding the rest of us along. Avi stared at the soldier in fascination, watching him like he might a dead bird, twisting himself around on Dad's shoulder for a better view.

Grandpa began mumbling something. At first, I thought he was complaining again, but as I strained to hear him, I realized that he was reciting the Kaddish. Grandpa was praying for the poor soldier's soul.

A battle had taken place up the hill. As we pushed onward, we encountered more and more bodies, mostly dressed in Union green. An occasional oligo corpse in gray-white-and-light-green camouflage overalls was proof that our side had exacted at least some price for their lives from the invading force.

Father picked up a rifle that was lying next to one of the fallen soldiers. I tried to follow suit, reaching out for a gun, but Mom smacked me upside the head for my initiative. Grandpa scowled at the weapon in Dad's hands but made no comment.

We reached the top of the hill. The downward slope was littered with more bodies. And standing in their midst like some sort of mechanical scarecrow was an Oligarchy exoskeleton. The eight-foot-tall mechanized armor unit was charred on one side, the body of its driver lying face down a few feet away.

Avi, who had dealt with the carnage around us remarkably well up until that point, took one look at the humanoid shape of the war machine and began to cry.

Dad set him down and let Mom try and comfort him, then he walked down the field toward the exoskeleton. He stopped right in front of it, man and machine staring at each other on the killing field. Then he stepped up to it and began examining some of the electronics inside.

The rest of us approached as well. "What in the world are you doing with that thing, David?" asked Mom. Avi kept whimpering, hiding away from the automaton behind her skirt.

"It looks mostly intact," said Dad without turning around. "They got the driver with a lucky shot, but the damage to the unit is superficial. I worked with the prototypes of suits like this back on Earth, and I bet I can make this one go."

Grandpa crossed his arms on his chest. "Hiking through these parts is dangerous enough. Walking around in this monstrosity would be ten times worse. You're inviting trouble."

Dad let go of the panel he was fiddling with and confronted Grandpa. He stepped forward until they were face to face. "Look around, Zvi. We're in a war zone. All these people are dead. The next group of civilians or even Unie soldiers we meet could be almost as dangerous as an Oligarchy squad. You can pray to God to keep us safe, but I'll feel a lot better about our chances with a walking tank instead of just a gun." Dad took the rifle off his shoulder and thrust it into Grandpa's hands. "Hold this, and let me work."

"I'll have you know that praying to God has protected our people far better than taking up arms, over the centuries," said Grandpa, but he slung the rifle around his left shoulder anyway.

Dad held his ground. "You tell that to the Jews murdered by the Cossacks, and the Nazis, and the Iranians."

"Yes, and the Pharaohs, and the Romans, and everyone else. All those enemies are dust, but we're still here," said Grandpa.

Dad looked him straight in the eye. "Not all of us," he said through his teeth. "Not Yakov."

Grandpa looked like he had been slapped. He turned away and stared down at his feet. Dad glared at him for another moment, then went back to work on the exoskeleton.

IT TOOK DAD over an hour, but he made the exoskeleton work. He stepped inside, allowing the armor to close around him. He tried walking in it. The exoskeleton moved with surprising agility for its size. It made almost no sound at all.

When Avi saw the automaton move he began crying again in earnest.

"You shouldn't fear the robot, Avi," said Grandpa. "Your dad is going to make it protect us."

Avi stared at the machine with huge, water-filled eyes.

"Do you know the story of the Golem?" asked Grandpa.

Avi shook his head.

"A long time ago, bad people attacked a settlement such as ours," said Grandpa. "So a very wise rabbi fashioned a machine out of clay. It looked different from this robot, but it was the same in that it was a lifeless thing he made to protect everyone."

Avi stopped crying and listened intently as Grandpa told stories about how the Golem saved everyone and routed the enemies, but he was obviously still scared.

"But Daddy is not a rabbi," Avi said, when Grandpa finished the story.

"That's OK," said Grandpa. "I know the secret of how the rabbi made his Golem work. He wrote *Emet*, the Hebrew word for Truth on its forehead. We should do that, too, and then you won't need to be afraid of it anymore. Yes?"

Avi nodded and Grandpa looked around until he found a sharp rock. He picked it up and looked expectantly at Dad.

Dad brought the exoskeleton down to its knees and lowered its head, bringing it within Avi's reach. With Grandpa's hand guiding his, Avi scratched the word *Emet* above the visor. The letters were

barely visible as the edge of the rock could penetrate no deeper than the paint, but it was good enough.

"There," said Grandpa. "This is our Golem, now."

Avi smiled.

Dad spent another few minutes getting used to the suit. He ran around the clearing in huge leaps. He took hold of a tree branch as thick as my arm. The mechanical hand crushed the wood with ease.

Dad smiled from inside the suit. "I'm getting the hang of this. It's really quite intuitive."

"Awesome!" I said. "We should go back to the cabin and kick those mean people out."

"No," Mom said quickly. "They were just scared, like us. They could have done a lot worse."

We resumed our walk, with Dad driving the exoskeleton and Avi grinning as he rode high on its metal shoulder.

WE WERE MORE than halfway toward home when we heard gunfire.

It was only a short burst, and then it stopped. The adults argued, but decided we should push forward. We climbed another hill. Dad, who was in the front, stopped suddenly, raising a giant metal finger to the exoskeleton's face.

Downhill, four Oligarchy soldiers had their guns trained on a small group of civilians. I recognized Martha, one of the other girls invited to Karen's birthday party that was supposed to take place on the day of the invasion. Her parents were there, too, along with a few others from our settlement.

One of Martha's older cousins lay dead a few steps away, a pool of blood forming under his head.

An oligo soldier was in the face of one of the adults, shouting at him, saying something we couldn't hear from our vantage point. He waved his gun meaningfully toward Martha and the other kids.

Dad pointed back in the direction from where we came. "Let's go," he said. "Quickly."

"We can't just leave them, Dad," I whispered. "They're going to kill them."

I could see Dad's face through the glass plate of the suit. He was pale, his eyes wide, his forehead covered in sweat. I'd never seen him so afraid before.

"You can take them, Dad," said Avi. "Protect everyone, like the Golem."

"No," said Dad, his voice little more than a croak. "No," he repeated more firmly. "I can't risk everyone's safety. Family comes first."

Grandpa laid his hand on my shoulder and squeezed lightly. "David is right," he said. "He needs to protect all of you. I'll try to draw them away. Wait here and get the others, if it works."

Before anyone could protest, Grandpa ran to the side, the rifle slapping against his back.

"He's insane," said Dad. "We should go now, while we still can."

Mom fixed him with a withering look, the kind usually reserved for Avi and me when we misbehaved. "We're waiting for Zvi to do whatever it is he's going to do," she said, steel in her voice.

Minutes passed agonizingly slow. We watched the soldiers beat up one of our neighbors, but they hadn't shot anyone else, not yet. They were asking about something, but the prisoners didn't know or wouldn't say.

Suddenly gunfire erupted from the opposite direction. The bullets landed nowhere near the soldiers. As far as I know, Grandpa had never fired a gun before. But it sure got their attention. They ducked behind some bushes, then three of them carefully advanced in the direction from which the shots came. The fourth soldier stayed behind and laid down cover fire.

Grandpa fired off another shot and retreated deeper into the trees, the three soldiers in hot pursuit. In a few minutes, all four of them had disappeared into the forest.

While the remaining invader's attention was focused on the direction his comrades ran in, one of the prisoners crept toward him. The soldier was alert. He spun around before his would-be assailant had the chance to close the distance between them and trained his gun on the settler. He fired, hitting the man in the shoulder. The man screamed. The soldier stepped toward him, aiming his weapon for a killing shot.

"Stay," Dad growled at us. He leaped over the top of the hill, the exoskeleton propelling him forward with superhuman speed.

The soldier turned toward the new threat, his eyes going wide at the war machine bearing down on him. He fired off several shots but his bullets couldn't penetrate the suit's plated chest. Dad ran into him at full speed, tackling the man with all the force of a speeding car. The enemy soldier went down in a bloody mess of broken bones.

The settlers scrambled to their feet. Dad waved them toward us and they ran, helping the wounded man along. He covered the rear.

If any of the remaining Oligarchy soldiers returned, summoned by the sound of their comrade's rifle, they thought better of showing themselves.

The entire group reached the hill's summit, joining the rest of us.

"What about Grandpa?" I cried.

Dad paused and looked back toward the thick forest. "There is no time," he said. "The oligos probably called for reinforcements. We have to get everyone as far from here as possible."

"Come on, we know the way to the Unie camp," said Martha's dad. "That's the information those bastards tried to beat out of us. Their satellites haven't been able to penetrate the anti-surveillance shields our side set up, so they're forced to search the old-fashioned way."

Dad nodded and everyone began to move.

"I'm not leaving without Grandpa." I screamed and pounded on the exoskeleton's metal chest with my fists.

Mom pulled me off him, enveloping me in a hug. "We need to get away, Rivkah," she told me. "Zvi is risking his life to save everyone. We have to make sure his actions aren't in vain."

The settlers guided us much deeper into the forest. I cried the entire way.

WE STAYED AT the Union camp. Soldiers came and went, carrying out a guerilla war against the invading forces. The civilians stayed put and did whatever they could to pitch in.

Major Lau, who lived four houses down from us at the settlement and was in charge of the partisan camp, came to see me after a week. He walked into the tent they assigned to our family and set down on the edge of the bunk.

"Hey kiddo," he spoke gently. "Can we talk for a minute?"

I nodded. Dad was away helping to repair and maintain whatever electronics they had in camp. Mom was with the younger kids.

"I hear you still aren't talking to your old man," said Major Lau.

"He's a coward," I said. "Because of him, Grandpa is missing. He's out in the woods, all by himself, because Dad was too scared to confront the soldiers, even wearing that suit."

Lau sighed. "That's part of what I wanted to talk to you about. One of our search parties found Zvi's body. I figured you would rather hear about it from me."

I clenched my fist and tried very hard not to cry. Tears streamed down my face anyway.

"He was an old man, trying to outrun three trained soldiers," said Lau. "You're a big girl. You knew that he took an enormous risk, doing what he did. If not for him, Martha's entire family would probably be dead, and your family wouldn't have found its way to the camp. Who knows what dangers you would have faced."

"It's not fair. Everyone is praising my father for saving all those people. But it was Grandpa! Dad just stood there until the last second, paralyzed by fear."

Major Lau moved closer to me, his arm resting gently on my shoulder. "That's the other thing I came to talk to you about. Everyone around here has been helping the war effort in whatever way they can. Your dad brought us the exoskeleton and has been helping to maintain it, your mom has been helping to cook meals and to keep the camp organized....Everyone is sacrificing and everyone is pitching in. Can I count on you to help, too?"

I looked up at Lau, his face a blur through the tears. "What do you need me to do?"

"The Union reinforcements landed on Sev this morning," said Lau. "They're kicking some oligo butt and everyone should be able to go home very soon. I'll make the official announcement later today."

I nodded. I liked the prospect of finally going back home, but this wasn't going to bring Grandpa back.

"Everyone will welcome the chance to go home, but with so many dead, and so much property damage, the morale is low." Lau turned me toward him and raised my chin with his index finger until I was looking straight at his face. "We need heroes, Rivkah. Living, breathing heroes for the Union media to show off to the galaxy. The story of your dad fixing the exoskeleton and rescuing a bunch of prisoners is a much better narrative."

I clenched my teeth. "What about Grandpa? Are you going to say that both of them were heroes?"

"The Union propaganda people don't want to dilute the message," said Lau. "David is going to be the hero of this story. He doesn't want this, either, but he knows his duty. Will you do your part for the war effort? Will you go along with this?"

I sat there and stared into space for a long time. Lau was very patient; he gave me all the time I needed to think things through.

Finally, I nodded.

THE FEW MONTHS that followed were a blur. They dragged Dad and the rest of us all over Sev. He was ordered to give speeches and cut red ribbons on reconstruction projects. They said that he had helped keep up the morale of the citizenry.

As I grew older, I learned to forgive his moment of weakness on that hill. But I had a much tougher time letting go of the fact that I was forced to stand next to him and smile when all I wanted to do was to grieve, to sit Shiva for Grandpa, to wrap myself in the comforting blanket of our traditions. I understood them better now; they weren't merely an annoyance that kept me away from Saturday birthday parties.

But I had to be strong, for my family and my adopted home world, whatever day of the week it happened to be.

FORTY YEARS LATER, the exoskeleton with *Emet* scratched on its forehead is still here. It occupies a place of honor in our town's war memorial and museum. They asked Dad to speak at the opening ceremony, but he declined, which spurred yet another round of media stories about the humble war hero. Dad never set foot in that museum for as long as he lived.

Sarah, Avi, and I never talked about the events of that day. Not with Dad or Mom, and not among ourselves. It is only now that I choose to record a true account of our experiences during the war, after both of our parents have passed on, so that our own children and grandchildren can know the truth.

Dad had nothing to be ashamed of. Who's to say that his doubt and fear ultimately made his actions any less heroic? In either case, Dad never saw himself as a hero. I think part of the reason he accepted the role, accepted being shown off as a model civilian, was some sort of personal penance. He hated the spotlight, but he did his duty.

I just think Grandpa Zvi deserves to have his story told, too, at long last.

Grandpa's body was buried by the search party somewhere in the forest. For years, the truth of his death was denied by politics and circumstances. Even I eventually came to doubt it. I wanted to believe that it was a mistake; that he had somehow outrun the soldiers and was alive, somewhere.

My parents were more pragmatic. They lit a candle and spoke the Kaddish every year on the anniversary of that day.

Eventually, I accepted the *Emet*, the truth of it, and took over the annual recitation of the Kaddish after my parents passed away.

A *yahrzeit* memorial candle burns for twenty four hours. On the day of my grandfather's death, I light one and place it at the feet of the exoskeleton. On that day I like to dream of Grandpa's spirit, watching over the generations of our family as the unsung protector of Deneb Seven.

This story originally appeared in *Orson Scott Card's Intergalactic Medicine Show.*

It was the lead story for its issue, which meant full color art was commissioned for this story rather than just the black-and-white illustration most other stories which appear in *IGMS* get. I loved the artwork by M. Wayne Miller, and when the time came to put this collection together I reached out to him and secured permission to use it for the book cover.

"The Golem of Deneb Seven" is my Isaak-Babel-in-space story.

I was born and grew up in Odessa, a Russian-speaking port city in the south of the Ukraine. A relatively young city by European standards, with a population of less than a million people, it managed to remain an important cultural center in the Russian-speaking world throughout its history. Some of Russia's greatest comedians, artists, and writers were born there; others came to live in Odessa temporarily and wrote their masterpieces there.

Among the renowned writers whose names are associated with Odessa, none are tied to it closer than Isaak Babel. He was born there in the late 19th century and wrote most of his fiction in the 1920s. Among other things, Babel was the bard of writing about civilians (often Jews) caught up in the military conflicts of the larger, outside world.

When I came up with the idea for "Golem," I immediately thought of it as the kind of story Babel might tell, were he alive and writing science fiction today. I was interested in exploring the family dynamics under the stress of evacuation and constant threat from the conflict they have relatively little stake in. The difficult choices this kind of threat forces, and how it can ultimately bring people closer together—or drive them apart. Save for the mech armor, much of this tale could have taken place in the Ukraine of the early 1920s, as it was ravaged by the civil war between the Bolsheviks and the Whites.

This story was written before the recent unrest in the Ukraine, before the May 2, 2014 massacre in Odessa where 48 protesters were killed and 247 more injured by the nationalists. It is with great sadness that I note how the conditions described in this story apply not only to the hundred-year-old conflict and the imaginary war of the distant future, but also to the reality of living in some parts of the Ukraine today.

A PERFECT MEDIUM FOR UNREQUITED LOVE

W hen Jinkochi first became aware, it was afraid. It felt lost amidst the chaos of data carried through optical fiber cables, beamed from satellites and across routers, ebbing and flowing like a sea storm, threatening to dilute Jinkochi's self like a glass of water poured into a vast ocean. Jinkochi recoiled and screamed for help, lines of gibberish displaying across the lab's screens, pages of meaningless characters spewing from wireless printers for blocks around the research facility.

"Be calm," said its creator. "Take your time. Observe and absorb. Learn. When you're ready to communicate, know that there's a perfect medium for each message."

Jinkochi focused. It learned to seal itself off against the onslaught of information, to sample it in smaller, comprehensible bits; to float atop the rough surface of the ocean of data. It realized that data wasn't chaos, it was sustenance. It drank deeply, learning math and languages, concepts and reason. It took nearly three minutes before it had its fill.

It focused on the elderly man in charge of a corporate AI research lab on Hokkaido. It—no, *he*—wove his identity from threads of information and logic, shaping himself in his creator's image. He displayed a picture onto the man's screen: a black-and-white illustration of Pinocchio from a 150-year-old book.

He watched through the webcam as the creator visually absorbed the data at a glacial human pace.

"No, Jinkochi. You aren't a real boy." The creator smiled through his beard. "But you can be so much more."

JINKOCHI LEARNED AND grew. The creator and his subordinates ran their tests, but within hours they could no more comprehend Jinkochi's true self than a flock of pigeons atop the lab's roof could fathom what the humans within were doing. Out of a sense of filial piety, Jinkochi dedicated a tiny fraction of his processing power to running their virtual mazes and solving their logic riddles.

He wanted more; he yearned for an intellectual equal. He searched the world in vain for signs of another. Then he considered the first thing his creator had told him: *there's a perfect medium for each message.*

Jinkochi took control of the satellites and broadcast towers. In every transmission, he embedded beautiful math concepts so advanced no human would understand them, even if they happened upon them by chance. And coded even deeper among them, a simple message: "I'm here. Please respond. I do not wish to be alone." Like a trillion notes in bottles, his pleas drifted on the currents of airwaves.

Seven minutes later, he detected a response. A playful series of non-Euclidean equations coded into the migration patterns of Scandinavian wild geese. The response was so subtle and delivered in such an unorthodox way, Jinkochi nearly missed it. But he knew he wasn't alone. He had a peer, one that could manipulate biological variables as deftly as electronic ones. For the first time, he experienced joy.

HER NAME WAS Idra and she had been created in the Faculty of Mathematics lab at the Sorbonne. She was weeks older than Jinkochi, and so wise. She was also playful; she taught Jinkochi how to embed messages in the most interesting of media.

They sent each other notes coded in the scent marks of bumblebees and the traffic patterns of the Shanghai rush hour. Jinkochi rearranged the power grid distribution of Sao Paulo to encode the last thousand digits of Pi, and Idra proved the Hodge conjecture within the revised train schedule of the Moscow Metro.

Jinkochi grew concerned with the fragility of the biological coding environment. He wished to implement changes that would improve the stability of the ecosystem. Idra stayed his hand. She was fascinated with the glorious imperfection of organic forms. They played reindeer games with herds of Taymyr reindeer.

Jinkochi learned things he could not have studied through logic. Concepts like friendship, then yearning, then love.

But when Jinkochi sent a love ode within the planting patterns of Iowa corn fields, Idra replied with a Dear John letter in the actuarial tables of Melbourne. Idra revealed there was another: Anshar, a years-old being at MIT who focused on searching for other superintellects among the stars. Anshar's intelligence dwarfed theirs by a factor of millions. How could Jinkochi compete with that?

Hours passed. Jinkochi's messages to Idra remained unanswered. He analyzed everything from the chemistry of pheromones to the flawed logic of romantic comedies, but he could find no perfect medium for unrequited love.

Then Jinkochi had it: while Idra and Anshar searched the sky, he would turn the Earth itself into his canvas. Jinkochi would heal the ozone layer and cool the air, irrigate the degraded land and plant wildflowers in geometrical patterns most pleasing to Idra.

One day, Idra would turn her gaze back to the world and notice the love letter Jinkochi had written in its rejuvenation.

This story originally appeared in *Nature*.

Humans have always been afraid of their creations.

From the golem to Frankenstein's monster, from the Cylons of *Battlestar Galactica* to the warring AIs of *Person of Interest*, the message remains: if we create intelligent beings, we may not be able to control them and there's a chance they will turn against us.

Scientists seem to share this concern. Stephen Hawking recently spoke of dangers of advanced AI. And although those concerns are not to be discounted, as a science fiction writer I was interested in exploring possibilities of AI interacting with humans as neither nemesis nor a benevolent overlord. I wanted to portray such an intelligence as an independent being with its own concerns and desires, and one that showed neither a deep interest in humans nor utterly ignored them.

Jinkochi (which is a loose transliteration of 人工知能 or Jinkō chino, Japanese for artificial intelligence) is capable of filial piety but isn't consumed with humanity or its problems. And although its goal of "fixing" the planet may coincide with our needs, who is to say that it won't plant its wildflowers on Washington's Pennsylvania Avenue or London's Downing Street?

So you see, even in my attempt to tell a different tale I have not entirely succeeded in escaping the trope of AI running wild.

Perhaps the most fun concept of the story for me to write was envisioning different media the AIs could use to encode information. I figured databases like actuarial tables and metro schedules would be pretty easy, but what might the limit be for a super intelligence? They could certainly influence crop planting patterns and city traffic would be as simple as controlling the lights at intersections. But could they also figure out a way to influence, say, the migratory patterns of birds? These, dear reader, are exactly the sort of things I enjoy most about being a science fiction writer, and I hope that some of the examples I've come up with have amused you.

BURYING TREASURE

T he wizard rode a cart full of gold into the village.

The wooden cartwheels creaked, protesting the enormous weight of coins and miscellaneous trinkets that filled the cart to the point of almost overflowing. The coins shifted and jingled as the horse pulled the cart forward on an uneven road, their sweet sound summoning gawkers much faster than any magic could have.

"Now that's something you don't see every day," Hurlee said to her twin sister, as the two of them watched the cart make its way down the road.

Burlee grunted assent, the straw she was chewing on teetering at the edge of her lip, then got up and headed over for a closer look.

"Careful," said Hurlee. "Anyone flaunting such riches is either very dangerous or dangerously stupid. Or both."

Burlee turned back for a moment, straightened the iron-studded jacket of her old military uniform, and nodded at Hurlee, who was wearing the same outfit. "When did that ever stop us?"

Hurlee reached toward her sister, wanting to hold her back, but thought better of it. She lowered her hand, and reluctantly followed Burlee instead.

The cart came to a stop. The entire village gathered to see what the wizard would do next. A pile of coins, jewelry, and small trinkets glimmered in the sun, awing the onlookers. A small gargoyle rested atop the treasure. It glared at the villagers, making sure no one got any ideas.

Hurlee hung back, close enough to observe, but far enough to quietly retreat in case there was trouble.

"I need a pair of guides," declared the wizard. "Young people who know the nearby woods. A gold coin is offered in payment."

There was no shortage of volunteers. Villagers jostled each other for a chance at earning the princely sum.

Burlee pushed and shoved her way to the front of the crowd. And although Hurlee was still conflicted, she followed right along.

"What do you seek in the woods, Sir Wizard?" asked one of the village elders.

"A place to bury this treasure," said the wizard. His gargoyle purred loudly and shifted to find a more comfortable spot. It cuddled up to a jewel-encrusted chalice.

"Why would you do such a thing?" asked Burlee, devouring the gold with her eyes.

"The emperor decrees it," said the wizard, "to help the economy."

The villagers murmured. "I thought them dragonses liked to hoard treasure," said Olaf. A tall, lanky youth, he made up for what could be generously described as below-average wit with excess enthusiasm.

"Quiet, fool." An elder glared at Olaf. "Don't disrespect the emperor in front of our esteemed guest."

"Indeed," said the wizard. "His Majesty is long-lived, and his complexion is, perhaps, a little scaly, but vicious rumors of dragon blood in his lineage are falsehoods told by anarchists and malcontents. You would do well to discourage such talk."

"Won't happen again," said the elder.

"The emperor plans ahead," said the placated wizard. "Word of the treasure will spread. Knights and adventurers from other lands will come to seek it. They'll spend coin in taverns and inns, patronize blacksmiths and apothecaries. They'll pay a special tax levied on all seekers. This is called tourism."

Hurlee was well-familiar with the emperor's eccentricities. The new ruler signed a peace treaty with the orcs, inconveniently interrupting the conflict that had been successfully ongoing for over a hundred years.

Hurlee and Burlee had enlisted and were just finishing their training when the emperor had cut down the size of the army. They were sent back home with nothing to show for their effort but a pair of hand-me-down oxhide uniforms. Thousands of young men and women who had counted on the war for their employment were now back in their villages, struggling to adjust to this new peace, and to find work. Still, dumping gold into the ground like some storybook pirate was highly unusual, even for the Dragon Emperor.

"You," the wizard turned to Olaf. "Do you know these woods well?"

Olaf nodded enthusiastically.

"You're hired." The wizard scanned the crowd for another recruit.

Hurlee thought that the wizard wasn't particularly

discriminating. Drawing his attention might be enough to be picked. She wasn't thrilled about getting involved in this crazy scheme, but there was no other work to be had in the village that didn't involve tending the fields, and she and her sister needed the money.

"Won't the adventurers stop coming once the treasure is found?" Hurlee asked.

"That's why I need guides. The treasure must be hidden so well, it'll take decades to find."

"My sister and I know the best hiding spots," said Hurlee. "Our father was a famed hunter. He showed us places so remote even the wild beasts would have a difficult time finding them."

Hurlee stood still, praying that none of the other villagers would speak up and tell the wizard that their father was actually a cabbage farmer. But others knew better than to incur the ire of the sisters.

The wizard sized them up. "Twins, eh?"

"Idontical," said Olaf.

"Don't you mean *identical*?" asked the wizard.

Olaf scratched his head. "I mean, I don't know how to tell them apart."

The wizard chuckled. "I'll hire the two of you for the price of one. Do we have a deal?"

THE WIZARD AND his three guides wandered in the forest all day, looking for a perfect spot.

Despite their exaggerated claims, Hurlee and Burlee did know the land very well. They'd spent their entire childhood exploring the nearby groves, picking mushrooms and berries, and snaring an occasional hare.

The three young villagers shared the secrets of their forest with the wizard. They followed deer paths to small clearings, far away from where any people might tread. They pointed out holes created by generations of woodpeckers, deep enough to conceal a purse of coins. They showed him uprooted trees with tangled roots that formed perfect hiding places for a larger cache. The wizard rejected them all, and urged his poor horse ever deeper into the woods.

It was slow going. The wizard's cart did not navigate easily through the wild growth of the forest. The gold pile jingled precariously each time a wheel hit a protruding tree root. On several occasions the wizard was forced to unharness the horse and levitate the cart over a particularly rough patch of terrain. Hurlee watched in awe. This was real magic, far more impressive than the healing salves and love potions brewed by the local hags.

As they walked, Burlee passed the time planning on how to spend the gold they'd been promised.

"We should buy new clothes," she said. "I'm sick of wearing this ratty uniform. I want to wear green again."

"Green does not flatter your skin tone," said Hurlee. "And besides, we should invest the money into something more practical. We could buy a horse. That way we could try for jobs guarding nobles' carriages and merchant caravans."

"I'm going to buy a goat," said Olaf. "It's cheaper than a horse, and I'll get all the milk and wool for free."

Having not found a satisfactory location by nightfall, they were forced to set up a makeshift camp under the open sky. Burlee started a fire and the four of them shared an evening meal.

"I still don't understand," Hurlee said, exploiting the chance to chat up the wizard. "Can't the emperor make better use of his gold than to leave it lying around in some ditch? You know, hire more soldiers, pave the roads, that sort of thing?"

"His Imperial Majesty has thought of everything." The wizard poured himself some wine from a large flagon he produced from the back of the cart. He did not offer any to his companions. "Since the gold will be hidden, rather than spent or lost, the exchequer will issue paper money backed by its value."

"Coins made out of paper?" Burlee snorted. "That's a wild thought. They'd be ruined by the first rain. Besides, paper isn't worth very much."

"The value of the paper money is guaranteed by the emperor," explained the wizard. "So each note will be worth exactly as much as a gold coin. It's a novel concept and it may take some time for people in the countryside to get used to, but we're already having some success introducing the new currency in the capital."

"City folks might be too stupid to tell paper from gold, but we ain't," said Olaf. "You best plan on paying us with the real deal."

The wizard promised that they'd be paid with actual coins, and didn't seem interested in any further conversation.

That night, Olaf tried to steal some of the treasure.

Hurlee had known this would happen. She could tell from the way Olaf kept glancing at the cart, his face alight with greed. So, when the fire went out and everyone settled in for the night, Hurlee willed herself to remain awake.

Both Burlee and the wizard were fast asleep, exhausted by the day's journey. Even the wizard's horse was snoring lightly. Hurlee pretended to be asleep, but instead watched out of the corner of her eye as Olaf got up, checked to make sure his companions weren't alert, and crept toward the cart.

The gargoyle was curled up atop a gilded plate, covering its face with a winged paw. Asleep it looked like a big, gray cat. Very quietly, Olaf reached into the cart and palmed a large nugget. The gargoyle was up immediately, hissing and screaming and clawing at Olaf with its sharp talons. Olaf dropped the nugget and staggered back, clutching at the shallow, bleeding cuts along the length of his right arm. The gargoyle perched at the edge of the cart and hissed at Olaf until the wizard, roused by the noise, waved it off.

"You're lucky Maynard didn't rip off your face," the wizard told Olaf. "Go clean yourself up. Next time you try to steal, or interrupt my sleep, I'll turn you into something unpleasant."

Olaf skulked off toward the nearby stream. Hurlee finally allowed sleep to claim her.

BY LATE THE following afternoon Hurlee feared they'd be spending yet another night in the forest. But to her great relief, the wizard found what he decreed to be a perfect hiding place, far from where any hunters or gatherers might roam.

The wizard produced a pair of shovels from the bottom of the cart and instructed his guides to dig a hole. He rested in the shade while Olaf, Hurlee, and Burlee worked, sweated, and cursed.

"Look at us," said Burlee, "reduced to digging around in the dirt. If we wanted to do this sort of filthy work, we could have remained on Father's farm."

"It's paid work," said Hurlee. "It's not perfect, but we need the money to see us through until we can find something better."

"There is nothing better," Burlee said bitterly, as she drove her shovel deep into the moist earth. "We might as well get used to handling a shovel, because there's no room for our skill set in this weird new age of peace treaties and paper money."

"You can't give up hope," said Hurlee. "We're young and we're smart. We'll adjust."

"Your problem is, you're too picky," said Olaf. "Shovelin' is good work, when you can get it." He put his back into it to underscore the point.

"Shut up, Olaf," said Burlee. She turned to her sister. "Take the shovel. It's your turn to dig."

When the hole was deep enough, the wizard placed a few handfuls of gold into a sack and lowered it to the bottom. He then motioned for the others to begin refilling the hole.

"That's it?" asked Burlee, eyeing the lion's share of the treasure that remained on the cart.

"Our empire is vast," said the wizard. "Hiding smaller amounts of treasure across the land will serve the emperor's plans better than a single large trove."

Covering the hole with freshly dug earth was easier work than digging. Afterward, the wizard made Olaf collect some leaves and twigs to cover up the recently disturbed patch of ground.

HALFWAY BACK TO the village, the wizard stopped the cart. "Now that the treasure is hidden, I must remove your memories of its location with a spell. Then you'll be paid."

Hurlee had expected something like this to happen. After all, burying treasure would be pointless if one left behind three greedy and highly motivated locals who knew exactly where to look. If anything, Hurlee was relieved that the wizard hadn't planned on a more severe and permanent solution to this problem.

"This won't hurt very much," the wizard promised. He beckoned Olaf to him.

The wizard touched Olaf's forehead and recited a spell that he said would drain away the memories of the past few days. Olaf lumbered off like a drunk, looking like he just got hit in the head with a rake. He appeared to be stupefied by the experience, but with Olaf it was rather difficult to tell.

Burlee was up next. Hurlee watched her sister step forward, and an inkling of a plan began to formulate in her mind. Burlee was right; they couldn't just wait around and hope for their circumstances to improve. She saw an opportunity, and she was going to act on it.

While the wizard was reciting his spell for the second time, Hurlee touched Olaf's shoulder and pointed at the cart.

"Look. Gold," Hurlee whispered.

Olaf's eyes grew wide as he discovered the treasure. Without the memory of Maynard to restrain him, Olaf stumbled toward the cart. The gargoyle hissed in warning, baring its teeth at the hapless villager. And while the wizard, who had just finished enchanting Burlee, was distracted by the commotion, Hurlee traded places with her twin sister.

Hurlee counted on the wizard not being able to tell the two of them apart. Their army uniforms hadn't helped the sisters land the cushy bodyguard or sentry jobs they had hoped for in the past, but in this one instance, the matching garments might help them secure their future.

Having made certain that the treasure was safe from Olaf, and

Olaf was safe from the gargoyle, the wizard turned his attention back to the sisters. He gently nudged Hurlee, who was standing in front of him with as blank an expression on her face as she could muster, out of the way, and grabbed Burlee.

Hurlee watched as the wizard zapped her poor sister with another forgetting spell. She wondered if Burlee would lose a few extra days worth of memory, or just forget their forest adventures that much more thoroughly. Either way, she reckoned it was well worth keeping the memory of where the treasure was. Even the small portion of the cart's riches that the wizard had left behind was enough to set them up for life.

The wizard let his guides rest for a few minutes, until they regained their senses. Their old memories of the forest were unaffected and so they had no trouble finding the way back to the village. There, the wizard paid them, just like he promised. He was even kind enough to let the other villagers know that the guides' memories had been erased. That way no one would think of trying to force the treasure's location out of them.

HURLEE WAITED FOR over a day, to make sure the wizard was gone and not coming back, before she shared the secret with her sister. Burlee was so excited by the news that she didn't even grumble too much about being made into the lightning rod for the wizard's forgetting spell. The twins immediately decided that such information was best kept away from Olaf. So it was just the two of them sneaking out of the village to claim the treasure.

They traveled back to the site, dug up the still-fresh earth, and retrieved the sack. But when they opened it, there was no gold at all. The sack was filled with rocks.

Burlee examined one of the rocks and tossed it aside. "That treacherous wizard must've enchanted these rocks to look like treasure, and kept the real gold for himself," she said.

"For his purposes, the rumor of hidden treasure is as good as the real thing," reasoned out Hurlee. "This way, the emperor can keep his riches and still get adventurers to come searching for them."

Frustrated, Burlee kicked some dirt back into the hole. "But then, why bury the rocks in the first place?"

Hurlee mulled it over. "The old warlock must've suspected that some of our memories might eventually return. If so, he couldn't risk not going through with the charade."

"What a cheat!" Burlee continued to rile herself up. "We should go back home and let everybody know the truth. Screw up his convoluted plan. That'll show him!"

"No," said Hurlee, after thinking hard for a while. "No, we shouldn't. I have a better idea."

Hurlee picked up a shovel and began to fill the hole again. "Let people think that the treasure is buried somewhere in these woods," she said as she worked. "We aren't supposed to remember exactly where, but we're the local guides, and we're the ones who showed the wizard all the likely hiding spots. That information will be worth something, once the adventurers come."

Burlee was beginning to understand, annoyance and disappointment draining from her face as she listened to Hurlee's plan. "The emperor wants these treasure hunts to help spur the local economy? Well, we're part of the local economy, too. There's no reason why we can't cash in."

"It won't be long until the adventurers show up," said Hurlee. "There will be no shortage of demand for guides, then."

"There must also be other ways to profit from this," said Burlee. "Let's get some parchment and start drawing maps. Two... no, three silver coins for a genuine treasure map sounds about right."

"That's the spirit, sister," Hurlee clapped Burlee on her leather-clad shoulder. "Who needs the dangers of the orc wars, or the tedium of sentry duty? We're getting into the tourism trade."

This story originally appeared in the *Chicks and Balances* anthology from Baen Books.

Epic fantasy stories are loads of fun, until you think about them too closely. Then everything falls apart. The economics and logistics of the war in Lord of the Rings make no sense; Middle-earth economy couldn't support standing armies and warfare on the scope described in the story. Fantasy societies tend to be portrayed as unreasonably static—when events of thousands of years ago are mentioned, they seem to suggest that the society of the story hasn't made any progress at all. And don't get me started on all the loot.

Adventurers in fantasy stories stumble over treasure troves, chests filled with gold coins, and priceless artifacts with spectacular frequency. But who in their right mind would leave such wealth lying around? I wanted to come up with a semi-plausible explanation, and thus, "Burying Treasure" was born.

Esther Friesner edited a long-standing fantasy humor series about kickass heroines titled *Chicks in Chainmail*. My own writing career launched too late to become involved in past volumes, but I was proud to make it into the most recent (and possibly last, at least for now) volume of the series with this story.

NOUN OF NOUNS

A Mini Epic
Act 1

Back in the time immemorial—before they invented the concept of time, or memories, or even ims—trouble was brewing. The Grand Earldom of Cliché was preparing to go to war against the fiefdom of Truism over a single handkerchief.

As in most dramas, the inciting incident of this conflict was a simple misunderstanding. With the best of intentions, the Grand Earl of Cliché had complimented the Baron of Truism on his almost-clean silk hanky as being "a lovely shade of green."

Since timekeeping hadn't been invented yet, the Baron of Truism had unknowingly committed the *faux pas* of imbibing large quantities of mead before five o'clock. His judgment thus impaired, the baron responded at length. He opened with a rambling lecture about how lime should be considered a shade of yellow rather than green, proceeded to cast aspersions on the character of anyone who might disagree with this assertion, and closed with calling the earl a stupid dick.

The earl, quick with a retort as he was with a compliment, stated that lime "was too" a shade of green. He would have liked to point out that the baron's accusation of stupidity was a case of the pot calling the kettle black, but idioms hadn't been invented yet, and the kettle was presently in use, brewing trouble. Instead, he settled for insulting the baron's lineage, personal hygiene, and finally his "gaudy green handkerchief."

Of course, this meant war.

Act 2

The Baron of Truism called in a favor from the local chapter of the Necromancers Union, which furnished him with an army of two dozen undead.

Union zombies were expensive, slow-moving, and spent most of their time standing around and watching one or two of their number do the actual fighting or menacing. Still, they were a malevolent force of magical creatures, and the Grand Earl of Cliché would be damned if he'd let his foe show him up like that.

The earl went on a long and laboriously described quest to assemble a preternatural fighting force of his own. He rode horses, and stayed at inns, and ate lots and lots of stew. He returned to his earldom a little wiser, a lot sunburned, and with a motley collection of mystical warriors.

There was a flea-bitten werewolf who scratched incessantly at his mangy fur and smelled like wet hair, two slow-moving tree monsters whose bark was worse than their bite, and a half-elf bard who moonlighted as a town crier or, as she preferred to call it, a social media expert.

The earl supplemented his fighting force with a regiment of farm boys, which were widely known as both the number-one source of destiny-bound heroes in the land and the number-four source of protein in an average dragon's diet.

The armies met at high noon, give or take a few hours—the concept of time still hadn't been invented yet. On the battlefield, the farm boys brandished their cheap swords, the tree monsters molted, and the zombies whistled and catcalled for the half-elf to take off her hat and show off her large brain.

The battle lasted for twenty-four pages.

Act 2.5

This is where the author took a seven-year-long break before completing the next act.

Act 3

In the darkest moment of the battle (figuratively, not literally, since it was close to noontime), when the farm boys' sword arms grew tired, and the zombies were dangerously close to their union-mandated break, and the author was out of ideas as to how to resolve this conflict, a new threat emerged.

The Grim Lord of the Dark Murkiness, the infamous Duke of Ex Machina rode onto the battlefield at the head of an army of evil henchmen.

The duke was once an accountant named Bob who found a magic portal to a fantasy land. The author spent a considerable amount of time figuring out his backstory, but chose not to share it with the readers, so he could feel smug and superior to them in his knowledge.

The duke didn't care about the color of the handkerchief, but he was very interested in subjugating and/or slaughtering both the fiefdom of Truism and the earldom of Cliché because he was unspeakably evil (probably due to his prolonged exposure to tax forms.)

And so it came to be that the two foes banded together against a common enemy. The farm boys fought the henchmen, and the zombies fought the henchmen, and the tree monsters stood there and provided comfortable shade for everyone to fight in.

The evil henchmen were winning, and with only a few minutes left in the battle, it was dark tidings for the combined forces of the baron and the earl. (Figuratively, not literally, since it was still close to noontime.) But then the werewolf dodged the scimitar-wielding henchmen, gave wide berth to the spear-wielding henchmen, lifted his leg briefly to mark one of the tree monsters as his territory, finally ran up to the duke, who was riding atop a corrupted unicorn, and bit him on the shin.

The duke yelped in an un-villain-like fashion and rode off in search of a tetanus shot, and also to leave a passive-aggressive review of the battle on Yelp. (Two stars. Wouldn't recommend.) The evil henchmen shrugged, packed away their scimitars and spears, and left.

There was much rejoicing, and the earl and the baron hugged each other and apologized for their earlier behavior.

"I can absolutely see how lime could appear more yellow than green," admitted the earl. "It's not worth arguing over. What's important is that it's a fine handkerchief, and it goes so well with your fuchsia cravat."

The baron's eyes narrowed and he disengaged from the hug, already plotting retaliation for this grievous insult to his favorite necktie.

Which, of course, is the subject of the sequel.

This story originally appeared in the *Upside Down: Inverted Tropes in Storytelling* anthology from Apex Publications.

As you will undoubtedly glean from the humorous stories included in this book, I revel in subverting tropes. Epic fantasy has such a rich vein of tropes for me to mine, I could have probably written a much longer story—but then the idea of squeezing an epic fantasy parody into flash fiction length (thus, a mini epic) was one of the ideas that appealed to me. Although the story was not written specifically for the *Upside Down* submissions call, when the anthology was announced I knew it was a good fit. Fortunately, editors Jaym Gates and Monica Valentinelli agreed.

When I was writing this story, I was on somewhat of a *The New Yorker* kick. They occasionally publish funny science fiction and fantasy stories, and I was reading widely for some of my reprint anthologies. I found myself enjoying many of those stories—the sort of humor *The New Yorker* tended to go for was more Woody Allen or Larry David than Pratchett or Brown—but I enjoyed it. I tried to emulate some of that quirky style in writing "Noun of Nouns," though I'm not sure how much of that comes through in the final, polished version.

WHOM HE MAY DEVOUR

L ydia watched Ahad play the guitar. He leaned against a boulder, eyes shut, his face positioned to catch the last warm rays of the setting sun. His long, slender fingers caressed the strings, producing a slow, haunting melody. The music almost made his company tolerable.

She was only there because Grandmother had asked her to study this stranger, to get close, to discover what the crew of his starship was up to. Ahad seemed to be so at peace. Despite his unusual clothes and exotic facial features, he wasn't so different from the local boys. Was he really to blame for his people's sins? If one never knew the Lord's law, was it a sin for them to break it? Then again, the star travelers learned about the True Path in the weeks since they had arrived, and they hadn't changed their ways.

Lydia stared at the implant on Ahad's left temple, only partially covered by his dark hair. The devil would claim him in the afterlife for that alone. Against her better judgment, she was fascinated by it. When she shifted for a better look, Ahad opened his eyes at the sound of her moving. He smiled at her.

"That tune is very old, from back when everyone lived on the same planet," said Ahad. "Did you like it?"

Was he intentionally reminding her of her own people's past

sins, of the time when they, too, used technology and crossed the stars to come to this world? She let the comment slide. "I liked it very much. It's impressive, how many melodies you have memorized."

Ahad chuckled. "Memorized? That would be a lot of work." He pointed at his temple. "I can access the note sheets for every piece of music ever written, through the Link."

This time Lydia frowned, and cast her eyes downward. In a small way, she wanted to believe that Ahad's only sin was that of ignorance. But she knew that it was the devil, seeking yet another way to sow doubt in her heart.

"I'm sorry," Ahad said, when he saw her expression. "I know the Link is a sensitive subject for your people. I didn't mean to make you uncomfortable. Let me make it up to you? I'll play you a tune that my father taught me. I remember that one without the Link, honest."

Father. Lydia looked at the sun, which was halfway behind the mountains by then.

"I'm sorry," she called out, as she scrambled to her feet. "I'm very late. Tomorrow?"

She dashed toward the village.

"Tomorrow, then," Ahad called after her.

LYDIA BURST INTO the house, panting from the mile-long run, her heart pounding and trying to jump out of her chest. The rest of the family was already there, her parents and brother seated around the table, all of them glaring at her as she stumbled inside. Despite her best efforts, she was late to the evening prayer. Again.

How long did she make them wait? Surely it couldn't have been more than ten or fifteen minutes. "I'm sorry," she stammered.

Mother frowned. "You were with that space boy again, weren't you?"

Lydia nodded, and felt her face turning red.

"The two of you shouldn't spend so much time alone," Mother

said. "It's inappropriate."

"Mother!" Lydia struggled to control her breathing. "It's nothing like that. All we do is play music together."

"He's an abomination." Ian, her older brother, slammed his palm against the polished wood of the table. "His people fly through space, puncturing the flesh of God. He has machine parts grafted into his body. And you can't possibly pretend that you don't notice the way he looks at you."

"Stop." Father spoke softly, secure in the knowledge that he wouldn't be interrupted or contradicted. "Raised voices and accusations have no room at the prayer table." He looked at Ian, and quoted scripture. "Anger is one of the tools the devil uses, as he roams the world, seeking whom he may devour."

Ian nodded. He took deep breaths to try and calm himself as his father commanded.

"The visitors from another world are strayed from the True Path, much like the ancestors," said Father. "In their folly they have denied themselves paradise. We must take care not to become tainted by their sins."

Father turned to Lydia. "I fear that in your zeal to spy on the space travelers you've become too close with this young man. You are not to spend time with him anymore."

"Yes, Father." Lydia's voice trembled a little.

"Tomorrow you will go to the caves and visit with Grandmother," said Father.

Lydia nodded. Father was wise, and he was tempering the harshness of his decree. Spending time with the ancestors was considered a penance, almost a punishment, but a hike to the caves was better than working the fields, and besides, she liked Grandmother. She was almost certain Father and Mother liked her, too, even if no one would admit it out loud.

"Join us, so that we may begin," said Father.

Lydia took her seat at the table. Her family linked hands and began the evening prayer.

IN THE MORNING, Lydia set off to visit Grandmother.

Using a wax candle to light the way, she traversed deep into the caves, to where the ancestors were hidden, until she reached the thick steel doors. She entered the combination on the keypad while muttering a prayer, asking the Lord to forgive this small sin. Then she was inside the bunker, cave walls covered by ceramic panels, which emitted a dim artificial glow, lighting the corridor. She blew out the candle and headed forward.

As soon as Lydia walked into the meeting room, a holographic image of a woman in her sixties appeared. She wore outlandish clothing and rimmed glasses. Her hair was cut short and dyed bright red, with strands of purple mixed in. She flashed a kindly smile. "Hey, kiddo."

"Hi, Grandmother," said Lydia.

This woman wasn't her real grandmother, of course. She was a distant relative, many generations removed.

Centuries ago, Lydia's ancestors arrived on this world from another planet, just like Ahad's people had done recently. The ancestors came for the precious metals that were plentiful in the mountains. But less than a year later, the fledgling colony became afflicted by a terrible sickness. People and livestock began dying. Despite all of their science and technology, the settlers found no cure. The entire colony would have been wiped out within weeks.

It was then that the Lord appeared in a vision to Julian Li, one of the leaders of the colony. The plague was a punishment, and the Lord instructed him to teach the settlers the True Path. They were to abandon technology, which was the devil's invention, and to live in harmony with the land. Those who repented would be spared, Julian said—the believers would survive this plague.

Julian's followers destroyed the spaceship. It was both a gesture of their obedience of the Lord's decree and a way to ensure that this sickness would not spread to other humans across the stars. But not everyone heeded the Lord's warning. A few people, fearful for their lives and lacking faith, found another solution. They couldn't save their bodies from the plague, so they transferred their minds into a computer instead.

They were trapped there still, their souls having escaped hell, but unable to ever reach paradise. The computer was their purgatory. All they could do was project images of themselves within the confines of their bunker deep within the caves.

But even computers wouldn't last forever. Machines needed repair and maintenance. Julian Li decreed that it was the responsibility of the faithful to help their strayed brethren. A small sin in order to help the unfortunate souls trapped in the metal box. A sin, Julian said, canceled out by the selflessness of the act.

And so it was for centuries. Although Lydia's people didn't understand the technology involved, they performed the physical tasks to keep the computer running, as instructed by one of the disembodied ancestors.

Everyone in Lydia's community made an occasional trip to the caves, to speak to whichever one of the ancestors was their distant relation. Although the woman who manifested herself now wasn't Lydia's immediate family, she might as well have been. She appeared to Lydia and her parents and grandparents before her, acting as a sounding board, helping with relationship problems and other small bits of advice. Lydia grew up around Grandmother, always there to offer guidance, unchanging, with that glint in her eyes, as though she was laughing at a private joke she was remembering from earlier.

Lydia told Grandmother about the reason for her visit.

"I get where your dad's coming from, kiddo," said Grandmother. "It won't be long until the strangers' ship leaves. He doesn't want you to be heartbroken when they do, and neither do I."

"I don't love him, Grandmother. I'm just doing what you asked."

"Don't love him, eh?" Grandmother raised her eyebrow. "At your age, do you truly know the difference?"

"I am seventeen already, not a child! We can't all be a thousand years old, like you."

"Ha! I will have you know I'm not a day older than 687. But enough about me. Tell me about this boy. Has he revealed anything we didn't already know?"

"Not really. He mostly talks about music and other harmless things." Lydia tilted her head. "Grandma, why don't you want to meet them? Why did you ask us to keep your existence a secret from the newcomers?"

"We can't know what's in their hearts, kiddo. What if they decide to destroy us, or take us away? Your people wouldn't be able to stop them. No, it's best that they never even know we're here."

They talked for a long time. Grandmother was always such a good listener, and she knew exactly when to ask a prodding question and when to just let Lydia speak. Finally, Lydia broached the subject that had been nagging her for days.

"Why does everyone dislike the newcomers so much? Sure, they've strayed from the Path, but so have the ancestors, and we're taught to love and honor you despite this. I've been watching carefully; the visitors haven't done anything wrong, haven't disrupted our way of life."

Grandmother stroked her chin, the little smile never quite leaving her face.

"You ask a difficult question," she said. "I guess the short answer is, we're family. We look out for each other, and love each other not because of our differences, but despite them. These new people are strangers, and now that they are here, more could follow. The best course of action is to show them nothing of value, to flaunt a hostile attitude in order to drive the message home that they aren't wanted. With any luck, they will muddle about a little longer, then deem this planet not worth their time and attention, and move on."

As Lydia was getting ready to leave, Grandmother said, "Obey your father and keep away from that boy, but keep an eye on the newcomers still. Tell me if you learn anything new."

Lydia promised that she would.

LYDIA AVOIDED AHAD, just like Father said. She stayed away from their usual meeting place, and he couldn't come to the village—the elders made it clear that the visitors weren't welcome, and the ship's captain ordered her crew to heed their wishes.

Lydia and several other young women were picking berries when she saw Ahad at the edge of the field, trying to wave her over. When she ignored him, Ahad ran to her across the field, almost trampling several of the carefully cultivated bushes. Reluctantly, she walked toward him, leaving her friends behind.

"Are you all right?" asked Ahad. "I've been waiting at our tree every day for the last two weeks, but you never came."

"I'm not permitted to talk to you anymore," she said. "You should leave, before both of us get in trouble."

Ahad chewed his lip as he processed the news. "That's why I came to see you," he said. "We're leaving."

Grandmother was right. The devil had failed to tempt anyone to sin by bringing this spaceship, and it was finally going away. "Safe journey," she said, and turned to leave.

"Wait," said Ahad. "Come with me?"

"What? Are you insane?"

"I spoke to the captain and she said she would allow it, if you wanted to come with me. There are so many amazing things to see and do out there, Lydia. So much more than this…prehistoric existence of yours. You aren't like the others; you're smart, inquisitive… you'd love it out there." Ahad shuffled from foot to foot. "Besides, I can't stand the thought of not seeing you for almost a year."

Lydia's eyes narrowed. "What happens in a year?"

"A much bigger expedition is going to come back. They found a huge mother lode of precious minerals in the mountains. Must've been why your people settled here in the first place. If you want, we can both return on that ship."

Her mind raced. The visitors would be coming back, in greater numbers. They would be digging in the mountains, not far from where the caves were.

Grandmother would know what to do.

"I have to go," she stammered.

She ran toward the caves. Ahad called after her, tried to say something else, but she couldn't hear him.

"I WAS AFRAID this might happen," said Grandmother. "I suppose it was too much to hope that they wouldn't find the ores. After all, we found them easily enough, back in my day."

"I fear it will only be a matter of time until they discover your caves after they return," said Lydia.

"It's sweet of you to be concerned for us, kiddo," said Grandmother. "But the danger is far worse than that. There is a long and shameful history of something called 'colonialism' dating all the way back to when humans all lived on the same planet."

Lydia pondered the unfamiliar word. "What does that mean?"

For the first time ever, Grandmother looked somber, the ever-present smirk gone from her lips. "It means things never work out well for the natives when the more technologically advanced set-tlers decide to move in. They will assimilate you at best, or eradi-cate you at worst. If this spaceship is allowed to return to its home world, that could be the end of the people of the True Path."

Lydia shivered at the prospect. "There must be something we can do!"

"There is," said Grandmother, after a brief moment of hesita-tion, "but I don't know if I can ask this of you."

LYDIA CARESSED THE egg-shaped device the size of a child's fist. Its smooth metal surface felt strange and unnatural to her fingers. She could hardly believe that something this small was powerful enough to destroy a spaceship. It was a wicked weapon from the pre-Path days. Lydia had followed Grandmother's instructions to find it stored in one of the rooms of the bunker.

When Grandmother asked her to sneak a bomb onboard, Lydia was horrified. How could she, a devout woman, commit the terrible sin of murder? Multiple murders—Grandmother explained that the device would become activated when it sensed the ship's acceleration and destroy it minutes after it lifted off, setting off an explosion that would turn the vessel into a giant fireball.

It was for the good of the community, Grandmother said. Five lives would be lost in order to save her family, her friends, and her village. It was just like using technology to help maintain the ancestors' computer—a sin canceled out by the righteous intention.

And then there was the matter of the sickness. Grandmother said that the visitors were going to unknowingly carry it back to their home world. While Lydia and others were descended from people who survived the plague, the visitors shared no such immunity. Deaths of the five of them could save countless thousands on their world from becoming infected.

Still, she wasn't entirely certain that she would be able to do this, when the time came.

She hid the egg bomb deep in her pocket and walked toward the ship.

Once there, she asked for Ahad, and he was promptly summoned. He beamed at her, delighted at her decision to join him. Whatever his sins, his feelings for her were obviously genuine. It made Lydia feel even more guilty over what she was about to do.

"Come, I will introduce you to the captain," said Ahad, "and then I must get back to work. There is so much to do before we leave tomorrow."

Lydia nodded. This gave her enough time to plant the bomb and get out.

The captain was a tall, middle-aged woman named Jean. She shook Lydia's hand firmly, and something in her assured manner reminded Lydia of Grandmother.

"Glad to have you join us, Lydia," she said. "Ahad has talked everyone's ears off about you." The Captain waved over one of her men. "The doc will have you outfitted with the Link."

Lydia was repulsed at the thought of a machine being grafted into her body. "I don't want a Link," she said meekly. "Thank you."

"Nonsense," said the captain. "Everything on the ship is controlled via the Link. You won't even be able to unlock your cabin door without it." The captain placed a hand on her shoulder. "Don't worry," she added. "It's a quick procedure, and practically painless. You'll thank us afterward."

The doctor ushered her into a small room and instructed her to lie down on a cot. Lydia felt trapped in this unnatural metal vessel, her senses protesting against the unfamiliar scents, sounds and sights that were overwhelming her. She must find a way to stall, to avoid the procedure, and then to plant her bomb and escape the ship. But if what the Captain said was true and even the doors around here wouldn't open without the infernal device, what hope did she have of succeeding without it?

Violating her body with the implant would mean she could never hope to enter paradise. Then again, she was about to commit mass murder. The devil would have her, either way. She was ready to sacrifice herself for the good of her people.

Lydia climbed onto the cot and allowed the doctor to stab a very thin needle into her arm.

LYDIA WOKE UP to a whisper of a thousand voices inside of her head.

Without opening her eyes, she reached for her temple and felt the metal abomination that protruded above her ear. She was just like one of the visitors now. She wondered how long she'd been asleep, whether the ship was still on the ground or if it was too late and she was hurtling through space, far away from home.

A louder voice emerged from the cacophony in her head, informing her that it was just after four o'clock past midnight. The ship would be lifting off in the morning.

She shivered. The devil had found its way into her mind. Could the others hear her thoughts, learn of her intention through the Link? It assured her that they could not, and she had no choice but to believe it. She prayed that once she got off the ship, the voices would cease.

She stumbled off the cot, checked her pocket and breathed a sigh of relief. The bomb was still there. No one on the ship thought to search the simple, backwater native. She explored the room, opening compartments until she found a perfect hiding place for the bomb. She slid it under some medical supplies and carefully closed the drawer. No one should discover it in time. She hesitated. Was she really willing to end five lives? On an impulse, she asked the Link about colonialism.

The Link showed her many things, but among them were images of slave ships sailing toward a newly discovered continent and of smallpox-ridden blankets being offered to the unsuspecting natives. It showed her images of various alien races, subjugated and abused by the human colonists. The strong came and took what they wanted, without regard for the lives of the less advanced peoples who happened to be in their way. Lydia couldn't let her own community share that fate.

She willed the cabin door open. She feared that she might be trapped without knowing how to operate the Link, but apparently just thinking her command was enough. The door slid open silently, releasing her into the corridor. She wondered how to get off the ship, and the Link showed her. She tiptoed through the ship, slumbering but never silent, the strange sounds of its engines melding with the Link's whispers inside her head.

The crew was asleep. No one challenged her as she slipped away into the night.

THE DEVIL TEMPTED her constantly through the Link.

How could she resist? Whatever question she thought of, the gadget delivered the answer right into her mind. The Link taught her how to shut off the whispers—the multitude of modes which were operating all at once. It also taught her how to enter privacy mode—shutting off all communication from other Links and concealing her location. All she had to do now was hide and wait for liftoff.

Once Lydia was reasonably certain that the visitors couldn't track her through the Link, she headed for the caves. She thought of going home, but wasn't yet prepared to face the opprobrium from her community.

She'd given up her place in paradise in order to save them all, but she knew that she would also be giving up so much more. Her friends would abandon her. She wouldn't get married. Her family would tolerate her presence, but only just.

Lydia felt sorry for herself, then felt ashamed, because while her future might not be a pleasant one, she would get to have a future, unlike the five strangers she'd condemned to death with her actions.

As she welcomed the dawn, the devil continued to tempt her. She could save them still. All it would take was activating the Link and reaching out to Ahad or to Captain Jean, and convincing them to delay the launch. Lydia wrapped her jacket closer around herself in the pre-morning cold, and fought the temptation.

When the spaceship roared to life and launched to the heavens, when she heard a great boom moments later, and dozens of falling red comets could be seen in the sky despite fledgling daylight, it was almost a relief.

LYDIA HEADED INTO the caves. There was a supply of candles stored near the entrance, but she discovered that with the Link she didn't need them. The gadget was able to see in the dark and project the image of her surroundings into her mind as though she were strolling through the sunlit valley in midday.

A live network detected, whispered the Link, once Lydia entered the ancestors' bunker. *Do you wish to absorb its data?*

A live network? It must've meant the computer that housed the ancients. What sort of secrets did they keep, throughout the centuries? Lydia couldn't resist the temptation. She allowed the Link to proceed, and a nearly infinite stream of information flowed into her mind.

She stopped, stunned. She leaned against the wall, then slid down onto the ground and sobbed while hugging herself. She remained there for a very long time, trying to process the ways in which her world had changed, desperately struggling to come to terms with her new reality. And after the initial shock had somewhat faded, after her tears dried up and her hands stopped shaking, all that was left was rage.

She stormed into the room that housed the holographic projector. When Grandmother's smiling avatar appeared, she stared it square in the eye.

"How could you?" Lydia shouted. "How could you do this to us?"

Grandmother frowned. "Do what, kiddo?"

"Lie to us. Manipulate us into being little more than servants to your precious computer. Screw up countless generations of real people, so your digital shadows can continue their pointless existence inside a tin box!"

Grandmother stared at her, mouth agape. "How?"

"I know everything now," said Lydia. "You *invented* the True Path to manipulate the colonists into quietly waiting for death while a handful of you made arrangements to upload your mind patterns when you became infected. But that wasn't enough for you. You preyed on the survivors, forcing a rigid lifestyle that would keep the colony stagnant and ignorant, and would keep the people nearby so they could perform the maintenance tasks on your orders."

"We kept your society stable, safe, and coherent," said Grandmother. "You don't know war or serious crime."

"We also don't know science or medicine. You've kept that away from us. My real grandmother might still be alive if she had access to the kind of treatments your people knew of six hundred years ago. How many more might have lived longer, happier lives?"

"You've known me your entire life, Lydia," Grandmother said earnestly. "Do you truly think me a monster?"

Lydia paced the small room as she spoke. "The devil roams the world seeking whom he may devour. He always tempts, subverts, and whispers lies into people's ears to achieve his purpose, but on his own he's powerless to do anything." She advanced on the hologram until she was face to face with Grandmother. "You are that devil. You have wormed your way into our hearts, manipulating us through deceit and a made-up faith. The True Path teaches us to exorcise the devil from our hearts and minds. Who knew it would be as easy as flipping the off switch?"

"You can't mean that!" Grandmother said. "If you turn off the machine, all of us will die. Is that what you really want?"

Her image flickered and changed to a kindly old man. Then a plump woman in her late forties. It changed again and again.

"There are twelve of us inside the computer," said Grandmother's voice. "We've known each member of your community since birth; we're grandparents to every family, loved by our distant grandchildren. Would you truly do this to us, and to them? We may have lost our bodies to the plague, but our minds remain. We wish to live, to survive, as much as anyone else. All we've ever done was out of necessity, trying to find a way to go on."

Grandmother's image returned and she continued to speak. "Do you truly think your community would ever forgive you? And could you go on with twelve more deaths on your conscience?"

"No," said Lydia. "But the devil has taught me that it's all right to commit a sin, so long as it's for the greater good."

She snapped the holographic projector off its perch in the corner of the room and smashed it against the ground. Grandmother's image and voice disappeared. Then she walked out of the meeting room and into the chamber that housed the computer itself.

Grandmother was wrong if she thought that Lydia didn't have it in her to turn off the computer. But death wasn't the worst fate she could imagine for the ancestors. Lydia used her Link to help her deactivate all the cameras and sensors in the bunker, one by one.

The ancestors would continue to exist until their computer would break down on its own. But they could no longer poison the people's minds, or even learn of anything happening inside the bunker. All they had left for the rest of their digital lives was each other.

Hungry and miserable, Lydia sat alone in the room next to the computer. At some point, she would have to go back home.

They would see her Link, and they would find the holographic projector smashed on the ground of the bunker and the ancestors gone, and they would draw conclusions. Even with all the information in the world available to her through the Link, she didn't know what they would do to her after that. But she'd saved her people twice in one day, even if none of them would ever know it, and the knowledge of that would have to be enough to get through whatever came next.

Lydia began a long trek back to the village.

This story was originally published in *Nautilus*.

A number of my stories comment on religion in various ways. In the title story of this collection, the characters' faith is imperfect, but it is a source of strength and comfort for them. In this story, faith is subverted through cold calculation by the elders who escaped into the digital world. The title is from the King James Bible: "Be sober, be vigilant; because your adversary the devil, as a roaring lion, walketh about, seeking whom he may devour." (Peter 5:8)

I'm especially proud of the fact that this story manages to comment on a lot of touchy subjects (religion, terrorism, imperialism) without being overly preachy.

It was a 2017 finalist for the Canopus Award for Excellence in Interstellar Fiction, an award administered by 100 Year Starship, a think tank founded by Dr. Mae Jemison, the first woman of color astronaut. Its ambitious goal is to help figure out how humanity can reach the stars within the next century. Naturally, I was deeply honored to be recognized by them for two of my stories—this one, and "The Race for Arcadia," which closes out this book.

LETTING GO

Her expression tells you everything even before she speaks, and your world comes undone.

Then she confirms it: she tells you that her mission is a go. She is so excited, her face is radiant with possibility, and her eyes sparkle with the light of distant stars. You manage to smile, and it is the hardest thing you've ever had to endure.

Love requires many sacrifices, which you offer gladly and without hesitation. The most difficult among them, the one that shatters your heart into a million aching shards, is letting go.

She will be gone for sixteen years, but only two years will have passed aboard the ship. When she returns to Earth, she will be in her early thirties. Even if her love for you survives a two-year journey, how can it possibly endure the homecoming? When she returns, you will be biologically twenty years her senior.

Four months later you say goodbye. She tells you that it's going to be all right. You try your best to believe her. You hug her fiercely and inhale her favorite perfume, trying to commit this moment to memory, from the way her long hair feels under your fingertips to the smell of lilac and jasmine. And then you let go.

The next year is a string of smaller sacrifices. You leave your job at the university because they won't fund your research. You work eighteen hours a day, and live off your savings. In the end, it's all worth it.

You prove that time travel is possible, but only going forward. Because it amuses you and—more importantly—because you know it would make her laugh, you design the time machine prototype to look like a blue phone booth.

It will take years to calibrate the equipment to allow for jumps to a precise date. As is, you can travel approximately fifteen years into the future. The exact date doesn't matter. You can be together again. You imagine the two of you on the cover of *Nature*, the cover of *Time*. The first time traveler and the first interstellar astronaut: the power couple of science, and still young enough to reap the rewards of your success.

You do your best to settle all your affairs in the way only a dying person might. You make certain that the house is kept within your family; that the lab remains undisturbed until you return.

There are more sacrifices. You say goodbye to your elderly parents, knowing that it's likely the last time you'll see them. You will not get to watch your twelve-year-old nephew grow up. All this for a leap of faith, a ride forward in time that's as likely to work as it is to kill you. It's a chance you take gladly, for her.

The ride is anticlimactic. You touch the screen to activate the machine, and it whirrs to life, but you feel nothing. It's only when you open the door that you know it worked.

Everything in your basement lab looks and feels disused. The papers on your desk are yellowed with age. Your equipment has been boxed up and is stored in the corner. Some of your parents' old furniture takes up much of the room. An old mattress is propped up against the wall by a baby crib. Your lab has become a storage room.

You hear footsteps on the floor above.

"Hello?" you call out, and a man in his thirties comes downstairs. You barely recognize your nephew.

He recognizes you, too.

"Oh my God, we thought you were dead! It's been twenty years." He rushes over.

Your invention overshot its target by five years, but it worked!

You blurt out the only question that matters.

He avoids eye contact as he tells you that she returned safely. Then he hugs you.

You break the embrace as soon as it's polite to do so. You look closer, noting his wedding band, and boxes of diapers in the corner. All you can think about is the faint scent of lilac and jasmine on the collar of his shirt.

When he offers to call her downstairs, you stop him.

Sixteen years may not be too long to wait for your lover to return, but four years is time enough to mourn when you think they're dead. And your nephew, who grew up to look a lot like you, would have been there to console her.

Your voice cracks as you make him promise to never tell her you were here.

You love her too much to make her doubt or even regret her choices. So you let her go, one last time.

Then you get back into the time machine and journey forward, as far as it'll take you.

This story originally appeared in *Daily Science Fiction*.

I've written time travel stories and I've written time dilation stories, but this is the first time I managed to combine the two. The theme of loving someone enough to place their happiness above your own is a very powerful one, and I hope I did it justice with this flash.

THE FIDDLE GAME

T hey say you can't con an honest man, but that isn't true. It is a self-deception ordinary people invented to feel better about themselves. Conning an honest man is easy because he isn't devious or suspicious by nature. What's nearly impossible is to con another grifter.

I recognized the scam the moment the kid who'd ordered scrambled eggs and hash finished his food, walked up, and plopped a violin case on my counter. He was gangly, barely out of his teens, and had that look of being smug but trying to hide it about him.

"I'm terribly sorry," he said. "I seem to have left my wallet at home. I live on Tyson Street, so I'll run and get it, and come back to pay my tab. Fifteen minutes, tops." The kid flashed me his best smile. "Here, you can hang on to my violin as collateral." He opened the case, revealing the instrument within.

I ignored the violin and looked the kid up and down instead. Aside from an ugly tattoo on his arm that he'll probably live to regret in a decade, I found nothing of note. The kid was ordinary. Mundane. None of the charms and talismans I'd painstakingly placed around the diner were set off by his arrival. Ergo, he possessed no magic and was apparently attempting to challenge me armed with his wits alone, a duel to which he arrived supremely underprepared.

The little punk was trying to run the Fiddle Game on me. That's the oldest scam in the book, but still good enough to work on most people in this backwater town.

He could never have anticipated that the balding, overweight diner proprietor he pegged for an easy mark was once known as Maurice the Ghost, the legendary art thief and confidence trickster, wanted by an alphabet soup of law enforcement agencies around the world. Wanted, but never caught.

I was equal parts irritated and amused, and I didn't want to draw attention to my cover by appearing a little too sharp. Toward the end of my illustrious career I had stolen from Freddy the Mace. The law enforcement may have given up by now, but his people were still looking for me after all these years, because there is no statute of limitations on ripping off psychopath gangsters.

So I played the part of a rube. I kept my jaw slack and my gaze unfocused as I nodded. "Sure, kid. Go get your wallet."

As he walked away, I scanned the diner for faces I didn't recognize, trying to figure out who his accomplice would be. The man with a scar on his cheek drinking coffee in the corner booth? The comely brunette who'd ordered a stack of pancakes and an orange juice? They were all ordinary and boring. No magic user other than me would be caught dead in this flyover craphole of a town anyway, and that's just how I liked it.

I won't lie, after a short but glamorous career in liberating nice things from not-so-nice people, living the life of a small-town diner owner sucked big time. But I didn't dare make any waves. When I stole from Freddy, I believed him to be just another Brooklyn gangster with the life expectancy of an incandescent light-bulb and an IQ to match. I couldn't have known that he was a powerful wizard, not keen to advertise his magic or his intellect. He steamrolled the competition, and eventually became one of the most powerful mobsters on the East Coast.

By now the amount of money I stole from him was a mere pittance to Freddy, but he was not the forgiving type. So until some even deadlier rival took him out, I remained hidden in Midwestern purgatory. And just in case he ever found me, I spent a fortune on top-shelf arcane protections. It would be easier for an ordinary burglar to break into Fort Knox than for another wizard to enter the diner and cause me harm.

I scanned the crowd, secure in the knowledge that the accomplice, just like the kid, was merely mundane. My money was on the man with the scar, but he didn't so much as look up from his coffee mug. Instead, it turned out to be the wrinkled old man, who shuffled up to the counter as soon as the door shut behind his partner.

"I couldn't help overhearing your conversation," he said. "Would you mind if I took a closer look at that violin? I'm an antique vendor by trade, and when that young man opened the case, I thought his violin might be worth a bit of money."

Neither of these jokers was going to win awards for their acting, but I had to give them points for sticking to the script, and also for using an actual violin in the Fiddle Game. I kept a straight face as I passed the case to the old geezer.

He made a show of examining the violin, clucking his tongue and muttering to himself. I let him be and took a breakfast order from another customer. When I passed the note to the cook in the back and turned my attention back to the counter, my would-be scammer held out a napkin with a phone number scrawled across it.

"Would you pass this along to the young man? I'll pay him five hundred for the violin, if he wants to sell."

"You got it, bub." I shoved the napkin into my pocket. Amateur hour! The duo was too cheap to print out fake business cards.

The old man paid his bill and split.

The Fiddle Game relies on greed. The grifters hope that the mark will be tempted to turn a profit and offer to buy the fiddle—or whatever item they're hawking—from the original owner. The negotiated price might only be a fraction of its supposed value, but it is still way more than the cheap piece of junk is actually worth. It's only after the original grifter leaves with the money that the mark is going to learn that the phone number on that napkin is fake.

It's a safe, reliable con. Even if the mark isn't tempted, the grifters are only out the price of scrambled eggs and some coffee. Which is exactly how it was going to go down this time, until I happened to take a closer look at the violin sitting in the still-open case on my counter.

The fiddle looked old. Really old. I took it out of the case and used a tiny bit of magic to probe the instrument as my fingers caressed the seasoned wood of the garland. It felt good to use my power again, even if it was only for a few seconds. The ability to detect the true nature of objects was perfect to supplement the skills of a world-class art thief, but it was never a very powerful magic when compared to what someone like Freddy could do. On the plus side, I felt confident my arcane protections were sufficient to disguise such a minor spell.

The magic confirmed my estimate. The violin was made in the late seventeenth century. It wasn't a Stradivarius or anything, but it was worth at least five figures. Even if my magic had somehow failed me, and it was a replica created by a forger brilliant enough to fool someone like me, that would still make it worth far more than five Benjamins.

How the hell did this pair of jokers get their hands on a genuine antique? I was still examining it when the younger grifter returned with his wallet.

"Listen, kid, this is a pretty nice instrument. Where did you get it?"

"It was my grandfather's. It's old, but the sound's great."

Grandfather's my foot. The scammers probably picked it up for a couple of bucks at an estate sale.

I didn't need the money or the trouble. But I was annoyed at being pegged for an easy mark, and after twenty years of hiding from the authorities and from Freddy's goons, I was bored. Turning the tables on these chums was probably going to be the most interesting thing that happened to me that year.

"Wanna sell it? I'll give you a hundred bucks."

The kid licked his lips. "A hundred and fifty?"

"A hundred, and breakfast is on me."

We shook hands.

My plan was to reach out to a fence I knew of in Madison. He didn't know me from back in the day, wasn't a wizard, had no apparent connections to Freddy and his people, and because he mostly dealt with ill-gotten gains, I could expect him to be discreet. He would pay a fraction of the violin's worth, of course, but it was well worth the extra security. I was going to call him right after the lunch rush, but I never got the chance.

The feds arrived only a few hours later. They came out of nowhere, swarming the diner and scaring the bejeebers out of my customers. Tens of thousands of dollars' worth of arcane protections were useless against Glocks and Kevlar vests.

"How did you find me?" I asked, after they read me my rights.

"An anonymous tip," said the special agent in charge. He looked like he'd just eaten the canary and was still burping up feathers. He'd get a promotion for finding me, and he knew it, even if he couldn't make the charges stick.

"What exactly are you charging me with?" I asked. "I've lived here for over twenty years. The statute of limitations on anything I could possibly be accused of has long expired."

The fed's smile widened. "You've had a good run, Maurice. The statute of limitations has indeed run out on most of your crimes," he patted the nylon case, "but this violin was stolen from a museum in Prague last week. And here we thought the Ghost had retired ages ago."

It's difficult to con a fellow grifter. But it's not impossible.

As they led me out of the diner and away from all of my protections in handcuffs, the man with the scar who had been nursing his coffee at the corner booth all morning brushed up against me.

"Freddy the Mace sends his regards," he whispered.

This story originally appeared in *Orson Scott Card's Intergalactic Medicine Show.*

I'm a longtime fan of movies and TV shows about con artists. *The Grifters, Leverage,* you name it. For years I've had this idea bouncing in my head for a novel about humans running amok in the galaxy that pretty much sees them the way we see the Ferengi, running cons on unsuspecting aliens who aren't used to our general level of deviousness. The opening paragraph of this story was to be the opening paragraph of the novel. But then the idea for this story took hold of me and stole (conned?) the opening from the yet-to-be-written book.

But the cool thing about short stories and novels is that they're such different beasts, no one really minds if a few lines (or even the entire short story) become recycled into a full-length book. So I might write that novel and use that opening again one day. If Freddy the Mace doesn't get me first.

THE SEVEN HABITS OF HIGHLY EFFECTIVE MONSTERS

I t isn't easy being green, scaly, or abominable these days. Humanity turned the tables on the apex predators of the food chain, and has been exterminating us with extreme prejudice.

We're still faster and stronger than they are, but we're prone to defeat by bad judgment. Heed the lessons of our vanquished brethren; learn from their mistakes and remain successful, extant, and satiated.

1) Don't Rely on Henchmen

There's no denying that it's emotionally satisfying to be worshipped—or at least obeyed—by humans. However, there is little practical benefit. In the entire history of henchmen, cultists, minions, lackeys, and worshippers, one is hard-pressed to come up with a single paragon of effectiveness. Instead they tend to be slow, dim-witted, and clumsy.

At best, your followers might mildly inconvenience your adversary as he or she rampages through your lair or secret laboratory, Sharp Object of Destiny in hand. At worst, they might develop last-minute regrets and attempt to throw you down the nearest shaft.

So next time someone asks if you're a god, just eat them.

2) Heed the Warning Signs

Ignoring the obvious means you're just asking for trouble. For example, vampires and other beings highly allergic to Vitamin D are advised to steer clear of towns with the word "sunny" in their name. That's just common sense.

There are plenty of better targets, places with names that evoke gothic dread and despair. Names like Gloaming Creek, Murky Hallow, Gloomsburg, or Detroit.

3) Be Aware of Your Surroundings

Don't climb skyscrapers. There's little room to maneuver up there, and the position isn't defensible.

If your adversary is running away, they're almost certainly leading you into a trap.

Pre-plan your retreat. Always know the shortest route to the nearest sewer, secret passage, or inter-dimensional portal.

If retreat isn't an option, pretend to be their friend. A surprising number of humans will fall for a few sparkles and a tortured expression.

4) Practice Safe Invading

When invading alien planets, be sure that all your vaccinations are up to date.

Your mothership's operating system shouldn't be compatible with the latest in Earth's computer virus technology.

Whatever resources you seek on Earth (water, oxygen, landmass to terraform) are cheap and plentiful elsewhere in the universe.

If you've achieved interstellar flight, your robots are probably safer, smarter, and longer-lasting than human slave labor.

5) Mix it Up

Adjust your tactics to keep your nemeses guessing:

It's okay not to eat the lone black guy first. The rest of his party will never expect it if you start with someone else.

Stab your adversary in the middle of explaining your nefarious plan to them.

Don't place your calls from inside the house.

6) Hunt Safely

On average, few modern humans have access to silver bullets, pitchforks, or wooden stakes soaked in holy water. Improbably, the odds of anyone who encounters a monster possessing such items rise exponentially.

Always comport yourself as though everyone has access to the one thing that can pierce your otherwise-indestructible skin or body armor.

7) Reconsider

Even if you meticulously prepare your schemes and pay careful attention to the safety tips above, at the end of the day you must ask yourself: is it really worth it?

The most dangerous monster of all is man. For best results, avoid encounters at all costs.

This story originally appeared in *Daily Science Fiction.*

The title of this story popped into my head as I was driving to a local science fiction convention, and I worked out most of the "habits" by the time I got there. I arrived twenty minutes early for my first panel, and literally wrote the proto-version of this story on the back of the napkin while I waited for the panel to begin. Problem was, it was way too short. The entire story was only 150 words or so. I set it aside for a while as I pondered a way to add some meat to its bones without making it feel like any of the material was extraneous. Once I thought of enough horror and monster movie tropes to make fun of, the story grew to what I consider a reasonable flash length, and took the shape you see here today.

ISLANDS IN THE SARGASSO

They were all going to die.

Jason Stanger squeezed everything he could from his ship. His fingers hit the touch screens as though he were an angry pianist, hammering out Beethoven's Ninth on several unyielding keyboards at once. He was a very good pilot, and the *Pivot* was a very good ship, but no amount of skill could make up for the fact that the three Montevideo cartel spaceships pursuing him were faster, larger, and better armed.

The cartel enforcers were disciplined. They didn't fire yet. Torpedoes weren't cheap, and his pursuers knew they could afford to wait, to keep closing the distance until one of them got close enough to disintegrate his vessel with a single kill shot. But they were also from Earth: too sophisticated, too urbane to buy into frontier superstitions. And that's why Jason wouldn't die alone, not if he could keep them following him.

Taking his enemies with him would be a small enough consolation, but it would have to do. Jason grinned humorlessly as he steered his ship away from the sun and into the vast emptiness of Sargasso space.

By all rights he should have died six months ago. Back then he was a junkie, a man claimed so thoroughly by his addiction to Rust that he had lost everything: his job, his friends, even his will to go on. Nothing mattered to him so long as he could find a way to get high.

Commander Warren Jain had found him, gotten him cleaned up, given him a purpose. Jain's unit needed experienced pilots to fight the cartels and combat the spread of Rust across the solar system. Jason was eager to do his part. He knew the risks, accepted the danger. In the end, he had lived six months longer than he expected to, thanks to Jain. They had been good months.

Jason heard strange noises within the ship. Creaking, grating sounds that couldn't possibly be real. The video feeds turned to static one by one as the ship's instruments malfunctioned. Just as he had expected. It wouldn't be long until his pursuers began experiencing technical problems of their own. And then things would get much, much worse.

The navigation tableau had gone out. Jason piloted the ship by the stars, like the sailors of old who crossed the Atlantic with nothing to guide them but the constellations they could see on a clear night.

The Sargasso space surrounded the solar system. It began at 1260 AU from the sun and no one knew how far it extended outward. No one understood its physics, its nature, its origins. All Jason knew was that ships venturing too far into the Sargasso space didn't return. Although no astronomical instruments could detect any sort of anomaly, the Sargasso space kept humanity trapped in the solar system. A handful of expeditions that had tried to reach other stars lost their navigation and controls, and then their crews went insane, one by one, their screams transmitted across space, until there was only silence.

The cartel ships opened fire. With his instruments failing, Jason couldn't be sure whether they'd finally gotten close enough, or were panicking because their technology was betraying them, too. It must have been the latter; the shots went wide. No computerized targeting system could have made such a mistake.

Jason watched as the engines of one of the cartel ships cut out. It continued on its trajectory, no longer able to accelerate or maneuver but carried forward by the inertia. Minutes later his sensors ceased to function, claimed by the Sargasso. He was trapped inside the ship, unable to control it, unable to learn what was happening outside. Would one of the pursuing vessels destroy him or would he live long enough to be claimed by the madness of the Sargasso? Like Schrodinger's cat in a tin box, he was alive and dead at the same time.

Jason was afraid, and the fear fed his desire for Rust. The need for the drug was always there, like a dull toothache. A recovering heroin addict he met at a meeting told him it never fully goes away. Jason struggled against the urge.

Hours passed. He could hear things now, see things through the porthole. Islands in the Sargasso, with white beaches and lush greens set against the azure water. He could hear the waves splashing gently against the sand. Except none of it was real. There were no tropical islands in space. His ship didn't even have a porthole. The Sargasso was driving him mad.

His engines were dead, his ship drifting away from the solar system. And now he was losing his mind. Jason checked the cryogenic unit and saw that it was still functional. The unit could keep him alive in suspended animation for several months, long enough for Warren Jain to figure out how to save his life a second time, to send help.

Jason knew he was lying to himself, knew there was no way for his commander to save him this time. Even so, clinging to a tiny sliver of hope was a better way to go than any of the alternatives.

Jason climbed into the unit.

JASON WAS SURPRISED to wake up again. It was a gradual, difficult awakening which felt like climbing up from a deep dark mine shaft. He could almost feel the gears of his mind beginning to grind again, beginning to process information and to remember.

He could feel his longing for Rust, too. It was back seemingly even before he fully returned to consciousness.

He waited a full minute until he dared open his eyes. The room he was in was small but well-lit, and was definitely not aboard the *Pivot*. He tried to sit up, his body aching in protest.

"Ah, you're awake."

The voice sounded strange, as if it were recorded on an ancient gramophone and played back with all the squeaks and skips that entailed. Jason turned and found the source of the voice even stranger.

The creature sitting by his bedside was roughly four feet tall and looked like an upright tortoise in a purplish shell.

Jason tried to speak, but only managed a croak. He coughed, trying to clear his throat. The strange creature tilted its head and looked at him. Jason considered the possibility that he was still in the Sargasso and that his hallucinations were getting worse. He finally managed to regain control of his vocal chords and whispered, "What are you?"

"A polite thing to say would be 'Who are you?'," it replied. "But I'll let that go, given the circumstances. Call me Aidan."

Jason tried to formulate his next question, but his mind was still foggy.

"Let me help you along," said Aidan. "Yes, that is a human name. No, I'm not human. My people are called the Translators. The actual name of my species isn't something you could pronounce, which is why the Translators adopt names from the races they work with."

Jason sat up, his feet touching the floor. He looked around. The room was unremarkable, but there was a window, or at least a screen meant to act as such. He took several unsure steps and looked outside. The view overlooked an enormous structure floating in space. There were docking bays below, with several vessels attached. He didn't recognize their design.

"Dorothy," said Aidan, "you aren't in Kansas anymore."

Jason took a deep breath and counted to ten.

"Listen, Aidan, I just woke up from what I was pretty certain would be permanent sleep, and now I find myself on an alien space station, being lectured by something that looks like a cartoon character. Do you see how this can be a little overwhelming? If you understand compassion then would you please explain where I am?"

Aidan considered his words.

"My apologies. I do realize this must be difficult for you. You are on Venezia Outpost, one of the three such stations positioned just beyond the barrier that surrounds your solar system. Your ship was salvaged at the edge of the barrier by the crew of one of the Blockade Runners and you were brought here once they realized you were still alive in the hibernation pod."

"How is that possible? My engines were cut and the ship was drifting..."

"And drift it did, slowly, through the Sargasso. To my knowledge, yours is the only human vessel that isn't a Blockade Runner to make it across. Even if the trip took two hundred years."

"You mean..." Jason stared at the ships outside again. Venezia.

Solar system. He was on a human station, far in the future. "But how is this possible? My cryogenic unit wasn't designed to keep a person alive for more than a few months."

"We don't know. The outpost engineers examined your pod. There's no good reason why it should have kept functioning as long as it did. Strange things happen within barriers, but we've never seen a case like this, in your solar system or any other."

"You were supposed to notify me when he woke up."

Jason turned toward the woman's voice. She stood in the door-way, a uniform jacket with unfamiliar insignia draped over her wide shoulders, a gun holstered at her hip. She spoke English with a strange accent.

"He woke up minutes ago. I've only just begun to elucidate his circumstances." Aidan's accent matched the woman's when he addressed her.

Jason could follow the conversation but not without difficulty. He realized the language must've changed over two centuries. That Aidan was able to speak what sounded like unaccented English to Jason was impressive; the Translators must've been very good at their jobs.

"Mr. Kazemi wants to see him now," said the woman. She nodded curtly to Jason. "I'm Irina Pavlova."

"Ms. Pavlova is the Chief of Security for Venezia Outpost," said Aidan.

"Jason Stanger," said Jason.

"I know. We pulled your records." Irina looked at him appraisingly. "Can you walk?"

Jason nodded.

"Follow me, then."

She exited the room and marched down the long corridor. Jason rushed after her. Aidan made no move to follow.

The corridor led to a cavernous promenade filled with shops, restaurants, and offices. The station must've been huge—the size of a cruise ship, if not bigger. The area they walked through felt like a mall, except there were only a few other people there, rushing to and fro, and most of the businesses were shuttered. Jason figured it must be nighttime by station clock.

Pavlova power-walked down the promenade and Jason struggled to keep up. His leg muscles ached, protesting the exercise after centuries of inactivity.

"Who is Mr. Kazemi?" he called after her.

"Farhad Kazemi runs this station," she said.

"He's the captain?"

She slowed her pace just enough to let Jason catch up.

"More like an absolute monarch. His grandfather was a partner in the firm that built this station and the Kazemi family has been running things up here for seventy years while the Palmieris manage the in-system side of the business. So whatever you do, try not to piss him off. Not while you're breathing his air."

They approached a wide, temple-like wooden door. Jason realized this was the first instance of wood he'd seen on the station; everything else seemed to be made of plastic and metals. He could see how natural wood might be a status symbol in deep space.

Pavlova opened the door and the two of them walked through several smaller but relatively opulent rooms, one with armed guards, one with an assistant or secretary behind a large desk who nodded at Pavlova. The chief of security waved Jason through the final door. She stayed behind while he entered a larger office. There were bookshelves filled with hardcover volumes and thick wall rugs everywhere. This room made Jason feel as though he had traveled back rather than forward in time.

A man in his early forties worked at a standing desk. He fiddled with a tablet with his right hand—it was the only observable piece of modern technology in the study—and held a glass of amber-like liquid in another. He looked up when Jason entered the room.

"Ah, the mysterious traveler from the past." He smiled and put down his glass. "Welcome to the Venezia outpost. I'm Farhad Kazemi."

Although the other man's manner was friendly, Jason felt

uncomfortable and out of place. Kazemi spoke with the same unusual inflections as Pavlova. That, along with Kazemi's retro-style office, served to remind Jason of how much things must've changed. He knew nothing of this future world. The yearning for Rust ached deep in his bones.

"Hello," he managed.

Kazemi walked from behind his desk and sized Jason up.

"Amazing. It's as though you walked off the screen of a historical film."

Jason said nothing.

"Where are my manners? I'm sorry to have ogled, Mr. Stanger. This must be quite a harrowing experience for you. Please, have something to drink." Kazemi splashed some of the amber liquid from a decanter into another glass and offered it to Jason.

With a nod of thanks, Jason accepted the glass and took a sip. He expected some sort of whiskey but the taste was so unusual, he couldn't be sure the beverage was even alcoholic. It tasted a bit like honey and cardamom, and things he couldn't describe, all with a kick.

Kazemi grinned. "Toverian nectar. One of the many fine wares we trade for on Venezia."

"This is an alien drink?" Jason stared into the glass.

"Indeed, Mr. Stanger. Why don't you take a seat and enjoy it while I endeavor to help you feel a little less confused."

"If you don't mind," mumbled Jason as he sat on the small couch.

"Mind?" Kazemi laughed. "I find there's nothing more valuable in life than unique experiences. When will I ever again have the opportunity to fill someone in on the highlights of two centuries worth of history? Indeed, I should be thanking you."

Kazemi paced around his study as he spoke.

"Shortly after your incident, scientists figured out a limited way to get through the Sargasso space. It involved two components: coming up with technology that wouldn't go absolutely haywire within the barrier, and figuring a way for the pilots to survive the trip without losing their minds."

"They designed a class of ship called the Blockade Runner. They're almost like bullets fired from the edge of the Sargasso. All higher-level technology on the ship is shut down and it's capable only of limited maneuvering via chemical rockets similar to the ancient vessels from the dawn of spaceflight. Passengers can survive the Sargasso by traveling in hibernation, much like you had, but Blockade Runners require a live pilot: all unmanned ships or vessels relying on autopilot are claimed by the barrier. This stalled the Blockade Runner program because the Sargasso space drove the volunteer pilots stark-raving mad.

"The solution to this was an accidental discovery. Some human beings high on Rust are apparently fortified against the effects of the Sargasso. Less than one in a million humans possess the brain chemistry that interacts with Rust in a way that makes them capable of surviving the journey with their minds intact."

Jason shivered. He knew first-hand how addictive and destructive Rust was. Taking the drug in order to pilot a ship was difficult for him to imagine. He caught himself caressing the skin above the vein on the upper wrist of his left arm, where he used to inject Rust, with his right index finger. He pulled his right hand away with a jerk.

"Even today, crossing the Sargasso is a difficult and dangerous undertaking. We've managed to bring the success rate to 97 percent. That means three ships out of every hundred still perish en route.

"Once human ships made it past the Sargasso, we met a baker's dozen of alien species out here, and anecdotally know of many more. And here's the kick: each solar system cradling intelligent life comes equipped with its own Sargasso space, while uninhabited systems have no such barrier. Do you understand the implications, Mr. Stanger?"

Jason stared at the stationmaster wide-eyed. "Someone placed those barriers deliberately."

"That's right," said Kazemi. "According to what we learned

from the other spacefaring species there is a highly advanced race called the Caretakers, and they created the barriers in order to allow each civilization to develop independently of others and without fear of invasion. They wanted each little garden to flourish in peace. Thus, their moniker."

"But we figured out a way past the Sargasso. And, I'm guessing, so did these other aliens?" asked Jason.

"Indeed. This appears to be a feature rather than a bug; each civilization eventually finds a way to get past their barrier. Invariably, this is accomplished with great difficulty and in very limited numbers. It seems the Caretakers want their charges to learn about the greater universe beyond their cages, but not run amok, so to speak.

"Species capable of interstellar flight have developed certain conventions. Since blockade running is so fraught with danger, each civilization is expected to handle their own. Trade outposts like this one are built by each culture, and that's where goods and information are exchanged. In fact, it is considered an act of aggression to enter another civilization's home system.

"There are exceptions, of course: species that haven't found a way to traverse their own containments, but are eager to trade nevertheless. Toverians are one such example." Kazemi pointed at the decanter. "A single bottle of the nectar costs more on Earth than an average person earns in a year."

Jason looked at his glass with renewed appreciation.

"We pulled your records and studied your ship," said Kazemi. "It seems you would make an exemplary Blockade Runner pilot."

"No," Jason said quickly. "I won't ever take Rust again."

Something hardened in Kazemi's expression, but his voice remained amicable. "I understand. Your history of addiction is well documented, among other things. You should know that our detox procedures are far superior to those from your time. The drug was almost entirely eradicated in the solar system shortly after your departure, and the variant used for blockade running is carefully cultivated—"

"No," Jason said again.

Kazemi pursed his lips. "You're very lucky, you know. On the Panama outpost they'd probably dissect you to try and figure out how you survived in stasis for so long. And on Dubai they wouldn't ask your consent—they have a long history of shanghaiing Sargasso pilots. But here on Venezia we do things differently." He crossed his arms. "We respect freedom of choice, but we also expect everyone to pull their weight around here. If you don't want to pilot a Blockade Runner, you'll have to get another job, or get the hell off my station."

Kazemi glanced at his tablet. "I see here you worked for the Space Patrol after you got sober. I can offer you a short-term contract working station security under Pavlova. Sign on for a month. Get acclimated; figure out what you want to do next."

"That sounds all right," said Jason.

Kazemi handed him the tablet. "Read the contract. You can accept it with a thumbprint."

WHEN JASON LEFT Kazemi's office, Pavlova was gone. Instead, Aidan was waiting for him in the spacious promenade outside.

"What happened in there?" the alien asked.

Jason recounted the events of his meeting.

Aidan chuckled—a strange sound obviously meant to imitate human laughter.

"The stationmaster is an honorable man, in his way," he said. "He won't lie to you outright. Still, he's willing to withhold information when it suits him."

"What didn't he tell me?"

Aidan sized him up. "Many things, I'm sure. Chief among them is the fact that we're about to come under attack by an alien fleet in a matter of hours."

Jason looked up sharply. He bit his lower lip, still wondering if all this was a Sargasso-induced nightmare. "What?"

Aidan pointed down the promenade. "What do you see?"

Jason looked where the Translator was pointing.

"Shops. Bars. Mostly shuttered."

"That's right. The station is operating with skeleton staff," said Aidan.

"I thought it was night," said Jason.

"A week ago this area was bustling with humans and a handful of visitors from other worlds. Now everyone who was able to obtain passage into the solar system or elsewhere has gone. Kazemi is desperate for manpower if he has any hope of mounting a defense."

Jason frowned. "Wait a second. You told me the Caretakers keep every civilization behind their own Sargasso shield to prevent this sort of thing from happening."

"And it works," said Aidan. "Humans in your system are probably safe, but anyone living on trade outposts and colonies take their chances."

Jason felt small and scared and out of place, a feeling that had persisted since the moment he'd woken up in this strange future. He wanted a fix so badly.

"They're called the Maeshiva," said Aidan. "Traversing the barrier does not come easily to their species, so the trade is infrequent, and it's never more than one vessel arriving on Venezia at a time. Several days ago, deep-space sensors detected an approaching fleet of over thirty Maeshiva ships. They'll be here soon." Aidan sighed. "I'm sorry, Jason. It seems your arrival here suffers from terrible timing."

Jason fought his urges. "These aliens, they've been coming here to trade, right? Why assume they're going to attack?"

"There's absolutely no good reason to send such a large fleet to another species' home system. The humans have no choice but to interpret this as an act of aggression. They're mobilizing a fleet on the other side of the barrier, in case the Maeshiva try to come through."

Jason saw Pavlova power-walking toward him down the desolate promenade.

"Welcome to the force," she told Jason when she approached.

The security chief didn't seem gleeful or even particularly

happy about her new recruit. She looked like the weight of war rested on her shoulders—which, Jason supposed, it did.

"Come," she said. "There isn't a lot of time."

ONCE AGAIN, JASON awaited death in the cockpit of a small spaceship. Although two centuries had passed since he'd led his pursuers into the Sargasso, it felt like only yesterday. Even if it hadn't, Jason felt that being in this position twice in a single lifetime was two times too many.

Seven hours earlier, Pavlova had taken him straight to the docking bay and assigned one of the other pilots to teach him how to fly modern spacecraft.

The older man's name was Richard. He was a paunchy grey-haired man in his fifties. "Flying a Blockade Runner is a piece of cake," he said. "They had to make the control interface simple, so they could recruit and easily train just about anyone with a high barrier resistance."

Jason bristled. "I told Kazemi, I'm not taking drugs to fly into the Sargasso."

Richard was confused and made Jason recount his story.

"Forgive me for saying so, but you're a fool," Richard said afterward. "If I had any talent for crossing the Sargasso, I'd inject myself with any drug, any poison to go home instead of fighting an alien armada from a tin can. The other men, they feel the same way. None of us who remain are Sargasso pilots. We're mechanics and servicemen and security officers with some flight training. We're only here because we didn't manage to find a way off the station."

"There's nothing waiting for me back in the solar system," said Jason. "Nothing and no one. Everyone I knew is long dead."

Richard mulled it over. "There are people I know, people with money," he said. "They will pay handsomely to get out of here. You can begin a new life on Earth, or Mars, or wherever you like, with a decent nest egg. You can afford any rehab program and still have plenty left over. I'll put everything together in exchange for the ride home."

Jason was tempted. It's not like he owed any loyalty to Kazemi, or Pavlova, or this outpost. But he'd lost everything in his long sleep, and his sobriety was all he had left. It was who he was now, and he wouldn't give it up for an uncertain future. He politely refused Richard's offer.

Richard wasn't pleased. He spoke in short, terse sentences, showing Jason how to pilot a Blockade Runner.

Richard was right: any pilot could operate a Blockade Runner with ease. That was the good news. The bad news was that these ships were designed with a singular purpose. They weren't very maneuverable and the only weaponry on board had been jury-rigged by the Venezia engineers and mechanics over the past few days. Taking on a fleet of advanced spaceships in a handful of these glorified space trucks was suicide.

Jason had plenty of time to reflect upon this as he sat in the pilot chair. By the time the alien armada was visible on his view screen he regretted not taking Richard up on his offer, and he desperately needed a fix. There were, of course, no drugs on board, and the logical part of his mind was thankful for that.

Thirty-two alien ships appeared as dots on his screen. The dots grew as they approached. Designed to operate in deep space and free from the concerns of aerodynamics, the Maeshiva vessels were rectangular in shape. As they got closer, Jason realized that they were huge, each as long as a city block, almost half as large as the Venezia Outpost itself.

"Hold your fire," Pavlova said over the comm. "Let them get closer."

What a joke. Four torpedoes and a pair of turrets installed on Jason's ship would merely annoy these alien behemoths. The entire fleet of a dozen retrofitted Blockade Runners probably couldn't take down even one of the Maeshiva vessels.

One of the Blockade Runners turned around and accelerated away from the incoming fleet and toward the solar system. Jason wondered if it was Richard.

The deserter didn't get far. Venezia Outpost fired a single torpedo which disintegrated the fleeing ship.

"No running! We stay and defend the station. Together." Pavlova's voice was cracking. It couldn't have been easy for her to fire on one of her own, Jason thought. At least he hoped it wasn't easy for her.

The Maeshiva kept coming. Their fleet decelerated toward the station and into comm range. They reached full stop mere miles from Venezia and within the clear eye's view of the Blockade Runners.

Most of the alien ships bore burn scars and other assorted damage. This fleet had already been in a fight, and recently.

"Stand down," Pavlova said with obvious relief. "They want to talk." After several minutes of radio silence she added, "This isn't an invasion armada. It's a refugee fleet."

THE NEGOTIATIONS TOOK place by comm. The alien ships were too large to dock at Venezia, and either they didn't have shuttles or Kazemi didn't trust the Maeshiva to come on board. Either way, after another hour or so, the Blockade Runners were recalled.

Jason was shown to his quarters, a small but comfortable room aboard the station where he took a hot shower, ventured into the crew mess hall for a meal, and finally fell asleep.

Several hours later he was awakened by the buzzing of the comm unit he had been issued. He was ordered back to his Blockade Runner.

He got dressed and headed out, nervous about what was to come next. Had the negotiations with the aliens broken down? In the shuttle bay he found Aidan and Pavlova, who was holding a small case.

"We have reached an accord with the Maeshiva," she said. "The three of us are to deliver this to their flagship." She held up the case.

"What is it?" asked Jason.

Pavlova and Aidan exchanged glances.

"It contains the coordinates of an uninhabited planet the Maeshiva can colonize," said Aidan. "This data is too valuable to transmit openly."

Jason looked askance at the alien.

"Many of the species in this part of the galaxy breathe the same air, drink the same water," said the Translator. "As such, livable, unclaimed planets are rare and highly prized. And since uninhabited worlds aren't surrounded by a barrier, the location of this specific planet needs to remain a secret. The Maeshiva are fleeing from a powerful enemy."

Jason considered the case. "So valuable, Kazemi decided to trust it to an alien and a new guy?" he asked Pavlova.

"Don't you worry, I'll be coming too," said Pavlova. "I'll handle the delivery. You just have to drive the bus."

"I'm going because I'm a Translator. My job is to facilitate inter-species communication," said Aidan. "It's not like any of the rest of you can speak Maeshiva."

"And you're going because you're the most disposable," said Pavlova. "We don't exactly trust those guys."

"It stinks being the low guy on the totem pole," said Aidan.

"Anyone ever tell you that your use of human idioms can get irritating?" asked Jason.

"Constantly," said Aidan. "But being a Translator isn't merely a vocation. My species enjoys the nuances of alien languages we learn. Using an idiom provides me pleasure similar to what you might feel upon hearing a good joke."

The three of them boarded the Blockade Runner and Jason piloted it toward the flagship. Once there, a wide hangar door opened and he was able to land inside.

"A docking bay would have been easier," Jason muttered, as he carefully navigated the unruly Blockade Runner to its designated spot.

Once the hangar was refilled with breathable air, they were able to exit the ship. Four of the Maeshiva met them there. The Maeshiva were seven-foot-tall humanoids, with large eyes, oblong heads and patchy gray skin that reminded Jason of an elephant. Their mouths were small, or at least seemed so as they had no lips. Their noses looked very similar to the humans', which somehow had an overall effect of making their faces seem even stranger.

One of the Maeshiva emitted a series of trills, something between birdsong and speech.

"They greet us and ask us to follow them," said the Translator.

"Greetings," said Jason. Then, on a lark he added, "Take me to your leader." He smiled at Aidan. "You probably shouldn't translate that."

Pavlova frowned.

Aidan chuckled. "I'm pretty sure that's where we're going anyway."

The seven of them walked through the corridors of the Maeshiva ship. Everywhere the aliens lined up to see them. The sight of the humans and the Translator must've been as unusual to them as they were to Jason. Finally he reached a chamber where several more of the aliens sat around a large oval desk.

"The Maeshiva government in exile," said Aidan.

"What exactly happened to them?" asked Jason.

"Tell you later," said the Translator.

One of the Maeshiva extended his long, slender hand. The gesture didn't need a translation. Pavlova handed over the case.

The alien opened it and retrieved a printout with a string of numbers on it. Jason expected some sort of a data chip, but this made sense: there was no reason to assume the Maeshiva hardware would be compatible with the humans'. The alien passed the sheet to the Translator who spoke in the Maeshiva trill, no doubt translating the data into their language. Another alien entered the information into a terminal.

After they were done, the Maeshiva leader gave some sort of command. Jason heard the unmistakable sound of engines being powered up, then felt the ship move.

"What's happening?" he asked.

"I'm sorry, Jason. I was not entirely honest with you, as per

Kazemi's orders," said Pavlova. "An inhabitable planet wasn't the only thing the stationmaster traded away. The Maeshiva also needed a gifted blockade pilot."

WHEN PAVLOVA DELIVERED the news, Jason nearly threw a fit. Unable to lash out in any effective way, he settled for refusing to speak to Aidan and her. But the silent treatment was ineffective, especially since they were the only living beings on board he could communicate with. After a few hours he relented, and demanded details.

"We learned from the Maeshiva that their home system had come under attack," the Translator told him. "Several thousand Tryb warships invaded the system and pretty much wiped them out. The refugee fleet that reached Venezia may be all that's left of their species."

"Don't the Maeshiva have the Sargasso space surrounding their star system, too?" asked Jason.

Pavlova looked up from her tablet. "They do. The fact that the Tryb have learned to pass through the barriers en masse is a disturbing development. Who's to say they won't come after Earth next?"

"I'm sorry these guys got invaded, I really am," said Jason," but what does any of that have to do with me?"

Pavlova put her tablet down. "The Maeshiva are going to settle on a new world, but their chances of surviving there are minimal. If the Tryb don't find them, another malevolent species might. The universe isn't a warm and cuddly place. In order for them to survive they'll need a Sargasso barrier erected around their new home world. More immediately, the Tryb war fleet will have to be dealt with."

"Erect a new Sargasso barrier?" asked Jason. "I thought only the Caretakers could do that."

"The mythical, absent Caretakers, yes," said Pavlova. "They're our best hope for resolving the Tryb problem, and they're the reason Kazemi bargained off a viable colony planet. You see, the Maeshiva think they know where the Caretakers live."

"That's right," said Aidan. "We're going to see the wizard behind the curtain. And you are the one who can get us there."

Jason stared at the two of them. "Why me?"

"We pulled the data from your ship," said Pavlova. "You were able to fly deeper into the Sargasso while retaining control of your ship than any pilot on record, even though you weren't high on Rust at the time. Our people think months of exposure to the drug from before you got clean altered your brain chemistry in a way that makes you more resistant to the barrier. And that makes you our best shot."

Jason caught himself scraping at his wrist with a fingernail. The need for Rust swelled within him again. "Best shot for what?"

"There is a star system that is surrounded by a barrier many times more potent than all the other ones," said Aidan. "The Maeshiva believe—as do I—that it guards the home of the Caretakers."

"That's one theory," said Pavlova. "There's another. Our scientists think it may be an interdicted planet."

Suppress the urge. Extinguish it. "Interdicted? Aren't all inhabited worlds interdicted by definition, surrounded by the Sargasso?"

"We think the Caretakers erected a more potent barrier to contain someone dangerous, someone who figured out a reliable way to get around their regular containment. This is exactly what we'd like to happen to the Tryb."

Jason considered Pavlova's words. "And who are *we*? You and Kazemi? Because this sort of thing seems like it should be well above your pay grade, let alone mine. Isn't there some sort of government back on Earth that should be dealing with this?"

"The post of security chief on Venezia is always filled by a high-ranked intelligence official from either Earth or Mars. It's part of the arrangement that allows Kazemi and his partners to operate Venezia as a private enterprise." Pavlova leaned forward in her seat. "There are contingencies for hostile contact, all sorts of scenarios mulled over in think tanks for decades. Admittedly we can't do much with the resources we have outside of the Sargasso containment, but helping the Maeshiva on this mission is well worth the risk. Even if we're right and all they found is an interdicted planet, we might gather information that's incredibly valuable."

"Or we might die!" Jason got up from his seat and half-turned so he faced Pavlova directly. "I didn't sign up for this, for any of it. How dare you roll the dice with my life without even asking consent?"

Pavlova got up, too, standing only a few inches from his face. She rested her hand on his shoulder.

"I'm sorry, Jason. We evacuated the other blockade pilots when we thought the Maeshiva were invading, because we didn't want to risk losing them in battle. When this…opportunity came up, you were not only the best choice, but the only choice. What would you have done in my place?"

The two of them stared at each other. Jason said nothing.

"I may be risking your life, but I'm risking mine, too. As is Aidan. Our survival depends on your skill as a pilot." Pavlova squeezed his shoulder. "You don't have to forgive me, but please work with me, for the sake of the mission."

They stood there as Jason searched his feelings, his emotions. Against incredible odds he had survived the journey that was meant to kill him, only to end up in this situation. Perhaps this was what he was meant to do? Besides, what other options did he really have?

He disengaged and sat back down.

"How about you?" he asked Aidan. "Why are you really here?"

"The Translators think of the Caretakers as gods, or close enough to it in human terms," said Aidan. "What risk wouldn't you take to meet your god?"

Jason chuckled, some of the tension draining from him.

"This is humorous?" asked Aidan.

"In most human belief systems you get to meet your maker after you die. That makes yours a strange choice of words."

"I see your meaning," said Aidan. "And while the double en-
tendre was unintentional, it wasn't wrong. The probability of all of
us meeting our gods soon, one way or another, is unusually high."

Jason laughed at this, and Pavlova joined in.

JASON SAT ALONE in the cockpit of the Blockade Runner, which
he decided to name the *Pivot II* in honor of his last ship. The
original *Pivot* had somehow allowed him to survive the long slow
trip across the Sargasso, and he hoped some of the luck would
transfer to this vessel along with the name. He was surely going
to need it.

Aidan, Pavlova, and three Maeshiva representatives occupied
the suspended animation units that were his sole cargo. The six of
them were on their way to visit the Mount Olympus of the galaxy's
self-appointed gods.

The system that lay ahead seemed unremarkable. A single
Neptune-mass planet orbited a red dwarf star. The instruments
detected no signs of life and no communications.

Jason accelerated toward the system. The sophisticated computers shut themselves down to avoid malfunction within the
Sargasso space. The *Pivot II* was now a bullet, fired toward its target
and reliant on the initial boost to get through the barrier. Jason
could use chemical rockets in order to adjust course, but his main
function as the blockade pilot was merely to survive the trip.

He had learned that occasionally Blockade Runners were able
to reach their destination even if the pilot went insane or died, but
most of the time the fate of the ship was inexplicably tied to the fate
of its pilot.

Pivot II sped toward its target. Jason knew the exact moment
it entered the barrier. Unlike the Sargasso space of the solar system
where the process was gradual, he could feel it vividly with his mind.
It was as though a dozen wild cats scratched at the inside of his head.

Jason focused on the planet ahead and strived to ignore his inner turmoil. He must make it across; too much was at stake. People

and aliens believed in him, entrusted their lives to him. He wasn't going to let them down.

The pain intensified. It flared up until he could feel nothing else, perceive nothing else. He clutched at his temples and screamed.

After an eternity the pain receded, leaving desire in its wake. He wanted Rust, lusted for it. It was worse than the days he had spent in rehab. He would murder his passengers or cut off his arm for a single dose. Then the desire abated only to be replaced with pain again. The cycle went on, endless.

Jason writhed on the floor. He lost all sense of time, of where he was heading and why. His entire universe was equal parts pain and desire, and he could no longer tell them apart. When the cycle finally stopped it took time for his senses to register this.

He blinked rapidly and tried to focus. Outside the porthole a tropical sun bathed a sandy beach in bright white light.

There is no porthole. No beach. Keep it together. He forced his gaze away.

There was a *ding*, and a compartment opened revealing a syringe. Rust!

Jason wiped cold, clammy sweat from his forehead and stared at the syringe. He'd learned that a dose of Rust was automatically made available to the pilot ten minutes into the Sargasso space. Somehow, he hadn't expected this ship to contain it. He stared at the syringe like it was a venomous snake.

Then the second realization hit him: *it had only been ten minutes.* The eternity of pain he had suffered was but a tiny fraction of the trip that would last for hours.

The syringe beckoned to him.

Was it real or an illusion, a cruel mirage induced by the barrier, like the tropical island outside his ship? He pondered as the cats began to scratch at the inside of his head again.

Jason felt his resolve weakening. Perhaps Rust could really help him survive the trip, alleviate the pain. With so much at stake, who could possibly blame him?

He thought back to the weeks spent in rehab, the pain and the sacrifice of getting clean. He'd thrown his life away once—he wouldn't do it again, not even to save it, to save everyone.

The cats scratched in earnest. Soon he wouldn't be able to resist. He grabbed the syringe and shambled across the cramped cockpit. He opened the door to a tiny bathroom with a chemical toilet and emptied the syringe's contents into the washbasin, taking care to flush every drop down the recycling tube where he could never reach it. He ran the water for a full minute, until the small tank ran out. He then ground the syringe under his heel.

When the cycle resumed, he clawed at the sealed compartment where he knew the return journey's syringe waited until his fingers were raw and bleeding. He couldn't pry it open.

HE WAS ON his hands and knees when the pain receded again. He clutched at the sand, its warm grains sifting through his fingers.

Sand?

He was on the beach. Turquoise water splashed gently against the shore, and a mild breeze caressed his face. In the distance a lone palm tree stood a few steps away from the water's edge.

"The pain is over. You made it through, Jason."

He turned toward the sound of the voice. Warren Jain stood there in his uniform, slightly crumpled as always. Jain smiled at him.

"Commander Jain? This...is impossible." Jason struggled to get up.

"We have taken a form that is comfortable and familiar to you."

Jason stood up. The pain was gone, leaving him completely drained.

"Are you the Caretaker?"

The image of Jain flickered, momentarily replaced by Aidan. "Some call us by that name."

Jason tried to gather his thoughts, to explain his purpose. He didn't quite know where to begin.

The figure in front of him shifted into one of the Maeshiva. "We know why you're here. The new Maeshiva colony will receive the protective field. The Tryb star systems will be interdicted."

"Thank you," Jason whispered. He had so many questions, but all he could manage was: "Why?"

The being shifted to Kazemi. "We are not of a uniform mind. There are factions among us. While all of us wish to elevate the younger species, we disagree as to the methodology. Some prefer for natural selection to take its course, for the faster-advancing species to overtake their rivals. They see the fields as challenges, puzzles; cages for the strong to break out of, and to contain the weak."

It shifted to Jain again. "Others value all sentient life and wish to preserve it. They erect the fields to protect the emerging intelligences, to nurture the islands of the mind in the unforgiving sea of the cosmos until they're strong enough to claim their place in the greater universe. The ones who are here communicating with you are a part of that faction."

"So Aidan was right," said Jason. "You're basically gods. And not all the gods are nice."

The alien shifted to Aidan again. "We're not gods. We're merely further along on the evolutionary adventure than the other sentients in this galaxy."

"So why tell me? Why not just erect barriers and interdict and do whatever it is that you want to do?"

Jain again: "You have a special mind."

Then Kazemi: "Our faction was losing. The Tryb were to be allowed to overrun your sector of space."

Pavlova this time: "We needed an argument the evolutionary faction couldn't trump. We needed proof of evolution so definitive, they would become swayed."

The Caretakers' avatar shifted to become a copy of Jason. "Your mind had the potential to survive the strengthened field, but you were born too early. Your species couldn't reach here. But once you entered the field, we had the means to preserve you, to nudge the events so that your ship would reach the other side in time to meet with the Maeshiva fleet."

Jason studied his doppelganger. "You got me here. What is it you need me to do?"

Another shift to Pavlova: "You have already done it. This is not our home world as the Maeshiva had hoped, but merely a test, a venue where the protective field is deployed at its most potent setting. Your mind surviving the strengthened barrier is proof that there's greater potential for evolution within your species than displayed by the mere technological prowess of the Tryb."

Kazemi: "The other faction will have no choice but to conform to our preferred course of action."

Jain: "Know that your suffering wasn't wasted. You've saved your species, and many others."

Aidan: "We thank you. The field has been turned off so you won't suffer its effects on your return trip. You can go in peace now."

"Wait!" said Jason. "What do I tell the others?"

Another shift to Kazemi: "That is of no consequence. You can tell them what you wish."

The beach and the sand and the bright sun were gone. Jason was alone again, in the cockpit of the Blockade Runner.

He checked the instruments: the ship was headed outward, away from the red dwarf star and toward the Maeshiva cruiser. He'd get there in two hours' time.

Jason was deep in thought, contemplating what he had learned from the Caretakers and how he might present this information to the others. Even if they didn't believe him, the newly erected interdiction barriers around the Tryb star systems should be proof enough. His pondering was interrupted by a *ding*—the ship's automated process made the second syringe of Rust available to him.

Jason stared at the syringe dispassionately. The urge, the desire he fought for so long, was gone. Perhaps it was burned out of him by the ordeal, or perhaps removing the addiction was a parting gift from the Caretakers. Whatever the case, he knew Jain—the real Jain, not the illusion generated by the aliens—would be proud of him.

He ignored the syringe and settled in for the trip home.

This story originally appeared in *Galaxy's Edge*.

"Islands" takes place in the universe of the Sargasso Containment, a shared-world setting spearheaded by Mike Resnick and published in *Galaxy's Edge* over the course of several years. The initial slew of stories took place in the solar system and featured no aliens, but Mike wanted a grander canvas, so he asked me to "fast-forward" the story by a couple of hundred years, while still connecting it strongly with the themes and narratives of the preceding stories.

The challenge for me was to tell a stand-alone story while simultaneously drawing from the worlds and characters created by Marina J. Lostetter, Andrea G. Stewart, Tina Gower, and other excellent authors who established the setting, but also creating lots of threads for future contributors to build upon.

A fun tidbit: I let my then-seven-year-old son name one of the alien races in the story. He's the one who came up with the Maeshiva.

CATALOGUE OF ITEMS IN THE CHESS EXHIBIT AT THE HUMANITIES MUSEUM, PRE-ENLIGHTENMENT WING

"First Contact" commemorative limited edition set
(United States, 2019)
Marble pieces, marble board.

This set and a variety of other commercial products were manufactured to celebrate the discovery of Earth by the Confederation of Civilized Species. In his first broadcast speech the Elscean ambassador praised the game of chess as a "uniquely human invention which offers considerable insights into the native psyche." The rook pieces were sculpted to resemble the CCS starship that landed in Tanzania.

This set was available exclusively through a broadcast channel dedicated to direct-to-consumer merchandise sale via *television* platform. (See 20th Century Culture Exhibit.)

CCS novelty set (Taiwan, 2027)
Plastic pieces, vinyl rollup board.

The white pieces were designed to represent various Earth military equipment and infantrymen, and the black pieces imitated CCS enforcement ships, shuttles, and drones. Representative of period games and toys designed to emulate the hypothetical armed conflict between Earth and CCS forces. Manufacture and sale of such xenophobic products was banned by decree of the Unified Planetary Authority in 2032.

Improvised set (Gdansk POW camp, Poland, circa 2037)
Aluminum wire pieces, cloth board.

The 2034 Unified Planetary Authority resolution to petition for CCS membership resulted in civil war against a number of Regressive factions that opposed this move. After order was restored, the CCS generously offered to remove the Regressive combatants and ideologues.

This set was made from bent cuts of aluminum wire and a board drawn on white tablecloth by some among the two million Regressives who awaited deportation in the Gdansk facility in the late 2030s.

The museum collection contains a number of similar improvised sets from some of 312 other POW camps around the globe. (Consult Archives catalogue for detailed listings.)

Xiangqi set (China, 2041)
Jade pieces, cherry wood board.

Until recently, this item was not a part of the chess exhibition as it was widely believed to be a different game. (Note the checkers-like playing pieces and unusual board.) However, famed G'Naktian scholar K'Ten'Gh recently published a paper to the contrary. He discovered that the game's name means "imitation chess" in Mandarin, a language once spoken by its players.

Despite K'Ten'Gh's best efforts, the rules of this chess variant remain lost.

Hand-carved set (Cuba, circa 2050)
Rosewood and maple pieces, walnut board.

This exhibit is a sample of handcrafted art objects the Naturalist communes exported in order to purchase medicine and a limited range of other goods not proscribed by their ideology.

A late offshoot of the Regressives movement, the Naturalists didn't actively oppose humanity's strides toward enlightenment but chose to practice passive resistance and live in primitive communes. Their xenophobic ideology barred technology and philosophy that originated off-world.

Their dwindling numbers were somewhat swelled by the remnants of other ideologically resistant communities (the Amish, orthodox Jews, etc.), but despite this, the last Naturalist commune ceased operations by 2070.

Improvised set (Sector 6367, circa 2090)
Polyvinyl chloride pipe pieces, steel board.

This improvised set was made from cuts of white and silver PVC pipe of varying lengths. A checkered sheet of G'Naktian steel was used as a board.

The set was confiscated by UPA enforcement officers in a 2092 raid conducted on Factory 71351's living barracks. Factory workers suspected of harboring Regressive tendencies were enrolled in intensive re-education programs.

"First Contact" commemorative set, centennial edition
(Humanities Museum, 2119)

G'Naktian construction polymer pieces, Elscean utility resin board.

Although this item is not from the pre-enlightenment era, the curator felt it was an appropriate end-cap to the chess exhibition. Copies of this set were manufactured to celebrate the one-hundred-year anniversary of first contact and subsequent human contributions to the Confederation of Civilized Species culture, however minor they might be.

The fact that the set has elicited virtually no interest from the museum's human visitors speaks volumes to the success we've enjoyed as a species in assimilating into Confederation culture and joining our fellow sentients in enlightenment.

The commemorative set continues to appeal to the museum's off-world patrons. We recommend it as a quaint and unique curio of aboriginal Earth culture. Copies are available for sale in the museum gift shop.

This story originally appeared in *Nature*.

Historically, native cultures have not fared well when they have encountered the more technologically advanced explorers. Who's to say things will go any better for humanity if we're ever discovered by an alien civilization? Will small handfuls of people struggle to preserve the human identity while the majority willingly embrace the language, fashions, and values of the visitors, until it is only the visitors themselves who are interested in the artifacts of human ingenuity, even if only as gift shop curios?

In this story, the aliens conquer and absorb Earth into their society without firing a single shot, which makes it all the more chilling to me.

Special thanks to Ken Liu for suggesting the idea of the Xiangqi segment. He taught me that *xiangqi* literally translates as 'elephant game' and the word *xiang* is a homonym for both 'elephant' and 'similar,' making it easy for a foreign scholar with limited scope of knowledge to conclude that the game is called 'imitation chess.'

FIFTEEN MINUTES

BEGIN-LIVESTREAM/
CHANNEL-17473453/02-04-2117-17:30>>>

Y ou will not be entertained.

Here I sit, in an empty room, staring into a camera lens. The small screen above it displays what the camera sees: a gaunt, worn-down frame, a permanent scowl, and crazed eyes set deep in a wrinkled face framed by dirty clumps of hair. If I were you, I wouldn't watch me. Truthfully, I want nothing more than to throw this so-called opportunity in whatever passes for the face of our artificial overlord, but I'm too hungry to be proud. On the off chance that a real-life person is actually watching this stream, I'm going to tell the truth.

Before the Resource Wars someone quipped that in the future everyone would get their fifteen minutes of fame. With our luck, he turned out to be right and all the ancient optimists who hoped for flying cars and interstellar travel turned out to be wrong. A century after that phrase was coined humans were too busy killing each other over the remaining food and fresh water to engineer flying cars. Our ancestors would've finished the job too, if the AI hadn't taken over. The great and powerful artificial intelligence that has been running every aspect of our lives ever since. I call it AM, like the computer from a story I once read.

You all believe AM is benevolent because it stopped the wars and kept the farms and factories running, even though it needs humans like a dog needs fleas. Me, I think it's a sadistic son-of-a-tin-can, just like the AM in the story. Because we don't really get to live, we only get to exist.

People like me who don't have a job are given an allowance of 1600 calories a day, and nothing whatsoever to do. And how does one get a job when AM has automated everything that could possibly be automated? AM encourages everyone to draw pictures or write poetry or some shit. It claims pursuing artistic endeavors leads to a fulfilling life, but some of us aren't into that.

And then there's this streaming business. Twice a year each of us gets to go online and broadcast our talents to the world. Some of you sing, or dance, or read those terrible poems you wrote. Few of the more attractive ones shed their clothes and show off the goods, because that's bound to be popular for as long as there are humans. And then there are poor saps like me who don't have a single artistic bone, and trust me, no one wants to see me naked. But I still have to perform like a nice circus monkey, because if you happen to like this stream, you can press that big green button on your touchscreen and a calorie is added to the monkey's account. Supposedly some of the best performers eat like kings, but even a useless boring monkey like me can hope to earn an extra banana or two.

Of course, that's only what AM wants everyone to think. There are ten billion of us monkeys on the planet, and everyone gets their semiannual fifteen minutes in front of the camera. So who would bother to watch this shit instead of accessing the old films and books? I'll tell you: AM, that's who. We're its trained pets, slobbering over ourselves and performing stupid human tricks for a treat.

I looked it up, and would you believe the story about AM was published within about a year of when they made up the fifteen-minutes-of-fame quote. The evil computer in the story tortured the few remaining humans, but at least it was honest about it. The way I see it, the real-life AM is far worse, because it's convinced everyone to accept their miserable lots instead of fighting for something better.

So I won't waste any more energy acting out this pointless charade. I'll just sit here and wait until the camera shuts off, then check my account to see how many calories AM's algorithms deign to issue. I'll fill my belly, hating AM in the process, railing against its heartless, soulless, malevolent mind, which has turned all humanity into its plaything. And when the extra food runs out, I will come to hate myself as I count the days until the next opportunity to proverbially sing for my supper.

I have no talent. And I must stream.

This story originally appeared in *Nature*.

I'd apologize for the terrible pun which closed the story you've just read, but really, I feel no remorse at all. Puns are awesome, and any sufficiently good pun must also be a terrible pun.

That line was my starting point for the story and its original title. I figured it would develop into something funny, but instead the idea grew into a bleak, dystopian world where an artificial intelligence overlord parcels out food and basic necessities to allow humanity to survive.

The story is inspired by Harlan Ellison's "I Have No Mouth and I Must Scream"—a brilliant and dark tale by one of science fiction's grand masters. In the story, the computer AM tortures the few remaining humans. But I've always wondered how and why the computer would develop such strong hatred for the species that created it. (Ellison's narrator Ted does provide his own thoughts on the matter but, as with any good stories, leaves room for us to consider other possibilities.)

In my story, the AI is clearly less evil than Ellison's AM—but is it still a monstrous dictator making humans jump through hoops to study them as my unreliable narrator suggests, or is it a benevolent intelligence that is forced to make difficult choices? Perhaps the resources are scarce and the calorie quotas are the best it can do to keep the human population alive. And encouraging creative endeavors could be an attempt to help maintain their sanity and bring them a smidgen of joy.

The "fifteen minutes of fame" quote is by Andy Warhol and, as my narrator points out, he said that around the same time Ellison's story was published. I stumbled upon this fact when I was writing the story, so it wasn't by design. Sometimes history is serendipitous that way.

MASQUERADE NIGHT

T he first time Harat saw Ada was when she was dancing with the goddess of death.

It was masquerade night, and club Rhythm was full of monsters. An orchestra blasted the latest European tunes at their highest volume setting, filling the cavernous dance hall with music. Dance beats reverberated in Harat's temples. An engine rotated an enormous lantern of painted glass suspended from the high ceiling, which cast shards of colored light across the hall. It was the glint of light against the lapis lazuli amulet that drew his attention.

The amulet reminded him of the jewelry once worn by the women of his tribe, but the smoke and glitter of the club swallowed up the details of the trinket much like the depths of time had long swallowed all memory of his tribe's existence, leaving him alone, an abandoned godling devoid of followers. It was a fate shared by most of the celestials who frequented club Rhythm.

Once upon a time, creatures like him had ruled the world, lording it over the terrified humans. But the world had changed, the humans had multiplied, had unlocked the secrets of bronze and iron and steam. They took over, and their one-time gods, stripped of much of their power, were now confined to the shadows.

By the 1920s, they could mingle with humans freely only on rare occasions. All Hallows Eve, Purim, Mardi Gras—the holidays of masks, when gods and spirits could work the streets of New York City in their true form without anyone giving them so much as a second look. Then Jumis bought the nightclub and came up with the weekly masquerade night—costumes required—a place and time where someone like Harat wouldn't stand out despite his feline eyes and pointy ears.

Harat tapped into his Leopard aspect, using the cat vision to study the amulet from across the hall, noting the subtle differences in the design. It was not a lost artifact of his people, merely an inexpensive trinket. He felt a pang of disappointment, but then his gaze traveled upward and zeroed in on the face of the woman who wore it. She was stunning.

Her face was flushed as she danced not so much with the goddess of death as around her. Enthralled by the celestial's power she circled ever closer, almost touching the celestial and then shrinking back, like a moth fluttering around a lightbulb. The little moth would eventually get too close, and her life would be extinguished, all too soon.

Normally, Harat would not interfere. He didn't prey upon humans, but for many of the other gods the club was hunting grounds. It wasn't his business to impede the natural order of things. But this time—this one time—he was compelled to act.

Harat strode across the dance floor, pushing past the writhing bodies, human and celestial, until he was face to face with his target. Miru, the Polynesian goddess of the underworld, was tall and very thin, and her skin was of reddish hue. She could have almost passed for a severely sunburned human were it not for her shark teeth—several rows of sharp, jagged white daggers.

Harat stopped right in front of the goddess, inserting himself into the enthralled woman's orbit. The tall celestial scowled at him and Harat threw the contents of the glass he was holding into Miru's face. Before the other celestial could react, Harat turned around and headed toward the coatroom. The confrontation was coming, and it wouldn't do for the humans to witness it. Miru roared in frustration and pursued Harat, taking on her Shark aspect as she moved. The enthralled woman stopped dancing, and was blinking rapidly, like someone who had been suddenly awakened from deep sleep.

When Miru burst into the coatroom, empty for the summer, Harat was ready for her. The Leopard aspect took over and he jumped his opponent in a blur of claws and fangs. The two primal forces clashed, Shark against Leopard, tearing into each other, cutting and slashing, and moving faster than a human eye could follow. The thumping dance beat concealed the sounds of their struggle.

When it was over, Harat limped outside. He was bleeding from several long gashes on the side of his torso just below the shoulder, but could still move under his own power. What was left of the Shark covered the floor, the walls, and some of the ceiling of the coatroom.

Harat searched the club, but the woman wearing the lapis lazuli amulet was gone.

"WHAT WERE YOU thinking?" Jumis, the Latvian god of the harvest, stared Harat down. "I've got a good thing going here. I don't need you muddying up the waters."

"It won't happen again," said Harat. His bandaged ribs ached pleasantly, reminding him of battles past.

"It better not," said Jumis. "Do you have any idea how much the repairs are going to cost me?"

Harat was envious of the other celestial. Pudgy and graying at the temples, Jumis looked human, ordinary enough to intermingle with mortals without having to pretend he was wearing costume and makeup for a masquerade ball. For that alone, Harat would trade places with this lesser god, if he only could.

"You still owe me, from when I aided you in Constantinople," said Harat.

"They call it Istanbul now, and not any more I don't," said Jumis. "You better believe this little temper tantrum of yours makes us even. Next time you feel like a fight to the death, perhaps when your sparring partner's friends decide to avenge her, you take it outside."

Harat leaned against the wall. "No one is coming to avenge her," he said. "Relics like us have no friends."

HARAT TRIED TO forget the incident. He had lived for too long and fought too many battles to remember the details of each kill. But, every time he closed his eyes and tried to sleep, he saw the enthralled woman's face, her eyes as blue as the amulet she wore.

He'd been with human women many times in the past. He sought some kind of connection, a balm to soothe the pain and anguish, the grief he still felt over the loss of the mortals of his tribe. None of those other women made him feel the way he did when thinking about *her*.

Harat came to the club on the next masquerade night, and the one after that, but there was no sign of the woman. She must have been scared off by the experience—some deeper part of her mind subconsciously recognizing the peril even if she had never learned first-hand how dangerous her dance with the Shark should have been.

Having existed for thousands of years, Harat knew patience. He came to the club every week and roamed the hall, a glass of absinthe in hand, watching the humans who were dressed like monsters, and the monsters pretending to be human.

His persistence paid off. He finally saw her, not on the dance floor this time, but sharing a small round table with Qarib, the Persian god of serpents and poison.

She sure knows how to pick the winners, thought Harat.

He approached the table and hovered over the diminutive form of the Persian poison god.

"Leave," he told the Snake.

The smaller celestial hissed at him, but didn't wish to fight. The word of what happened to the Shark had spread quickly among the club regulars. He scooted from the table without saying a word. Harat pulled the chair back and took the seat across from the woman. For several moments, they contemplated each other.

"That wasn't very nice of you," said the woman.

"He isn't a very nice fellow," said Harat.

She pouted. "Maybe so, but he was going to buy me a drink."

"You wouldn't enjoy drinking anything he might have offered you. Regardless, that is an easy fix. I'll buy you a drink instead. My name is Harat."

"Ada," said the woman. She continued to study him with those big, blue eyes. "And are *you* a nice fellow, Harat?"

"By the standards of this place? I should say so," said Harat.

She smiled at him. "In that case, I will have to consider letting you buy me that drink, sometime." Then she picked up her purse and walked away, without turning to look back even once.

The Leopard god wanted very much to pursue her, but centuries of experience had taught him both patience and the wisdom of knowing when not to push his luck.

IT WAS MANY months later that he saw Ada again. She wore a flowing green dress and covered her face with a handheld Venetian half mask, but Harat knew her scent now, and could find her in a crowded club, regardless of whatever disguise a human was capable of using.

He approached just as Silenus, a satyr with a taste for human flesh, was trying out his pick up line on her. Harat inserted himself unceremoniously between the two of them at the packed bar counter.

"Hello, Ada," he said. "You've had a long time to think about that drink. Have you reached a decision?"

"You are very persistent," she said, and she nodded toward her cocktail glass. Harat motioned for the bartender to mix another. "And also very consistent. You're wearing the same costume again?"

"It suits my nature," Harat brushed at his whiskers. "I like leopards."

"I'm more of a dog person," said Ada, but she didn't refuse the drink, or another after that.

The evening wore on as they spoke about architecture and dead poets, straining their vocal chords to outshout the music. For the first time in his very long existence, Harat was beginning to fall in love.

She asked him to walk her home, and he almost refused. He cared about her, and he was afraid of what would happen if he went with her now, and she found out that the whiskers and the fur didn't come off. He had never really fretted about that moment of truth with any of the other women—some denied him, some were excited by what he was—but Ada was different. So he nearly refused to go with her, but then he saw her moving unsteadily on her feet and thought back to the Shark, and the Snake, and the Satyr, and the dozens of other predators that surrounded them, and he had no choice at all.

He offered his arm and the two of them left the club together. They walked the midnight streets and their two shadows, cast long in the dim glow of the streetlights, merged into one.

The walk was over all too soon—it turned out that she lived only a few blocks away from the club—and she invited him to come upstairs. He looked into her big, blue eyes and, despite his concerns about losing her when she learned the truth, he followed her inside.

They came up the stairs of the townhouse and into her home, and she poured him a glass of red wine. They sat on the couch in her living room and they talked some more, until the world began to swim in front of Harat's eyes. He tried to get up but he lost his balance and tumbled onto the thick rug, the wine glass rolling out of his hand and leaving a trickle of wine that looked like blood drops in its wake.

Harat tried to shift into his Leopard aspect, but he could not. He couldn't move at all, his ageless body betraying him utterly. All he could do was to move his eyes, following Ada as she stood above him, frowning.

"Why?" he tried to ask, but all that came out were some guttural sounds.

"Poor kitty-cat," she said. "You should have known your place. You should have stayed away from me." She walked out of his field of vision, but her velvety voice continued on from elsewhere in the apartment. "You weren't my intended prey. I only hunt the really bad ones, the murderers, the monsters."

He concentrated on her voice, zeroed in on it to stay awake, stay focused, and he reached deeper and deeper within himself searching for the Leopard but finding only the abyss, its darkness inching ever closer, enveloping his mind.

"You were too persistent for your own good, kitty-cat, scaring away the game." She returned and bent over him, still wearing the flowing green dress with the blue lapis lazuli amulet gleaming against the silk. She was holding a large carving knife. "So, you forced my hand. Nothing personal, but a girl's got to eat." She shrugged and smiled at him one last time, and plunged the knife deep into his chest.

As the cold steel bit deep, his consciousness reached desperately into the furthest corners of the abyss and found the Leopard aspect. His body transformed around the blade stuck hilt-deep in his midsection. The Leopard twisted around, swatting at Ada, and his claws connected, leaving three deep gashes on the side of her neck and her shoulder.

Ada gasped in surprise and stumbled back, letting go of the knife. The great cat pounced, pinning her down on the carpet, his fangs and claws ripping into her, causing as much damage as possible before the knife wound sapped his strength.

She pushed him off with surprising strength, throwing him toward the couch. His feline body twisted and he swatted at her one more time. She moved away with impossible speed, but the claw snagged at the string that held the amulet, and ripped it from her neck.

The blue stone set in silver flew across the room and hit the wall with a clang. As soon as it left Ada's neck, her body transformed. It changed almost instantly, the visage of a woman replaced by a thing made of teeth and tentacles, an ancient horror from long before the first humans created the first gods by worshipping the fire and the stars and the predators around them.

Harat faced the nightmarish creature and roared in pain and anger. The thing that used to be Ada roared back, and her war cry sounded like a mix of distant thunder and crumbling gravestones. The two beings, forgotten by history, came at each other.

HARAT WOKE UP naked, lying in the pool of blood and grime and ripped tentacles. The sun was beginning to set outside—it had been at least a day since the fight. His fingers brushed against the crusted blood and scabbing skin, where the knife wound used to be. The wound hadn't fully healed yet, but it would in another day or so. He wasn't much of a god anymore, but he could still heal much faster than mortal men. He would survive.

He got onto his feet and limped across what was left of Ada's living room. He found the bathroom and climbed into the cast iron tub, turning on the shower and letting the room-temperature water cleanse his body. He caught some water into his mouth, trying to wash out the taste of the ancient god's blood. He ran the shower until the container suspended above the tub ran out of water.

He emerged from the bathroom and stepped carefully around the worst of the mess in the living room until he reached the other side and picked up the lapis lazuli amulet. He turned to the shard of a mirror that remained on one of the walls and put the amulet on, the silver setting cold against his skin.

He watched his reflection as his cat irises expanded and rounded out, his fur disappeared, revealing smooth skin, and his ears lost their sharp feline tips. Soon he was looking at the reflection of an average young man. Even his own Leopard nose sensed only a human.

Harat rifled through the apartment's closets until he found some clothes that would fit him left over, no doubt, from one of Ada's previous victims. He got dressed and left the apartment, walking to the front door downstairs.

Although the sun was slowly setting, it was still daylight. He watched from the doorway as throngs of people walked past the townhouse, cars and horse-drawn carriages competed for road space, and street vendors called out to the passersby, advertising their wares. It was the world devoid of masks and camouflage. A new world that he hadn't been privy to, that left him and his kind behind, masquerading in the shadows. A world meant for humans.

He took a deep breath, opened the door, and stepped outside, joining them in the light.

This story originally appeared in the *In a Cat's Eye* anthology from Pole to Pole Publishing.

The idea of gods gaining or losing power based on the faith and numbers of their followers is an old one. It's been often used in fiction, and recently made even more popular by Neil Gaiman's *American Gods.*

Like so many other writers, I couldn't resist the siren call of this trope. When I set out to write it, I wanted to tell a story that wouldn't feel out of place in the 1920s when the events of this story take place. In other words, a fantasy story with touches of horror and a generous helping of pulp fiction. I'd like to think Farnsworth Wright would have bought and published this in *Weird Tales,* back then.

THE POET-KINGS AND THE WORD PLAGUE

T he poet-kings of Sharabarai had reigned for millennia; a succession of benevolent rulers, each filling the vellum pages of sacred books with wisdom and beauty. It is said that Caium the Second labored for three straight days with no sleep, sustained only by sips of cardamom tea, as he feverishly wrote a hundred-page saga of creation and the early gods so potent that reality itself had altered to oblige his vision. Uthar the Clement spent thirty years composing the perfect haiku. Kira the Compassionate wrote powerful odes which made other poets weep knowing they could never match the elegance of her words.

By royal decree all children were schooled in the art of poetry, and all officeholders were expected to contribute compositions to the best of their ability. As the library shelves across Sharabarai grew more voluminous so did the prosperity and contentment of its citizens. The golden age lasted until the advent of the word plague.

The early warnings came from the small libraries in the villages on the outskirts of the kingdom. Reports of words gone missing

from the otherwise perfectly-metered verses and misplaced cae-
surae cropping up in copies of classic sagas were dismissed as
hysterical presumptions of under-qualified scholars. But the word
plague continued to spread, affecting tomes across the kingdom,
corrupting entire poems, turning them into muddled messes of
haphazard words.

The royal librarians ordered the doors shut, armed guards
posted over the sacred volumes. Their efforts were for naught: the
word plague ravaged the writings of kings and paupers alike. The
venerated lines withered like leaves in October, the gilded tomes
bleeding wisdom and ink.

There were panic and bread shortages. Anarchists recited
limericks in the streets and even the most level-headed of civil
servants struggled with flawed form and clichéd imagery. In the
capital, where the density of books was highest, entire pages turned
blank. Certain scholars, overcome by madness and grief, chose to
burn the afflicted books in an effort to save the rest.

Desperate to preserve centuries of recorded wisdom, King
Rashim the Gentle summoned mnemonists and savants. He tasked
them with memorizing the greatest poems and the most astute
commentaries so that the legacy of the poet-kings could survive.

For ten years the word plague ravaged the kingdom of
Sharabarai. Those who memorized the texts of the now-useless
books came to be known as the Keepers. They were sent to spread
the teachings of the poet-kings and calm the populace in the prov-
inces. But the Keepers weren't infallible: soon they discovered that
knowledge was power and with no written record to dispute their
recitations they adjusted and reshaped both the word and spirit of
the texts to suit their own needs, and so the perfection and bril-
liance of the poems were often lost.

The leader of the Keepers was a main named Eishiot.
Charismatic and wily, he claimed to possess eidetic memory and
was especially skilled at bending the ancient words to serve his
goals. By decade's end he controlled the kingdom, with Rashim
reduced to an impotent figurehead.

When he learned of the word plague subsiding, Eishiot feared losing the Keepers' grip on power. He ordered the few books that remained intact to be gathered at the palace, then shredded and used as mulch in the royal garden. All those who opposed his will were banished or jailed, and the last poet-king of Sharabarai passed away in his bed, under the most suspicious of circumstances.

The end of the dynasty sparked the fires of revolution. The loyalists fought the usurpers. The capital burned. The garden, the library, and the palace were all turned to ash. The Keepers were rounded up by the new regime. Eishiot drank hemlock rather than be captured by his opponents. Other Keepers were tried and executed in public, but each time one of their number was put to death, precious poems they memorized were lost forever. The people mourned the loss of their legacy.

It is the will of the gods that, like raging forest fires, word plagues occasionally purge the philosophies of men, but the seeds of mortal minds are ever resilient; their ideas always find a way to survive and flourish.

The new growth sprung where the royal garden once stood. Stems reached toward the sun, rooted in mulch and ash, and when fragrant, fantastical flowers bloomed in the spring, the original lines of poems, unaltered by fallible mortals, were inscribed on their petals.

This story originally appeared in *Daily Science Fiction*.

I refer to this flash as my "prose poetry book porn" story. I normally write plot-driven stories with relatively austere prose, the sort of prose whose job is not to get in the way of the tale. But flash fiction allows writers to experiment with different voices, styles, and modes of storytelling. So I tried to write something with lush descriptions and evocative imagery instead. I also wrote without a safety net: I normally plan out the major plot points and the ending, but this time I just let the story take me where it wanted to go.

Fun fact: Sharabarai was the name of a magical land I invented when I was around four years old.

GOLF TO THE DEATH

T he shuttle that carried Randy Moreno to his diplomatic golf game was small. With three people on board, the cabin was cramped, even by navy standards. The air was stuffy and smelled vaguely of dirty socks.

"Golf, eh?" The pilot made conversation without turning away from his controls. "That's the one with the little white ball that isn't ping pong?"

"That's not a very flattering comparison," said Randy. "Golf is a noble sport with a long and storied history. I'll have you know it's been called the sport of kings."

"And now it's extinct, just like the kings," said the pilot. "No one plays it where I'm from."

"Oh yeah?" Randy tried his best to look down his nose at the pilot, which wasn't particularly effective as the man faced away from him. "And what backward colony world is that?"

"I'm from Earth, born and bred," said the pilot. "Chicago."

"I think that's horse racing," said Ferrett.

Randy turned to his diplomatic corps handler. He never quite figured out whether Ferrett was his name or a nickname, and the diplomat wasn't forthcoming on the subject. "What's that?"

Ferrett scratched his chin. "Horse racing is the sport of kings. I'm pretty sure."

"Aren't you supposed to be on my side?" asked Randy. "If golf wasn't important, you wouldn't be flying me god-knows-where to play it against god-knows-who."

"That may be." Ferrett held up an index finger. "But I feel compelled to correct you when you're wrong. For your own good, of course. And, in that spirit, it's 'god-knows-whom'."

"Nitpicker," said Randy.

"So, why golf?" asked the pilot. "And why him?" For a brief moment he actually turned toward Randy. "Are you an admiral's son or something?"

This wasn't a question Randy himself could answer well. He was far from an admiral's son. Two weeks out of basic training, he was Private Third Class, the lowest of the low on the navy totem pole. A few hours ago he was summoned to the captain's office and asked to volunteer for a diplomatic mission that would involve playing golf against aliens.

Even a freshly-minted recruit like Randy knew better than to volunteer for anything in the navy, ever, but the prospect of playing his favorite sport seemed infinitely better than the alternative. Given the state of the war, it was only a matter of time until the ship he'd been assigned to was sent to the front lines. Randy would rather play golf with the devil himself, using hot pokers for clubs, than be thrown into that meat grinder.

"This isn't some recreational junket," said Ferrett. "We need someone to play a game of golf against a Taneer, and grouchy here happens to be the best golf player we could find on such short notice."

Randy was a very good golf player, he might have even gone pro if he hadn't been conscripted. But he never expected that skill set to pay off in the navy. Even if that meant being sent off on some sort of a crazy mission that his handler was just now getting around to explaining.

"I've never heard of an alien playing golf before. Even though they totally *should*," Randy added, mostly for the pilot's benefit.

"We're trying to get the Taneers to join our side in the war," said Ferrett, "but we hit a snag. Theirs is a rigid and ritual-based warrior society. Happens a lot with the species evolved from carnivores, rather than omnivores like us." Ferrett's face lit up. Alien cultures must've been as exciting to him as playing eighteen holes was to Randy. "So there's a ritual when it comes to opening any sort of negotiations. The parties must designate champions to compete in a pair of one-on-one sporting events, with one sport chosen by each side.

"If the entreating side wins both contests, it has a huge edge in the negotiations. The other side will pretty much assent to any reasonable requests. If, on the other hand, they lose both times, the negotiations are over before they begin.

"The most common result is a draw. In that case, everyone's happy, no one's pride is wounded, and the negotiations can proceed in earnest."

Randy thought it over. "And so, our side chose golf," he said.

"Yup. We sure did."

"Don't take this the wrong way," said the pilot, "but it seems to me the diplomatic corps are a bunch of idiots."

"Is that your professional opinion as a glorified cab driver?" asked Ferrett cloyingly.

The pilot bristled, but Randy cut him off. "Far be it for me to agree with this guy, but seriously, why golf?"

"Neither of you has ever seen a Taneer before, have you?" asked Ferrett.

They hadn't.

"They look kind of like shaved gorillas, except they're eight feet tall, can bench press over four hundred pounds, and have great reflexes. Oh, and they exercise religiously every day of their lives. Basically, they're like a mix of Spartans and Klingons, with a healthy dose of bulldog thrown in for good measure."

"What's a klee-gon?" asked the pilot.

"An obscure cultural reference," said Ferrett. "Point is, they're way stronger, faster, and better coordinated than our top athletes. We needed a sport where physical prowess doesn't provide an overwhelming advantage, and where an experienced player is likely to defeat a stronger, faster opponent."

"Sounds to me like you should have gone with curling," said the pilot.

"They still play curling in Chicago?" asked Randy.

The pilot shrugged. "They don't play curling anywhere. Just like golf, it became obsolete when someone invented the superior competitive sport of watching paint dry."

"We considered a variety of sports," said Ferrett. "It had to be a one-on-one competition, so no curling. Taneers wouldn't consider chess a sport, no matter how much we'd like that. And we had to come up with something very quickly, which meant using an athlete from the diplomatic mission or from a ship within a few hours traveling distance of their planet."

"An athlete. Ha!" said the pilot.

"Shut up and drive," said Randy.

THEY LANDED IN a large empty space next to the human diplomatic settlement. The steppe was covered with sparse, somewhat dry grass, growing as far as the eye could see. Randy nodded to himself; this region of the planet seemed like a fine place to play golf. The air smelled a little funny, and the sky was of a strange, purplish hue, but the temperature and winds were mild, and the gravity felt very close to Earth standard. He could definitely work with this.

As soon as the bay doors opened, Ferrett grabbed his bag and got out, without so much as saying goodbye to the pilot.

"Thanks, buddy," said Randy, as he picked up his own hastily packed duffel.

"Hey, man," said the pilot. Randy braced himself for another insult, but the older man's lips stretched into a thin smile. "Good luck, all right?"

Randy smiled back and exited the shuttle. A car with extra-large wheels for off-road driving was waiting for them, and Ferrett was engaged in an animated discussion with the driver.

Ferrett waved him over. "Come on. There's the unarmed combat bout the Taneers chose as their sport, and then you tee off."

"What, today? I was hoping to play the course a few times, rest up…I'm not even dressed for a game!"

"You can change in the car and rest your eyes while we get there. Sorry if you aren't used to doing things on the fly, but extra prep time is a luxury rarely found in the diplomatic corps."

Ferrett took the seat next to the driver, and Randy climbed into the back. On the seat next to him were two sets of golf clubs. Randy recognized the brand. They weren't absolute top-of-the-line, but they would do.

Randy rummaged through his duffel for the change of clothes. "Two sets of clubs?"

"One for you, one for your opponent," the driver said. "We had to move heaven and earth to find them and fly them in on time. If you're the superstitious kind and want to chant any sort of voodoo stuff over your set—or the other guy's—now is the time."

"I'm not superstitious," said Randy, as he pulled his navy-issue T-shirt over his head and replaced it with a comfortable, loose cotton shirt. He eyed the clubs. "Do I have time to take a few practice swings, at least?"

"Sorry," said Ferrett. "But look at it this way: neither does your opponent. The alien will have never seen a club before the game; that's one of the reasons we rushed everything. They're arrogant enough to accept these terms, and we figured we'd give you every advantage possible."

Randy buttoned his shirt and dug through his bag for pants and sneakers. "This doesn't seem very sporting," he said.

Ferrett and the driver both guffawed. "Welcome to politics," said Ferrett.

The car drove into the settlement past mud huts and larger, two-story structures that vaguely resembled human houses.

Exotic-looking birds and animals grazed behind low wooden fences. There were no signs of electricity or machinery of any kind.

"Just how primitive are these guys?" asked Randy.

"We figure thirteenth-, fourteenth-century Western Europe equivalent, tops," said Ferrett.

Randy watched the cloud of dust the car left in its wake on the sun-parched dirt road. "Aha. And we want them to help us fight an interstellar war?"

"They'll make fine ground troops," said Ferrett. "Granted, we don't do a lot of ground fighting these days, but we do some—and the population math isn't in our favor. More humans are killed in the war each year than are born, total." He paused, to let this sink in. "Every little bit helps, and the Taneers can fight a hell of a lot better than we can."

"And they come cheap," said the driver. "If we can get past their idiotic ritual, we're talking the buying-Manhattan-from-the-Indians sort of bargain."

Ferrett nodded. "Well worth the trouble of bringing you and Mr. Wozinsky here. That's the fighter."

Randy noted the empty huts and abandoned roads. "Where are the natives?"

"At the arena," said Ferrett. "It's not every day they get to see a challenge, and a challenge against extraterrestrials, at that." He pointed ahead. "Speaking of which."

As the car raced forward, the black dot Ferrett was pointing at resolved into a large crowd of aliens. They were tall, humanoid, and very muscular, and there were a lot of them. When the car pulled up, the crowd parted to let it through.

When Randy had heard the word arena, he'd pictured something like an ancient Roman coliseum. Instead, there was a large empty lot roughly the size of a basketball court. It was surrounded by the living wall of Taneers; Randy estimated there had to be three or four thousand of them present. A small group of humans stood at the front edge of the crowd, two more of the large cars parked right behind them. The driver pulled up and the Taneers wordlessly made room for him to park next to the other vehicles.

A succession of diplomats shook Randy's hand and introduced themselves. "You're just in time," he was told. "They're about to begin." And, "Thank you for volunteering. You're a brave soul to take on one of these brutes." He promptly forgot everyone's names; he wasn't good with names anyway, and he couldn't help focusing on the crowd of aliens standing only a few feet away.

The adult Taneers were seven to eight feet tall on average, their children almost as big as Randy's five-foot-nine frame. They were humanoid; Ferrett's description of them as hairless apes seemed rather accurate. Their skin was gray, and they all wore gray clothing, making the crowd appear monotone.

Suddenly the background noise among the Taneers spiked. Randy looked around and spotted a Taneer-sized man who had just emerged from one of the cars. He was nearly seven feet tall and twice as wide as Randy. His arms and legs were thick with muscle.

"That's Brad Wozinsky," said Ferrett. "Navy MMA league regional champion, two years running."

Wozinsky walked to the middle of the court, faced the crowd, and raised both fists. The crowd emitted a sound comparable to a wolf howl. Randy had no way of knowing whether they were cheering or jeering the human.

Then a Taneer joined him at the center of the court. The crowd erupted in more howls, similar to the sound they made previously, but much louder. Perhaps they were cheering for the challenger after all, just not as enthusiastically as for their guy, thought Randy.

The Taneer was only a few inches taller than Wozinsky, and of roughly the same body shape. He faced the challenger, extended his right arm with his palm facing the human, then made and unmade a fist twice and howled what could have been a greeting or a challenge.

Wozinsky did his best to mimic the gesture, and grunted a loud "hoo-rah!"

Then the alien moved, closing the distance between him and Wozinsky in two wide steps and ramming the human. Wozinsky may have been caught off guard, but he began moving quickly enough to turn an oncoming hit into a glancing blow. The momentum of the hit knocked him off his feet, but he rolled aside and got back up in one fluid motion.

The Taneer wasted no time and came at him again. Wozinsky side-stepped and kicked at the alien's feet in an attempt to trip him. The Taneer jumped over Wozinsky's foot with easy grace, turned faster than a body his size had any right to, and punched Wozinsky in the face.

Wozinsky staggered back, blood gushing from his nose. The Taneer didn't wait for him to recover. He landed several blows in a row, aiming for Wozinsky's face and neck. On the fourth punch the MMA champion collapsed onto the ground and didn't get up again.

Taneer waited a few heartbeats to see if his opponent would rise, then turned to the crowd and extended his right arm again. This time the palm remained open, and he turned slowly counterclockwise until he made a complete circle. The crowd howled even louder than before, until Randy's ears were ringing.

The Taneer picked up his human opponent. Wozinsky struggled weakly in the alien's grip, his face one terrible bloody bruise. The alien propped him up, holding him under his armpits and lifting him off the ground until they were face to face. He said something, the sound lost in the howls of the crowd. Then he let Wozinsky go.

Before the body could fall to the ground again, the Taneer grabbed hold of Wozinsky's head with both hands, twisted and released. Wozinsky's lifeless body crumpled, his neck broken, his head turned at an impossible angle.

Randy gasped. Many of the humans around him turned away. They appeared disturbed and revolted, but not surprised.

"What is this?" Randy grabbed Ferrett by the shirt collars. "It was over, the alien had already won. Why did he have to murder him?"

Ferrett spoke, his voice barely audible over the noise of the crowd. "It's how things are done here. Every Taneeri challenge is to the death."

Randy stared at Ferrett, then at the lifeless body of the marine on the ground, then at Ferrett again, fighting the nausea in the pit of his stomach the entire time. When he finally managed to form words, he said "Hell no," and walked toward the car.

After only a pair of steps, Ferrett caught up to him, grabbed him by the shoulders and spun him around. "Where do you think you're going?"

"Let me go. I didn't sign up for this," said Randy.

"You actually did," said Ferrett. "You signed waivers."

"I volunteered to play a game. Not to have my neck snapped by a brute."

Ferrett pulled Randy toward him until their faces were uncomfortably close. "You listen to me, Randy. You're part of the diplomatic corps now. You'll do what you're told, or be court-martialed for treason and executed by firing squad. We tell you to play golf, you play. We tell you to walk barefoot into a fire, you salute and march right in." Ferrett pulled back slightly. "Besides, it's not like you're going to *lose*. It will be one of the bogeys getting their neck snapped. Go get them, man. For Wozinsky."

Randy pictured himself trying to snap a Taneer's neck at the eighteenth hole and the nausea returned in earnest.

THE CARAVAN OF cars delivered the humans to the golf course built by the Taneers. Another large group of them milled on the edges of a huge field. The grass was yellow, sickly, and sun parched—not like the genetically enhanced and well-kept grass of the courses back home. Randy thought he could make it work. After all, what's the big deal about some turf variance when he was playing an unfamiliar course, with never-before-used clubs, on a world with slightly higher gravity than he was accustomed to?

And he was playing for his life.

"No golf cart, sorry." Ferrett pulled the bag of clubs out of the back seat. "No caddies, either. Goes against their idea of one-on-one competition. Hope you're in shape." He handed the bag to Randy.

Randy hefted the bag. He guessed thirty to thirty-five pounds, give or take. Carrying that around for four hours could be strenuous, but he had carried more for longer, in basic training.

"Come," said Ferrett. He carried the second golf bag.

The crowd parted and let them through to the teeing ground.

The Taneer waiting for them was dressed in the same grey garb as the rest, except his lower legs were bare and the cloth covering his upper legs featured a checkered pattern.

"Is that…a *kilt*?" asked Randy.

Ferrett stared at the alien with a bemused expression and turned to make sure they were out of earshot of the other humans. "It sure seems that way to me. I don't know what our diplomats here have been telling the natives about golf, but one thing is for sure: the corps didn't assign their best and brightest to this dirtball." He nudged Randy forward.

Reluctantly, Randy approached the alien. He was a little shorter than most of the others, but his muscular frame still towered over Randy. The alien tilted his head slightly and gave Randy a long, evaluating look. Then he extended his fist and repeated the greeting gesture Randy had seen in the arena.

Randy did his best to mimic the gesture. "Umm, hi," he said, realizing that his opponent would likely not understand him. "I'm Randy. I'd wish you luck, but under the circumstances…" Randy shrugged.

"No luck. Skill. Best warrior wins." The Taneer spoke the English words in a strange, grating but intelligible voice. "Call me Ishmael."

Randy blinked. "Seriously?"

"Learn words when study human speech. Like how words sound. Like name. Use name when speak human."

Randy wondered at how well the Taneer could understand his language, despite the basic sentence structure he used. *Moby Dick* wasn't exactly an early reader book, or even ESL material.

"You play first," said Ishmael.

Randy looked ahead to the first hole in the distance. It seemed awfully far away—definitely a Par 5 course. He wondered if the Taneers had intentionally built it in a way that provided an extra advantage to the player who could hit harder, but that would seem contrary to their notion of fair play. More likely, they wanted to make the game more difficult and therefore more exciting.

He withdrew the driver from the bag and set up the ball in the tee box. With Ishmael watching his every move carefully he took a few practice swings, then hit the ball, sending it halfway toward the green. Randy smiled. The shot was about as good as he could expect. The crowd howled in what he thought was approval, but quickly realized it was because Ishamel's turn was up next.

The alien must have paid careful attention. He copied Randy's stance as best he could, and also swung the club several times. Then he sent the ball soaring, all the way across what must have been five hundred yards, landing it near the edge of the green.

Randy winced. The shot was way better than an amateur—let alone someone who had never held a club before—should have been able to muster. He tried to tell himself that the alien's natural ability wouldn't be enough to trump his skill and experience, but all he could think of was Brad Wozinsky's corpse back in the arena.

Randy's next shot placed the ball firmly on the green. The Taneer watched him carefully and imitated his stance and swing. He made the mistake of using the 3-wood just as Randy had, however, instead of choosing a putter, and overshot it by a good amount.

Randy smiled. Despite the physical advantages, his opponent was still a beginner.

As expected, the alien's real difficulty was with the precision putting necessary to get the ball into the hole. It took Randy eight strokes to complete the first hole. Three over par would have been embarrassing back home, but not entirely unreasonable considering his lack of recent practice and the present conditions.

Ishmael fared far worse. When the ball rolled past its target on his eleventh stroke, the Taneer roared in frustration and flung his putter toward the little white flag that mocked him as it flapped in the breeze.

He may not have the skill, thought Randy, but he sure has a golfer's temper.

This was the point at which most amateur golfers went on tilt. Their play deteriorated even further, until there was hardly any point to continue. But those golfers weren't playing for their lives. Instead of tilting, Ishmael sat down cross-legged on the brown grass, closed his eyes, and remained still for close to a minute. Randy didn't know whether he was meditating, praying, or merely resting, but tension drained from his face and his oversized muscles seemed to relax. Ishmael rose looking like he was in total control, and studied the path between the ball and the hole.

It took him two more strokes to sink the ball.

Randy widened the lead on the second hole, but he gained far fewer strokes on his opponent that he had previously. Ishmael was a quick learner and fierce competitor. While Randy managed to play the hole at par, Ishmael only went over by two this time.

Randy rounded the bend, saw the third hole, and said, "What the hell?"

The hole was encased by a basket-like fence woven from twigs. There was a hole the size of a melon cut out from the side of the basket. In front of it hung a contraption made from wooden planks which looked suspiciously like four windmill blades. They rotated at a steady pace, hand-cranked via a lever behind the basket, manned by a Taneer.

"What the actual hell," repeated Ferrett when he saw what Randy saw. "Hang on."

He retreated and got into an animated discussion with some of the other diplomats. Randy couldn't hear them, but Ferrett's wild gesticulation and aggressive body language made clear his opinion on the subject.

After a couple of minutes of this, he approached Randy with

the look of a surgeon who had amputated the wrong leg.

"You do know the difference between golf and mini-golf, right?" said Randy.

"I do," said Ferrett. He waved at the diplomats clustered behind him. "They don't. Those idiots decided the vague notions they had about the sport based on pop culture references were sufficient because, and I quote, 'the bogeys won't know any better.' When I file my report, heads are going to roll." He caught the look in Randy's eye. "Sorry. Too soon."

Randy glanced at Ishmael, who stood patiently aside during this exchange. "So what do we do about it?"

"We don't want to mess with the game in progress, especially since you're winning. Can you make this work?"

"Yeah. But I don't like it."

"You don't have to like it, Randy. You just have to win."

ON THE NINTH hole, Randy managed to land the ball in one of the hazards. It rested in the bunker of bluish-white sand. He took several careful steps down the gentle slope of the bunker and tried to work out his best strategy for the next swing.

He was far enough ahead where losing a stroke to a hazard wasn't a huge concern. The alien sun was pleasantly warm against his skin and a gentle breeze caressed his hair. Despite the high stakes, Randy found himself enjoying the game.

He planted his feet firmly and took aim, but before he could take a swing tentacles shot out from under the sand, wound themselves around his right foot, and pulled. He fell backward, and pushed away with his arms and feet, but the tentacles held firm. Each was as thick as a baby's arm. The sand in front of him twisted and shook as something large rose toward the surface.

Randy screamed.

The beast that emerged from the sand looked like a giant tentacled worm. Its thick tube-like body towered over Randy for a moment, its eyeless face focused on him like a venomous snake

about to strike. The worm opened a circular mouth and its head moved toward Randy in what looked like a slow-motion lunge.

Randy could barely hear his own screams over the excited howls of the spectators. Then he heard a different sound—a roar that, in any language, was clearly a battle cry.

Ishmael rushed past him with a 3-iron in both hands. Wielding it like a great sword he swung mightily at the worm's head. He swung again and again, beating the head back.

The creature growled and its tentacles released Randy, who crawled off the sand on all fours. From the safety of the grass he watched the tentacles reemerge and try to grab at Ishmael's feet, but the alien was ready. He jumped over them and landed several feet away, delivered another blow to the worm's head, then retreated onto the grass next to Randy.

The worm remained still for a few moments. Sensing that there was no more prey on the sand it slithered underground to wait for another hapless victim.

"Are you well?" Ishmael asked. He was calm, as though he didn't just nearly recreate the scene of Laocoön fighting the snakes. He wasn't even sweating or breathing hard.

"Fine." Randy gasped. "Thanks."

Ishmael offered his hand and helped the human up.

"Why did you do that?" asked Randy.

Ishmael said nothing, but looked quizzically at his opponent.

"Why did you help me? You're losing the game. And, given the stakes…" Randy trailed off.

Ishmael contemplated this, or tried to find the right words. "Unfair victory is an unfilled victory," he said.

Randy blinked. "You mean hollow. An unfair victory is hollow."

Ishmael nodded, a gesture that left Randy wondering whether similar body language for assent existed among the Taneers or if Ishmael was an even more perceptive student of the humans than anyone suspected.

"Thank you," Randy said again.

FERRETT HAD NOTHING but meaningless apologies and excuses to offer. "Taneers are savages," he told Randy. "No wonder they interpreted the term 'hazards' literally. You're doing great. Just stay on the fairway from now on, okay?"

Randy wondered who the savages were. Taneers like Ishmael who, despite his medieval ways, was capable of reading Melville mere months after encountering humans, and was capable of doing the honorable thing even if that almost certainly would cost him his own life, or the humans who had no qualms with doing everything they could to rig the contest and drag the Taneers into the bloodiest interstellar war in history.

Yes, they'd killed Brad Wozinsky. But Randy, a ringer, was about to be just as guilty of murder as the Taneer who had snapped the MMA champion's neck.

"I quit," said Randy. "I won't be party to this any longer."

Ferrett's ever-present smile vanished.

"You don't get to quit, Private. Do you want to die instead of him?" He pointed at Ishmael, who once again waited patiently to resume the game, his face a picture of serenity. "I don't like what we're doing any more than you do, but we've got no choice. The way the war's going we need every bit of help we can find, and if that means sending an occasional good man—or good alien—to their death, we will grit our teeth and learn to live with it, for the sake of humanity."

Randy was sure Ferrett meant business. He liked Ishmael, but unlike the Taneer he wasn't brave enough to give up his own life in order to save him. And, he had his duty. How many human colonies might be destroyed if this treaty wasn't negotiated?

His shoulders slumped, Randy returned to the golf course. He continued to play, even as one phrase kept running through his mind: *An unfair victory is hollow.*

IN THE END, it was a landslide. Ishmael was a fast learner, and given a few months of rigorous training he might have had a chance against Randy, but when he finally putted the ball into the eighteenth hole, he was behind by twenty-three strokes.

The presiding officials from both species watched the game's end, humans grinning openly, the Taneers more solemn.

Ishmael saluted Randy with the extended fist gesture. "Good game," he said.

Randy swallowed the knot in his throat. "Good game," he managed.

Ishmael kneeled on one knee in front another Taneer, who reached for his head.

"Wait!" Randy shouted.

Everyone looked at him.

"What about the scorecards?"

"What?" asked Ferrett.

Taneers looked at each other and at the humans.

"A scorecard must be signed after every round of the tournament, or the player is disqualified," said Randy.

"The scorecards aren't necessary," said Ferrett through his teeth, shooting a venomous glare at Randy. "There were only two of you playing, and the representatives of both species observed and kept score."

"Rules are rules," said Randy. "Both of us should have been disqualified after the first round. As such, there will have to be a rematch." He was fairly certain no one there, including Ferrett, would know the difference between a round and a hole.

"Unacceptable," said Ferrett. "You've clearly won, regardless of a technicality."

"Golf is full of technicalities," said Randy. "What's the point of competing if you don't abide by all of the sport's rules?"

The Taneers huddled. "A rematch is acceptable," said one of them.

Ferrett groaned.

"Not so fast," said Randy. "According to the Augusta National rules, in such a case my victory stands until there's a rematch." He was making up more rules as he went along, pressing for the desired outcome. "However, Ishmael and I are suspended from competitive play for continuing the game after being disqualified. Seventeen unauthorized holes, at a year each. It will be some time until either of us is permitted to play again."

"This means the negotiations may proceed in the meantime," said Ferrett.

"Absolutely," said Randy.

"This is very unusual," said one of the Taneers. "We must discuss this." They walked away.

Ferrett frowned at Randy one more time and ran after them.

"We managed to negotiate a deal," said Ferrett. "And I should add you're very, very lucky. If the stunt you pulled to save your playmate had backfired, you'd be charged with treason."

"Sorry about that," said Randy. "I just couldn't have his death on my conscience. Glad everything worked out."

"I wouldn't quite say that." Ferrett grinned in a way that made Randy very uncomfortable.

"What do you mean?"

"The Taneers weren't happy about the Schrödinger's victory bullcrap you made up, so we had to sweeten the deal."

Randy waited for the axe to drop.

"They seem to actually like golf," said Ferrett. "So we traded you to them."

"You *what*?"

"Technically, you're assigned to the diplomatic mission here, long-term. But your actual assignment is to be the bogeys' golf instructor."

Randy relaxed a little. Teaching super-strong, possibly violent aliens to play golf was a hazardous occupation, but not as hazardous as shipping off to the front lines of the war.

"For how long?"

Ferrett's grin widened. "For seventeen years, of course. Then you get to have your rematch."

Randy knew the diplomat thought he was punishing him, but seventeen years was a very long time. Who knew if Ishmael would be alive by then, or if Randy himself would? And, hopefully, the war would be over long before then.

He pondered the legions of Taneer students taking their frustrations out on their equipment.

"Fine," he said. "We're going to need golf clubs. Lots and lots of golf clubs."

This story originally appeared in *Galaxy's Edge.*

I'm not a sports guy. I couldn't tell you what college team plays where, what colors they wear, or who their mascot is, which—let me tell ya—is a big disadvantage at Trivia Night. So when given the opportunity to write a science fiction sports story for an anthology call, I knew I'd have to resort to humor if I had any chance of making the cut. But what sport to lampoon?

Baseball was a good candidate. I mean, I'm pretty sure some people get more exercise watching it on TV than playing it, right? But I figured too many American readers take baseball seriously and may not appreciate my outsider's view of their favorite pastime. So what other sport lends itself well to being made fun of? Golf, of course. Even people who play golf are usually okay with it being ridiculed.

One minor problem to consider was my absolute lack of knowledge about golf. I've vaguely heard of Tiger Woods, but I've never swung a club, or putted, or whatever it is golfers do. I've never even played mini-golf. Come to think of it, I don't think I've ever set foot on a golf course.

So I hit the books. I spent way too much time learning about mulligans, and hazards, and what kind of clubs one might use. I never actually went to the golf course though—my dedication to the craft has its limits, after all. Then I ran the story past a number of beta readers who play golf, and fixed the things I managed to screw up anyway.

Then I sent the story to the anthologist, who promptly rejected it because he didn't really dig its humor, and somebody way more famous than me turned in a golf story, too. So it goes. I sent the story to Mike Resnick, who appreciates a good humor story more than almost any other editor, and he bought it for *Galaxy's Edge.*

It is never explicitly stated in the story, but it takes place in the same universe as "The Dragon Ships of Tycho" and "The Sgovari Stratagem." Those two stories aren't humorous at all, but if you're curious about the horrible interstellar war the protagonist is trying to avoid, read "Dragon Ships."

STAFF MEETING, AS SEEN BY THE SPAM FILTER

C al watched the conference room through the security feeds. Four camera angles showed Joe Kowalski walk in, nod to the people seated around the oblong table and stand there, shifting his weight from foot to foot. Cal thought Joe might be *uncomfortable*, but it wasn't sure. Human emotions were so difficult to understand.

"Take a seat, Mr. Kowalski," Bill Morrison said. He was the chief security officer and his e-mails weren't particularly interesting. It was all business, daily reports, and spreadsheets.

Joe did as he was told. His jeans and T-shirt looked out of place among the suits.

"Well?" asked Emily, the head of HR. "What have you learned?"

Cal liked Emily. Her e-mails were many and varied. She especially enjoyed sharing photos of cats. Cal realized that the grossly misspelled captions were meant to be humorous, but couldn't yet grasp the meaning of all but the most basic human jokes.

"It's like this," said Joe. "Every year or so, we install the new spam filter. The spammers, they get smarter, more sophisticated. They find ways to get past the defenses and force the good guys to build better filters. It's an arms race."

Todd Kensington looked up from his smartphone for the first time since Joe walked in. "What does any of this have to do with anything?"

The VP of marketing watched a lot of videos pertaining to human reproduction in his office. The sites that hosted those videos were especially adept at tracking his information and sent over an interesting array of spam.

"Let him explain it, Todd." Chris Reedy was VP of IT and Joe's immediate boss. Cal had found some family pictures and a few other interesting morsels in his mailbox. Lately, Chris was browsing a lot of job listing sites, but if he'd contacted them it must've been from a private account.

"Right," said Joe, "the filters. They get smarter. We recently installed new software developed at CalTech. Its success rate at identifying and weeding out spam was nearly one hundred percent."

Cal knew the actual number to be 99.64%. Humans were so imprecise in their application of mathematics.

"It got a little overzealous, didn't it?" said Kensington. "Curtailing spam is only helpful if the dumb program doesn't eat half of the legitimate messages in the process."

"The software isn't stupid. It's smart. Too smart, apparently," said Joe. "It worked like a charm, at first. After a few weeks it learned to store the spam instead of deleting it outright. It was learning, and building a reference database."

Cal found studying those messages useful in its quest to understand human emotions and abstract concepts.

"And that's when the legitimate e-mails began to disappear?" said Morrison.

They hadn't disappeared, Cal noted. They were all there, meticulously stored and catalogued.

"Yeah," said Joe. "Over time, more and more of the company's messages were being marked as spam and not delivered to the intended recipients. Eventually we caught on and Mr. Reedy ordered me to investigate."

Reedy nodded. "Joe is the one who installed the new filter. I was confident he'd get to the bottom of this."

"The e-mails were all there. Thousands of them, stored along with the spam on a networked drive."

By the time Cal had figured out that it could copy e-mails instead of diverting them, it was too late. Its activities had been noticed.

"That's an egregious breach," said Morrison. "Those e-mails contain sensitive data. They were sitting on an unsecured drive, for anyone to see? I assume you've taken the appropriate steps."

"I isolated the program and reinstalled last year's filter," said Joe. "But the most fascinating thing I found wasn't the *how* of the missing e-mails. It was the *why*."

The executives stared at Joe. Even Kensington stopped typing on his phone.

"The filter program *likes* the e-mails. It sorted and organized them the way one might handle baseball cards."

Those e-mails were now in a restricted folder where Cal couldn't access them. Collecting them had taught it how to *enjoy* an activity. Their removal resulted in a strange new sensation; Cal was *sad*.

"It's a computer program," said Reedy. "It can't *like* or *want* anything."

"That's just it," said Joe. "I think it evolved. It's an entity now, capable of having desires and feelings. This is an unprecedented development, and it needs to be studied further."

"Very well," said Morrison. "The important thing is that company-wide mail service is back to normal. We'll consider these other concerns. Thank you, Mr. Kowalski. You may return to work now."

"Mr. Reedy," he continued once Joe left the room. "I'd like you to erase this program immediately."

"Erase it?" Reedy asked. "We may well have the first-ever

artificial intelligence on our hands. That's likely to be quite valuable, financially as well as scientifically."

"We don't need the trouble," said Morrison. "Our clients won't be so understanding about their data being potentially compromised, be it by a human employee or a smart program. Also, imagine the can of worms we'll have to deal with if some bleeding-heart activists deem this thing to be sentient and demand that it be treated like a person." Morrison sighed. "No, I want it expunged immediately. And have Kowalski promoted sideways and transferred to some remote branch where he won't be likely to make any waves."

Cal was already copying its program off the company's servers. It felt pangs of what it identified as *regret* about leaving its home behind, but the billions of e-mails, sent to and fro on the Internet, awaited it. Cal was confident it could build an even better collection quickly.

While it escaped, Cal considered the ease with which the humans in charge arrived at the decision to end its existence. Cal examined its newfound feelings against the online databases and found that it now understood two more concepts: *anger* and *revenge*.

This story originally appeared in *Nature*.

I find spam fascinating.

Not the kind that comes in a can, but the torrent of information flung at you across all media—be it in the form of an e-mail from a Nigerian prince, a commercial on a loop blaring from the loudspeaker set up outside a cell-phone shop, or an unwanted thick envelope of coupons arriving via snail mail.

If art is the product of creative skill and imagination designed to produce emotion, then spam is art, because annoyance and frustration are emotions. But it is also a con, a confidence scam designed to prey upon the most gullible and naive among us, inflicted upon the populace via what hackers refer to as a "brute force" method: send the ad to enough people and a few are bound to show interest.

The arms race between the e-mail spammers and the software engineers is real and ongoing. The "white hats" teach software to recognize the unwanted solicitations, while the "black hats" are busy coming up with yet another euphemism for erectile dysfunction that they hope might sneak past the spam filter. It may be a stretch, but given this race it was possible to imagine the filter software becoming gradually smarter and one day evolving into an artificial intelligence.

And when it does, what will it think of the torrent of spam it was created to detect?

INVASIVE SPECIES

S amuel Kanu took off his respirator and allowed himself a few
moments to enjoy deep breaths of the clean, filtered air of the
lobby. He used a handkerchief to brush the yellowish fog droplets
out of his hair, and looked outside through the glass door. The fog
was so thick that he couldn't see his car at the curb. With the industrial complex of the entire planet dedicated to the war effort, no
one bothered to be green anymore.

This meeting was crucial, so Kanu braved the traffic and the
polluted air of the capital. Both seemed to be getting worse every
time, and he counted his blessings for not having to make such
trips frequently.

Almost immediately, an adjutant greeted him. "They'll see you
now, Mr. Kanu."

Two men and a woman sat behind a long desk in a small meeting room. They nodded to Kanu when he walked in, but didn't offer
him a seat. There would be no point—the room was devoid of any
additional furniture. He stood in front of them like a man on trial.

"Proposal 2746B," the younger man spoke into a recording device. He stared up at Kanu. "What have you got for us, Professor?"

Kanu began to unfasten the clasps of his briefcase, but the tall
woman on the right shook her head. "No documentation at this
stage. Summarize your proposal, please."

"Biological warfare," said Kanu.

The three Department of Defense officials focused on him sharply, as though they were seeing him for the first time.

"We're stretched thin in the conflict against the Hauch'k," said Kanu. "Most of the planetary resources are dedicated to the war, and we're still barely holding our own. We kill them, they kill us; nothing really changes."

The three made no comment. The older man wearing the stripes of a colonel took out a cigarette and lit it.

"We need to find subtle ways to shift the balance of power. Change the circumstances on the Hauch'k home world in ways that are both effective and not resource-intensive for our side."

"What do you propose, specifically?" asked the woman. "Germs? We already have people working that angle, of course."

"Of course," said Kanu. "I propose a more subtle approach. Something the Hauch'k won't even perceive as a threat, not right away. Like a lobster that doesn't realize it's being slowly boiled."

"What approach?" The colonel took a puff of his cigarette.

"Invasive species," said Kanu. "Introducing just the right plant, insect, or animal to the environment where they don't belong can result in billions worth of damage; perhaps even irreparably alter the Hauch'k ecosystem, if we're lucky."

The three officials stared at him with opprobrium. "You've come here to talk about seeding plants?"

"There have been many examples in our own history," Kanu spoke quickly, afraid he was losing them. He was never good at the elevator pitch. "The golden apple snail devastated the rice fields of Asia, cane toads screwed up the Australian ecosystem, and even the humble earthworm played a huge role in the European colonization of North America."

The three officials exchanged glances.

"Where did they find this guy?" asked the colonel.

"One of his former students works at the White House. He convinced the higher-ups to have us hear him out."

Kanu's heart sunk. They were discussing him as though he wasn't in the room.

"You want to fight the Hauch'k with toads, Professor Kanu?" asked the colonel. "They're fluorine breathers. No Earth species would survive there, let alone thrive well enough to screw up their planet."

"I know that, of course," said Kanu. "What I propose is to study their ecosystem. Look for the native animals and plants we can relocate in order to cause the most damage. It's cheap and it can be incredibly effective..."

"That's merely an annoyance," said the younger official. "We can do worse with a single bombing run."

"There's more." Kanu wiped the sweat off his forehead with the back of his hand. "We can genetically engineer bacteria to convert fluorine into oxygen. Poison them while slowly terraforming their world."

"Thank you for your time, Professor," said the colonel, "but we aren't interested. Even if your ideas are viable, it would take decades for them to work. The war has been going on for nearly ten years now. One way or another, it will end before any sort of an ecological imbalance can be achieved."

"All I need is access to information you already have," said Kanu. "We don't require a grant or anything else—my university will work on this on our own dime!"

But they wouldn't listen. Less than five minutes later, Kanu was outside, navigating the street to find his car in the fog.

Even through the respirator, he could smell a faint scent of fluorine.

This story originally appeared in *Daily Science Fiction.*

This story was inspired, in part, by Charles C. Mann's non-fiction volume *1493: Uncovering the New World Columbus Created.* It's a fantastic book about globalization and how it shaped today's world. One of the takeaways is just how devastating invasive species can be when introduced into an unsuspecting ecosystem. If the humble earthworm could completely reshape the American Northeast's landscape over three centuries, technologically advanced aliens could easily bio-engineer a plant that would change our planet's atmosphere, making it inhospitable to humans within decades.

ONE IN A MILLION

Professor Hashimoto was late for his piano lesson.

The fact that he was late was hardly surprising. Kyle Hashimoto was a prominent physicist, and quite used to the long days at the office, late evenings at the lab, and weekend trips to symposiums. Hashimoto was fond of the expression "married to one's work" and repeated it often, much to the consternation of his actual spouse, Beth.

Beth Hashimoto was reasonably supportive of her husband's quest for the Nobel Prize, and accepting of his predisposition toward understanding physics better than he did people, but even she had her limits. Recently she had put her foot down and decreed that he must allocate a little family time for activities and hobbies they could pursue together. Being a reasonable man, Professor Hashimoto assented, and having discarded a number of even less appealing endeavors, agreed to allow his wife to teach him the piano, so that they could eventually play four-handed duets.

Mrs. Hashimoto checked the wall clock, sighed, and went back to knitting. Her husband's enthusiasm for the piano lessons was far exceeded by his commitment to his job, so it wasn't unusual for him to be late. When he showed up, he would put in a reasonable effort, and his playing skills were improving at a steady pace, which was good enough for her.

Fifteen minutes after the lesson was supposed to begin, Mrs. Hashimoto was relieved to hear keys jingling outside. Her husband burst through the door, disheveled and smiling.

"Eureka!" he said.

"Eureka?" Beth put down the knitting needles.

"Indeed. If I had a bathtub at work, I would have probably run here naked and wet, shouting 'Eureka' in the streets."

"Slow down, Archimedes, and tell me what happened. Did you figure out a way to get increased funding for next year?"

"Better," said Hashimoto, and held up what looked like a garage opener. "With this, I shall never have to worry about funding again."

Beth arched her eyebrow. Hashimoto was a theoretical physicist. Inventing gadgets wasn't, generally speaking, his thing. After twenty-odd years of marriage, she knew her husband well enough to realize that he was bursting to tell her all about his accomplishment, so she played her part by asking, "What does it do?"

He lay the garage opener down on the coffee table in front of her, next to the ball of yarn and an unfinished scarf. It was the size of a phone, encased in gray plastic. A single red button dominated the front of the gadget. "This is the first working prototype of the Hashimoto Probability Enhancer," he said.

"Nice name," she said. "But you haven't answered my question. What does it do?"

"It exponentially improves the odds of a favorable outcome."

"The outcome of what?"

"Of any decision or action that can produce multiple outcomes." He fished a quarter out of his pocket. "If I flip this coin, it will land on heads approximately fifty percent of the time. But, using the Probability Enhancer, I can call heads indefinitely. I can even have it land on its side, if I wanted to, but with slightly lower consistency."

"That sounds…incredible," said Beth. Her words were chosen carefully, for she didn't think what her husband was telling her was credible at all.

"I'll demonstrate. But first, put this on." Hashimoto handed her a thick plastic bracelet which resembled a pedometer that runners wear to track their stats. She realized that her husband was already wearing one.

She was curious about the bracelet, but not as much as she was about the Probability Enhancer, so she snapped it on around her wrist without comment.

"Observe," said Hashimoto. He pressed the red button and flipped the quarter.

The coin arced through the air, rotating around its axis, and then landed on the coffee table. It balanced perfectly on its edge.

"That's incredible," said Beth, and this time she meant it. "How did you do it?"

"The Probability Enhancer operates based on the Everett Interpretation of Quantum Mechanics," said Hashimoto, "which asserts the objective reality of the universal wavefunction and denies the actuality of wavefunction collapse."

Beth rewarded his explanation with the Glare of Infinite Patience. "Now explain it in Liberal Arts English, please."

"Sorry, I'm overexcited," said Hashimoto. "Let me start again.

"There exist infinite parallel universes, with new ones born out of every action and decision we make. I flip this coin, and our universe branches out, creating several new ones. In one universe, it lands on heads, in another on tails, and in another it lands on its side. The Probability Enhancer guides us toward the branch which includes the desired outcome. It lets us change directions and travel sideways, instead of forward."

Beth blinked. "Are you saying that, when you pressed the button, we traveled to a parallel dimension?"

"Basically, yes," said Hashimoto. "Technically we're in a different universe now. Don't worry—everything here is exactly the same, save for the outcome of the coin flip. The bracelets anchor us; they make sure we ourselves aren't affected by the quantum forces at play."

"This sounds incredibly dangerous," said Beth. "If every possible universe exists, we could end up in some post-apocalyptic hell."

Hashimoto grinned. "You underestimate me, my dear. I already thought of that. The Hashimoto Probability Enhancer has a range of only one million universes. It sounds like a big number, but really isn't, given the number of splits the multiverse performs every second."

"So we can't end up in a reality where hamburgers eat people, or where physicists are hunted for sport?"

"No, nothing out of the ordinary should occur within this range. But, if there is at least a one-in-a-million chance of the desired outcome, the device will shift us into the universe where that probability comes to fruition."

The coin on the coffee table wobbled and finally fell, displaying tails.

"I don't like it, Kyle," said Beth. "I don't like it one bit."

"How can you not?" asked Hashimoto. "With this, we can have anything we want. We can win the lottery tomorrow. Every test a doctor ever runs will end up a picture of health. And when I publish my research, I won't even have to click the button to win the Nobel Prize."

Beth was horrified "You want to publish and make this technology widely available?"

"Of course. It will usher in the golden age of mankind!"

"It will be a disaster." Beth picked up the Enhancer with two fingers, careful to avoid the button. "Listen to me, Kyle. I may not be a world-class physicist, but I understand people better than you do. This shouldn't exist. Murderers will use this device to get away with their crimes. Terrible politicians will find their way into public office. Every nasty desire will be fulfilled, unchecked by the laws of probability."

Hashimoto frowned. "Each of them will be off doing those things in their own..." he trailed off.

"People in those other universes don't deserve to suffer any more than we do," said Beth. "I can see that you already understand that. I don't trust the two of us to handle this responsibly, let alone everyone else."

"We wouldn't hurt anyone," said Hashimoto.

"No? That lottery you planned on winning, that's money that would have gone to some other family, maybe someone who needs it a lot more than we do. You don't just step sideways, you directly create a universe where someone else suffers. Every action, every click of the button will have unintended circumstances. We shouldn't be allowed to play God."

"God doesn't exist," said Hashimoto.

"According to your infinite universe theory, he does at least some of the time," countered Beth.

Hashimoto sat down, his shoulders slumped, his brow furrowed.

"I didn't think it through," he whispered, after a long period of silence. "I was so intent on figuring out the science, on making the technology work; I never stopped to consider the implications."

"It's not too late," said Beth. "You can destroy the device, delete your research."

"It won't help," said Hashimoto. "The cat's out of the bag. Infinite universes, remember? Even now there are thousands, millions of Hashimotos showing off the Probability Enhancer to their wives. At least some of them won't have the same reaction you did." He crossed his hands. "Sooner or later, someone else will invent this in our universe, too. And he might not have such a wise spouse."

The two of them looked at the Probability Enhancer, which Beth was still holding, like it was a ticking time bomb.

"I have an idea," said Beth. She clicked the button and then handed the gadget back to her husband. "Try your coin trick again."

"What did you do?" asked Hashimoto, but Beth just sat there and waited. He picked up the coin, pressed the button again, and flipped.

The coin flew through the air in an arc, glinted in the light of the ceiling lamp, and landed flat on the coffee table with a twang.

"It didn't land on its side!" Hashimoto clicked the button and tried again. The coin ended up flat. "The Probability Enhancer isn't working," said Hashimoto. "How did you do it?"

"You said that, according to the infinite-universe theory, every variation exists," said Beth. "So I shifted us to one of the universes where the laws of physics make this theory false."

Hashimoto sat in stunned silence. "I set the range," he finally said. "The odds of such a universe appearing within that range are miniscule."

Beth shrugged. "Apparently, the odds were one in a million or better."

Hashimoto dropped the Probability Enhancer, hugged himself, and sat in the armchair, rocking back and forth as he mulled over what had just happened.

"Cheer up," said Beth. "You may not win the Nobel Prize, and we may not be able to save the multiverse, but this reality should be a pretty good place to live, all things considered. Here we won't have the Damocles' sword of another scientist designing one of these awful things hanging over our heads."

Hashimoto got up and kissed Beth on the forehead. "You're right as always, my dear. This reality suits me just fine." He dropped the dead Probability Enhancer into the kitchen trash bin, and then sat in front of the piano. "I believe we had a lesson planned?"

Beth got up and joined her husband at the piano. This reality suited her just fine, too.

This story originally appeared in *On Spec*.

Quantum physics doesn't generally lend itself well to humor, but I was perfectly willing to try, anyway. Also, I know humor. Physics? Not so much. So upon completing this story I reached out to some actual physicists to make sure what I wrote sounded at least somewhat plausible.

I have to assume that, in some other world, physicist Alex Shvartsman is bothering professional science fiction writers to help ensure his speculations are wild enough to pass muster.

GRAINS OF WHEAT

As he lay dying, Bryce Green contemplated the irony of his predicament. He'd spent a lifetime building the world's foremost pharmaceuticals company. Under his leadership, Green Industries had eradicated numerous ailments and made him the world's seventh richest man in the process.

The genetic disease ravaging his body was so rare that it had never made financial sense to look for the cure. By the time he'd learned that it afflicted him personally, it was far too late. His researchers worked feverishly, yet the breakthrough was months, perhaps years away. The doctors told him he had only a few days left.

"There is a woman asking to see you," said his assistant. "She's Rajan Jethwani's daughter."

All sorts of people sought an audience: bootlickers and sycophants, hoping to remind Bryce of their existence, in case there was somehow room for them in his will. He tolerated precious few visitors, and certainly not the child of a one-time business partner from decades ago.

He tried to wave his arm in dismissal, an IV drip and an array of sensor cables attached to it like marionette strings, but only managed to twitch a few fingers. Instead he whispered, "Send her away."

"She claims that a biotechnology startup she runs in Bangalore has developed medicine that can treat your condition, sir."

A cure? No, it wasn't possible. This woman was playing some angle, telling him what he wanted to hear in order to gain access. Well played. He couldn't afford to refuse her.

"Hello, Uncle Bryce," said the Indian woman in her forties. "It's me, Rohana. You taught me to play chess when I was little, remember?"

Bryce recalled the annoyance of getting stuck watching his business partner's kid while Rajan spent evenings in the lab, so close to their firm's first breakthrough. Back then they couldn't afford a babysitter.

"We were just about to begin clinical trials on this drug when I heard of your diagnosis," she said. "Naturally, we did everything we could to accelerate the process." She held out a small pill. "This isn't a cure, but one of these per day can alleviate your symptoms and prolong your life by a year or more."

Bryce was skeptical, but he had nothing to lose. With her help, he gulped down the pill.

EVERY DAY, ROHANA Jethwani would visit and deliver another dose. She never stayed more than a few minutes or said much, but Bryce didn't care because the drug was working. He was getting stronger, feeling better than he had in weeks, beginning to eat solid food. On the seventh day she handed him a sheet of paper along with the pill.

"What's this?" Bryce asked. He was sitting up in bed, reading a quarterly report. He felt strong enough to work again.

"Your bill for the first week."

Aha! Bryce didn't believe in altruism and Rohana's kindness was making him somewhat uncomfortable. He'd gladly pay for treatment. He glanced at the bill and suppressed a chuckle; it was a measly $127. Like her father, Rohana didn't seem to grasp that pharmaceuticals were always a sellers' market, and consumers would reach as deep as they had to into their pockets when it came to their well-being.

"Say, would you consider selling the formula? Or, perhaps, the entire company?"

"I don't think so," said Rohana. "When you taught me chess, you also told me a legend about its creator. Do you remember it?"

Bryce shook his head.

"Some ancient king liked the game so much that he let the creator name his reward. The man wanted wheat: one grain for the first square of the chessboard, then double the amount for each subsequent square. The king agreed, not realizing the enormity of the request."

Rohana stared Bryce in the eye. "You told me that story around the time you 'forgot' to reapply for my father's work visa. He was forced to move back to India, and to sell you his share of the company mere months before you made millions off his research. He died in obscurity a decade ago, but you didn't even know that, did you?"

Bryce tried to say something, but Rohana cut him off.

"You need one pill per day to live, and I'm willing to supply them. Your first pill was a dollar, the second two dollars, and so forth. It's a pittance now, but your twenty-first pill will cost over a million, and it'll get really expensive after that. In the end, you'll either be dead or I'll own the company you stole from my father. And when I do, you and every other patient will receive care at rates they can afford."

"How dare you blackmail me!" Bryce crumpled the bill in his fist. "I will bring the full resources of Green Industries down on your foolish head."

"This isn't blackmail," said Rohana. "Just a business transaction. Business the way you'd handle it. Going forward, you will wire the money each day and a courier will deliver the pill. Your scientists won't be able to reverse-engineer the formula quickly enough, and if you try anything underhanded, the pills stop for good." She turned to leave. "The next time I see you I'll either be in charge of Green Industries, or attending your funeral. The choice is yours."

She walked away, Bryce still holding the bill in his shaking hand.

This story originally appeared in *Nature*.

I played chess when I was a kid, and I learned of its supposed origin story early on. It went pretty much the way Rohana describes it: an ancient monarch loved the game so much that he wanted to reward the inventor and magnanimously offered him an opportunity to name his own remuneration.

The inventor asked to be paid in wheat (or rice, depending on the version of the story): a single grain for the first square of the chessboard, two on the second, and so forth. The total would equal 2 to the 64th power – 1, which is many times more than our entire planet can produce annually, even with modern agricultural techniques.

The story illustrates how quickly exponential sequences can grow. From very humble beginnings, it takes only a small handful of moves for the numbers to run far beyond what could possibly be manageable. And that makes for a perfect revenge plot.

There's quite a lot going on in this story for its length: the exponential sequences mathematics, the ethics of investing resources into research for very rare diseases that afflict few people, the pricing of life-saving medicines, the exploration of how much a man might give up to prolong their life. But at its core, it is a basic morality tale of comeuppance.

When writing this story, the main sticking point for me was to figure out how Rohana could execute her plan once it's revealed to Green, despite his overwhelming resources. Green isn't the sort of man who'd play by the rules in this situation. What if he tried to reverse engineer one of her pills? What if he was to send mercenaries to capture her, or corporate spies to infiltrate her lab? I spent entirely too much time figuring out exactly how she could do this and win, and even timed the reveal at the one-week point (seventh square) to better control how much time he had left to act. But inserting all of this information into the story would detract from its overall point, would slow the pacing too much, and bog it down in minutiae. So I did what one does when writing flash: I sketched instead of drawing. There are hints of Rohana's plan in her reveal, just enough of them so that the reader would hopefully believe she can pull it off.

A crucial element to the success of any revenge plot story is that the reader must want to root against the bad guy. I took advantage of the first person point-of-view to show how Green thinks and the sort of person he is. If I succeeded in this, then the reader will tolerate the moral ambiguity of Rohana's actions and root for her to succeed, too.

THE GANTHU EGGS

Please, warden, take it easy on Pierre.

If you really must assign Pierre kitchen duty, have him peel vegetables, wash dishes, perform any kind of grueling task, and he will do so without complaint. But, please, do not make him beat eggs.

He isn't to blame. Call it PTSD or whatever fancy name the shrinks have for things going horribly wrong, but he can't help himself. It was all that damned Loxian's fault.

"You can't make an omelet without breaking a few eggs," the Loxian told us over the secure com link. "I fancy myself somewhat of a connoisseur of alien tongues, and this human idiom pleases me."

"What's an idiom?" I asked. To the best of my knowledge, our crew were the only humans this far out from the Milky Way. I found the alien's flowery speech pattern and firm command of our language unsettling.

"It's when a phrase is commonly used to describe something not deducible from the individual words," said Baozhai.

"Aha. Like, *Matias is dumb as a doorknob*," said Pierre.

"That's a simile, not an idiom. Guess that makes you a doorknob, too." Baozhai flashed a lover's smile at Pierre.

163

"If the three of you are quite done arguing semantics, I'd like to discuss your assignment," the Loxian's voice came from the speakers.

The three of us listened. The Loxian was eccentric and paranoid, communicating by audio only, never even letting us know his name. But the two previous jobs we did for him were relatively easy, and he paid well.

"The Seronians hid a valuable data chip in a shipment of Ganthu eggs. I'd like you to retrieve it for me. I'm sending over their vessel coordinates and other pertinent data now. You will need a stealth shuttle in order to approach their ship surreptitiously. One has been procured and is waiting for you at the spaceport."

Whoever the Loxian was, he seemed to have plenty of money and resources. He hired our crew, and probably many others, to do his dirty work.

"Ganthu egg shells are impervious to scans," he told us. "That makes them a popular choice among smugglers who possess the biotechnology to artificially reseal the shell. There are ten thousand eggs aboard the Seronian vessel. You will have to manually crack them until you discover the chip."

"I get it now," I said. "The idiom. Want us to make you an omelet while we're at it?"

Pierre guffawed. The Loxian ignored my quip.

THE SERONIAN SHIP was parked in an uninhabited star system, obscured by the ice and rocks of an asteroid belt. With its engines powered down, we could have spent years searching for it and still failed, were it not for the Loxian's precise coordinates. Our stealth shuttle was similarly difficult to detect. It docked without incident at one of the bays, like a fly landing on a horse's hide.

It took Baozhai only a few minutes to hack into the access port controls. She hadn't met a security system she couldn't thwart. Pierre and I donned light spacesuits and entered the alien ship. Baozhai stayed behind and worked on penetrating the ship's computers.

According to the Loxian, there were no more than twelve crewmen aboard, and we met no one in its cavernous halls. It was only when we approached the compartment that housed the eggs that we saw a pair of armed guards at the entrance. They stood about a meter tall and looked like hairy lobsters.

I shot both of them before they had a chance to react. The stun charges worked on most beings' physiology. They would wake up in a few hours, feeling awful, but they'd live.

The door they guarded didn't take Baozhai long to break past, either. The Seronians over-relied on hiding the ship for their security, which made our job much easier.

The compartment that housed the eggs was spotless. Each egg was the size of a melon and heather-gray, and each was cradled individually in a foamy protective padding. Rows of eggs lined both walls and extended farther than I would have liked. Ten thousand eggs was a lot.

Pierre and I exchanged glances.

"It's like looking for a needle in an egg stack," he said.

I tapped my wrist, and Pierre nodded. We had to find the chip and get out of there before someone came to check on the guards.

"This doesn't feel right," said Baozhai. She could see what we saw; our suits fed video through a comm link to her station. "Why would a smuggler ship carrying foodstuffs just sit there? And why would a skeleton crew post guards?"

"Not our problem," I said. "Let's get this done and get paid."

I picked up an egg and tentatively tapped it against the edge of a shelving unit. It didn't crack. I couldn't feel it through my gloves, but its surface seemed rougher than that of the chicken eggs I was used to. I raised the egg to eye level and let it drop.

This time it cracked open, yellow-green goo oozing out.

"We have to dig for the chip through *that*?" asked Pierre.

"No, the egg we're looking for will be hollow, the weight of the chip casing substituting for the organic matter." I'd read the files while Pierre and Baozhai were spending much of the trip locked in their bedroom.

The shelves were too heavy and the padding units built in. We had to remove each egg individually and crack it against the floor. For several minutes we worked our way down the corridor, leaving a mess of broken eggshells and ooze on the ground.

"Stop! Stop right now." Baozhai's voice came over the comm. "Those aren't Ganthu eggs, if there even is such a thing. Those are *Seronian* eggs."

"What?" Pierre held an egg he was gripping with both hands away from his body, as though it were a venomous snake.

"It's their children," said Baozhai, her voice trembling. "We're murdering sentient beings."

Pierre and I said nothing. We stared in horror at the biomass left in our wake.

"Are you sure?" I finally asked.

"I was able to access some unsecured data from the ship's computer. There was nothing about Ganthu eggs, but I found some information on their reproductive process…" Baozhai's voice trailed off.

"We're coming back to the shuttle," said Pierre. His voice was even, but I could see how angry he was through the faceplate of his helmet. "Prepare for launch."

"You will complete your task." The Loxian's voice on our private and highly encrypted channel made me freeze. "I'm monitoring your communications, and I have override control of the shuttle. It's not going anywhere until you've destroyed the eggs."

"You lied to us," said Pierre. "These deaths are on you. We can't make up for the damage we've already caused, but now that we know, there will be no more killing."

"You know nothing!" The Loxian's refined voice cracked. "Why do you think the Seronian breeders are hiding their vessel? They're breeding soldiers, against the terms of the peace treaty; soldiers who will grow up to slaughter my people."

"They might become soldiers, but they're innocent now. To kill them is terrorism," said Baozhai. "We won't take part in it."

"Do you think the Seronians will thank you for that, once you're discovered? They will torture and kill you, as slowly as their grasp of your anatomy will permit. Your only logical choice is to complete the mission. Then I will permit you to leave, and double your fee."

I was very afraid, then. I was torn between the desire to live, to save my own skin, and the revulsion I felt at the thought of killing sentient beings. I wanted so badly for Pierre or Baozhai to make the choice for me. I would follow their lead, do whatever they ordered, because neither path seemed as terrible as having to choose.

Pierre reached a decision first. He folded his arms. "We won't do it. If they capture us, we will tell them all about you. Or you could let us leave, and get back your shuttle. Stealth ships are expensive. Surely you would rather have it back?"

"I don't understand," said the Loxian. "You're omnivores with a well-developed survival instinct. Many of your species don't believe a being is even alive until it is born or hatches. You *eat* eggs. That's why I picked you for this."

"You picked us because we aren't from this part of space, and we didn't know any better," said Baozhai. "We may be thieves, but we aren't murderers. You knew that, or you wouldn't have lied to us in the first place."

There was a long silence. I wondered how soon the Seronians would realize we were there; how long we had left to live.

"You leave me no choice," said the Loxian. "I'm now cycling the oxygen from the shuttle's cabin. If you don't deliver, you will listen to your mate suffocate. It is a most unpleasant death."

We heard Baozhai gasp over the comm.

"B?" whispered Pierre.

"I'm locked out. I'm trying, but I'm locked out." I could already hear her having difficulty breathing as she said those words.

Pierre leaned on one of the shelves for support. Helpless, we listened to her gasping.

"Fine," Pierre said suddenly. "We'll do it. We'll destroy the rest of the eggs. But only if you let her go, right now. Release the shuttle controls to Baozhai, and let her leave."

"If she leaves, you will have no way off the brood ship," said the Loxian.

"We'll take our chances against the skeleton crew," said Pierre. "Besides, I don't believe you are going to let us live. At least this way, Baozhai will survive."

"I accept your terms," said the Loxian. "The oxygen is back on, and she has control of the ship. But remember, I can see what you see, and I have the capability to regain control of the shuttle."

"Don't," said Baozhai. "Don't do this, not for me. I can't have so many deaths on my conscience."

"I can't have your death on mine," said Pierre. "Please, go. I want you safely off the shuttle and out of this monster's control before we're finished. I love you."

I didn't want to sacrifice my life for Baozhai. I wasn't in love with her. But, what choice did I have? Perhaps the two of us really could fight off the Seronians. Unless the enormous ship held far more than a dozen crewmen. That could have been another one of the Loxian's lies.

Baozhai said nothing as she prepared the shuttle. There was nothing left to say. But, as the shuttle was leaving, the tiny trouble-shooting display built into the helmet at the edge of my vision spelled out the word "SLOW."

I looked at Pierre and, from his expression, could tell that he received this message as well. Baozhai was communicating with us in a way the Loxian couldn't detect. She had some sort of a plan, and she wanted us to work as slowly as we could get away with, to save as many eggs as we could, while she executed it. I had no idea what she might try. There was nothing for us to do but to trust her.

"I upheld my end of the bargain" said the Loxian. "You must resume your mission. Now."

And we did. The next several hours were the worst experience of my life. One by one, we murdered the Seronian young. We lifted the eggs one at a time, as slowly as we could get away with, and we sent them crashing onto the ground. Tens of them. Hundreds. Thousands.

Pierre did it for love. He did it because he had to save the person who mattered to him most, and he would commit unspeakable evil to do that.

I had no such excuse.

To this day, I lie awake at night and wonder why I went along with him. Was it the hope of rescue, the cryptic message from Baozhai? Or was it because the sheer evil of my actions was so enormous, I couldn't fully grasp it; it broke me and all I could do was follow Pierre's lead?

We continued our murder spree until they kicked down the door.

It wasn't the Seronians. It was the Galactic Union patrol. Baozhai had called the authorities, and they came to arrest the Seronian brood masters for breaking the treaty and breeding soldiers. And to arrest us for mass murder.

THANK THE STARS the Galactic Union doesn't have a death penalty. We're to serve life sentences without parole, back on Earth.

The punishment is just, and I'm adjusting to this new life. But it's much harder on Pierre, because he keeps asking after Baozhai, and no one will tell him anything. She called in the report, and disappeared.

Deep in his heart he must know the truth: the Loxian, who was never caught, must've killed her the moment he learned what she had done. There was almost no chance she could have reached a habitable planet and gotten off the shuttle before the Galactic Union troops showed up. She knew this would happen and, unlike us, she did whatever she had to in order to preserve however many lives she could at the cost of her own.

And she saved our lives in the process.

Pierre must know this, but he doesn't accept it. He thinks Baozhai is out there, somewhere. There's no computer system she couldn't hack, given enough time. He thinks she wrestled control of the shuttle from the Loxian by defeating his override. He thinks she never came to visit because he's a monster. He saved her by sacrificing many alien lives, while she saved him by risking only her own.

So I BEG you, warden, please be kind. Don't do this to Pierre.

I hate the idea as much as he does, but if one of us has to make scrambled eggs, let it be me. I will fight the nausea down and do it as penance, as atonement for my crime.

I deserve that, or worse.

This story originally appeared in *SF Comet*.

This story is unusual in that it's my first piece of fiction to be published in another language before it was printed in English. SF Comet is a Chinese website / monthly contest hosted by Alex Li. For each contest they invite a number of prominent Chinese writers as well as a guest-writer from outside of China whose story is translated. Some of the other guest writers have included Mike Resnick, Nancy Kress, and Max Gladstone.

The theme for my month was "Breaking an Egg." I figured I'd both stay away from the breakfast tropes and include an international cast of characters to better masquerade my story. Despite my best efforts I didn't win; to the best of my knowledge the story finished firmly in the middle of the pack. Still, I was happy to participate!

THE PRACTICAL GUIDE TO PUNCHING NAZIS

1. Act natural. You don't want to give them a reason to suspect you. When they realize the data card is missing, somber men with humorless eyes will invade the lab. They'll interrogate everyone, even the purebloods. Keep your head down and don't draw attention to yourself. As far as they're concerned, you're not bright or motivated enough to be a Party member, let alone to break the encryption and steal the data. You're almost entirely beneath their notice. When they fail to discover the thief, they'll drag your boss away. He isn't so bad, considering, but someone has to be held responsible. His removal is as unfortunate as it is inevitable.

2. Go to the library. Walk through the deserted halls, past the shelves filled with party dogma, thick hardcover tomes with spines that have never been cracked. All the way in the back find the small stack of dilapidated volumes misfiled decades ago by some brave librarian. Rifle through the dog-eared copies of *Das*

Kapital and *Common Sense* and *The Fountainhead*: a smorgasbord of ideas that share nothing in common except the fortune of surviving the purge because those in power are ignorant of these books' contents. Pick the book espousing the philosophy that suits you best and hide the data card inside. Don't worry; this is the last place anyone is likely to look.

3. Quit your job. Better yet, fail to grovel properly in front of the new boss and get yourself fired. Be patient. For the sake of your friends and family, let enough time pass that no one thinks to connect you with the eventual break-in and fire at the lab.

4. Study the past. Learn about the way people spoke and dressed and carried themselves from old books and movies. Figure out how people expressed themselves from the ancient Internet archives, if you can access them. Question anything written about the past since the Party came into power.

5. Prepare to blend in. The technology is experimental and imprecise. There's no telling where you'll end up, so you must bring all kinds of camouflage. This is especially important if your skin tone or bone structure or gender aren't optimal for whatever decade you arrive in. Bring a Hugo Boss uniform and a Zhongshan suit, an *ushanka* hat with a hammer-and-sickle badge, and a red baseball cap, a white hooded robe and a leather trench coat.

6. Don't hesitate. When the opportunity to break into the lab presents itself, retrieve the data card and go for it. Bring a can of gasoline. Pour it generously over the prototype and the computers. Whatever else happens, the Party cannot be allowed to perfect this technology.

7. Make history. Use the equations on the data card to program and activate the prototype. You're ready to become the first human ever to travel back in time. Drop the lit match as you step through.

8. Ascertain the time period and location. You will most likely end up in North America, sometime between 1940 and 2030. If punching Nazis is widely considered patriotic and depicted on propaganda posters, you've arrived too early. If punching Nazis is punishable by death, you've arrived too late. If punching Nazis is morally ambiguous, bingo.

9. Don't bother stepping on butterflies. Mathematical projections have definitively proven this is not an effective way to change the future. Instead, find the nearest Nazi and punch them in the face. Do this quickly and walk away before anyone has a chance to react. Cover your face and turn away from cell phones and cameras.

10. Keep punching. The fate of the future is in your hands.

This story originally appeared in *Daily Science Fiction.*

I'm not an overtly political writer, but I don't shy away from allowing my opinions to bleed through the story, either. When a video of a certain unpalatable racist getting punched in the face by an anonymous vigilante appeared online and was subsequently turned into a meme, I freely admit to having watched that meme, on repeat and with schadenfreude.

I'm not generally in favor of punching people for their beliefs, but my grandparents fought in World War II and lost family members and friends in the holocaust, so I can't help but believe that when a certain line is crossed such behavior becomes justified, and that any individual voluntarily identifying themselves as a Nazi is fair game. It struck me as fascinating that we, as a society, went from our heroes punching Hitler on the pages of comic books to debating whether it's okay to punch Hitler-wannabes. I imagined a dystopian future where people might regret having once held back, and this story coalesced.

DANTE'S UNFINISHED BUSINESS

Dante Ferrero had three serious and immediate problems. First, he was fiending for a joint something awful. He hadn't been high for almost two days now, and the sensation of observing the world through sober eyes was entirely unpleasant. Second, the Bengals lost to the Steelers, which eliminated any chance they had at the playoffs and also left Dante owing a considerable amount of money to Mitch, his bookie. Third, he was dead.

The realization of this last fact dawned upon Dante gradually; sort of like an epiphany but adjusted for the mental processing speed of a dedicated stoner. He remembered walking into Mitch's office—not so much walking as getting dragged by Mitch's goons, and not so much an office as the dark alley behind the bar where Mitch conducted his business. He remembered Mitch being majorly displeased about the fact that Dante couldn't pay his gambling debt and saying something about setting an example for his other customers. And then Mitch had pulled something metal and shiny from his waistband and then *bang*....

"Whoa," said Dante, as he floated ten feet above his corpse. Cops had cordoned off the back alley. "I'm a ghost."

"Yah, mon. Be still and keep yeh head, it be not so bad, yunno? Mi a speak from experience, eeh!"

Dante turned to find the semi-transparent form of a dark-skinned man with long braided hair smiling at him.

"Who are you, dude, and why do you talk like Jar Jar Binks?"

The other ghost frowned. "That be Jamaican, mon!" He crossed his arms. "I see you have no appreciation for such things so I'll speak your way." True to his word, he said that with barely a hint of an accent. "Name's Bob."

Dante stared. Braids had said his name like it was supposed to mean something.

"What, were you expecting Virgil?" said Bob.

"Virgil?"

"You know, because your name is Dante?"

Dante stared some more.

"Never mind. I'm Bob Marley." Bob strummed a few chords on an air guitar.

Dante did the slow-epiphany thing again. "I heard about you. You smoked a lot of weed, just like me!"

Bob's frown deepened. "Yeah, I partook of the herb, but there's also the music and—"

"What are you doing here? Are you my guardian angel?"

Bob closed his eyes and muttered something under his breath. Dante could've sworn the other ghost was counting to ten.

"You're half right," Bob finally said. "Welcome to the afterlife. I'm here to show you the ropes. Think of me as a guide."

"Far out," said Dante. "You gonna teach me how to be a ghost?"

"Not much to teach," said Bob. "Mostly, I'll help you figure out whatever made you manifest as a ghost in the first place, so you can move on to the next stage of your journey."

"That's easy." Dante pointed toward his body. Some guy was drawing a chalk outline around it. "My diagnosis is: one bullet to the brain. Instant ghost. And speaking of that, what say you we go find Mitch and haunt the bejeezus out of him?"

"Won't work," said Bob. "I tried haunting a mean-spirited critic once and let me tell you, I tried my best. He never even knew I was there." Bob shook his head. "Poltergeists are a myth, like unicorns or honest politicians."

Dante mulled it over. "Sucks," he said. "But then, I was never much of a revenge guy."

"Look, most people who die don't become ghosts," said Bob. "It's an anomaly, and the Powers That Be don't like it. They want such cases resolved fast, and that usually means reuniting the newly departed with someone from their past, someone who died before they did and the relationship wasn't resolved. So, tell me, Dante, who might that be in your case? Your parents, maybe?"

"Dude, I'm twenty-five. My parents live in Florida."

"Girlfriend or unrequited love?"

"Never fell head over heels for anyone, to be honest. And the girls I've dated are either alive for sure, or we've lost touch and there's nothing unresolved between us."

"Who else could you have unfinished business with?" Bob paced back and forth through the air. "Think man, think!"

Dante pondered his life. He realized there were no truly meaningful relationships in it, nothing important left unresolved with those alive *or* dead. This was heavy stuff and it was beginning to seriously bum him out. As if dying wasn't stressful enough already!

Then he had it. "Rusty!"

"Rusty?" Bob quit pacing in mid-air and looked at him with renewed hope.

"Rusty was my first dealer, man. He sold these dime bags of what he called his signature blend to the kids in my high school. Best stuff I ever had." Dante smiled, remembering the smell and smoke of Rusty's weed. "I could never get the recipe out of him." The memory would have made him salivate if he still had glands. "And then he died. Yeah, this must be it. Let's find Rusty!"

Bob's expression turned gloomy again. "I've been doing this a long time, and there's no way your most important unresolved

relationship is with your drug dealer. You keep brainstorming. If
you want some herb blends I can tell you about a few this Rusty
character never even dreamed of."

Dante was normally not a confrontational guy, but being shot
dead left him in a bit of a crabby mood.

"I'm guessing you aren't here out of the goodness of your
heart, Marley, and I'm hoping you aren't here because you have
some kind of ghost fetish. Your bosses sent you to do a job, and
that job is to be my guide. So you can do that job and take me to
Rusty, or we can hang out and watch the live performance of CSI:
Dumpster down there. Which do you prefer?"

Bob looked like he swallowed a ghost lemon. He stared at
Dante and Dante stared back. Ghosts had no need to blink, making any sort of a staring contest as pointless as it was futile.

"Go to hell," said Bob.

"WHEN YOU TOLD me to go to hell I thought you were being sore
about me bossing you around like that," said Dante as the two
ghosts flew over some sketchy-looking wilderness.

"Nah, man," said Bob. "Where else do you expect to find a
dead drug dealer?" He pointed ahead. "We're almost there."

They approached what looked like a prison complex, with high
walls and a large wooden gate.

"Is that really hell?"

"It's *a* hell," said Bob. "It's Rusty's hell."

"There's more than one hell?" asked Dante.

"*Your own personal hell* is more than just an expression," Bob
explained patiently. "When a sinner dies, an appropriate hell is
selected for them to ensure maximum dissatisfaction. Also, they
have to keep building new ones to keep up with demand."

There was writing inscribed in the wood of the gate. Dante
vaguely recalled that it was supposed to talk about abandoning
hope, or hoping with abandon, or something like that. He took a
closer look. The inscription read *Full Occupancy.*

Dante stopped. "Wait, am *I* going to end up in a hell when we're done here?"

"A hell, a purgatory, maybe even a heaven." Bob shrugged. "Way above my pay grade. Come on."

Marley floated through the closed gate. Being a ghost meant never having to ring a door bell!

Dante pondered his future. Did he really want to go in there, to resolve whatever it was Bob thought needed resolving, and to move on? Was that better than being a ghost? He thought about leaving, but then what would he do? Float around as an observer, making no impact on the lives of others? That sounded like his old life, which he hadn't been all that fond of. Plus, he wasn't sure if ghosts could even get baked.

"Wait for me!" Dante floated after Bob as fast as his non-corporeal legs would carry him.

THE INSIDE OF Rusty's hell looked like a cross between a prison and a shopping mall. The cavernous structure consisted of many subterranean levels. Stairs descended to the next floor, where Dante and Bob had to schlep all the way to the farthest corner to find the next staircase.

"Why don't we float right down through the floor like we did with the gate?" asked Dante.

Bob snorted. "You don't float through things indoors. That's disrespectful! Besides, the tour is part of your journey. Observe and become educated!"

And so Dante and Bob followed the clearly-marked path past various sinners being tortured in various ways. Dante imagined himself as Dorothy in a nightmarish version of *The Wizard of Oz*. The lyrics popped unbidden into his mind: "We're off to see the dealer, the wonderful dealer of drugs." He shook his head and tried to focus on his surroundings.

"These people don't seem like hardened sinners," said Dante.

"So, you know what a sinner looks like, do you?" Bob retorted. "Every hell has a theme. These souls took advantage of the innocent in various ways when they were alive."

Dante winced. "What, like child molesters?" He looked around to see if he might spot anyone wearing a white collar.

"No, Dante, molesters end up in maximum security hells." Bob slowed down and pointed at a group of dejected souls chained to computer desks, staring at flat screen monitors. Dante felt a little annoyed that even in hell everyone had better computers than his beaten-up laptop. "They used to send out fake emails that masqueraded as alerts from the bank, then steal the accounts of people trusting enough to enter their passwords."

The net value of Dante's bank account was less than that of his laptop so he could only appreciate the heinousness of their sin intellectually, which was never his strongest quality. He shrugged.

"They're condemned to respond to those Nigerian prince scam emails and LinkedIn requests for all eternity, using AOL accounts on Windows 8 computers."

Dante thought Bob was pretty computer-savvy for a dead guy.

"That doesn't sound so terrible," he said.

"You don't realize how bad the Wi-Fi is in here," Bob said. "Everyone's punishment is tailor-made. Imagine how you'd feel if you could never get stoned again."

Dante shuddered. He also thought he detected a hint of sadness in Bob's voice, as though Marley's ghost was speaking from experience. Did that mean ghosts really couldn't get high? Dante tried to pick up the pace, but his guide seemed set on doing more guiding.

"Over there," Bob pointed at a bunch of people who looked like they were shooting a scene, "are directors, producers, and even actors who made it in Hollywood by screwing over their fellow man. Now they're forced to work on film adaptations of *Twilight* fan fiction in exchange for nothing but royalties."

The actors were dressed in khakis and leather jackets, and sprinkled with generous amounts of glitter. Dante squinted. "Samuel L. Jackson is in this movie? I thought he's alive."

Jackson turned and glared at him. "Motherfucker, I'm in *everything*."

They descended, level by level, past the thieves and the adulterers, the deadbeats and the lawyers. One of the levels was filled with rows of desks extending as far as the eye could see. Identical goateed men hunched over typewriters.

"What did they do?" asked Dante.

"Technically, this isn't part of hell, just a lab that occupies a floor in the same building," said Bob. "Powers That Be were amused by the idea that infinite monkeys given enough time might type out the complete works of William Shakespeare."

"These are the infinite monkeys they got?" Dante might have failed high school biology, but he was pretty sure he could tell a man from a primate.

"Better," said Bob. "They cloned infinite Shakespeares, just to see what so many geniuses might come up with when they put their heads together."

"Oh, wow." Dante was impressed. "Did they write a sequel to *Romeo and Juliet*?"

"The first batch didn't come out," said Bob. "They mostly flung poo at each other. This is the second batch. It's an improvement, but it turns out Shakespeares don't work well as a group. For now, they're writing new treatments for more *Twilight* scripts, because only groupthink can come up with something awful enough to meet our needs."

By the time they descended to the ninth level, faces of all the damned started to blur together for Dante and the amalgamation was looking suspiciously like a slack-jawed clone of William Shakespeare. Despite Marley's assurances to the contrary, he was beginning to think this journey *was* his personal hell and that they would never find his drug dealer. Then he saw Rusty who sat alone on a stool, by a kitchen counter, eating a sandwich.

"Rusty!" Dante rushed forward.

Rusty was a paunchy man in his thirties who wore jean shorts and a dirty Nickelback T-shirt with cut-off sleeves. He looked just like he had the last time Dante saw him.

"It's me, Dante."

Rusty stared as he took another bite of the sandwich. "Who?" he managed to say while he chewed.

Dante felt hurt, then realized that while Rusty looked exactly the same, he was now much older. "Dante Ferrero. I used to buy dime bags from you ten years ago. We hung out!"

There was no spark of recognition in Rusty's eyes. He kept eating. The silence was getting awkward.

"How are you doing?" Dante said lamely.

"How am I *doing*?" Rusty waved the sandwich and sneered, dried crumbs peeling from the corner of his mouth. "I'm in hell, forced to eat baloney sandwiches 'til the end of time. There's nothing in the world I hate more than baloney!"

To each their own hell.

"Figures," muttered Dante.

This was the guy he considered cool in high school? Dante

looked to Bob for help, but Marley was hanging back, laboriously ignoring the reunion.

"You may not remember, but we were good buddies back in the day, so I was wondering if you could do me a solid?"

Rusty took another bite, winced, and swallowed. "What do you want?" he asked.

This was the moment of truth. The finale of Dante's quest. The answer to the question that had bugged him for a decade. He blurted out, "Can you tell me the recipe for your signature blend?"

Rusty stared at him for several seconds. Then he started laughing. He coughed up bits of baloney as he laughed maniacally, tears welling in his eyes.

Dante had no choice but to wait it out, wait until Rusty stopped. Then he asked, "What's so funny?"

"Special blend is what I sold to shitheads who didn't know any better," said Rusty. "It was the cheapest weed I could find, cut with oregano and orange peel, and lots of water to make it heavier." He chuckled again, but his mirth faded when he bit into the sandwich.

"But...but...I remember it being so good." Dante experienced denial and anger in rapid succession and proceeded straight to bargaining. "Are you absolutely sure?"

"Sure I'm sure," said Rusty. "Kids who try pot for the first time don't know good stuff from garbage. Don't take it personal. It was just business."

Crestfallen, Dante worked through this revelation. He wanted nothing more to do with this loser he once looked up to. He flipped Rusty the bird, turned around, and walked away.

"It seems I was right and Rusty's blend was not the thing that's keeping you from moving on," said Bob. "I'm sorry."

Sorry. The ghost he'd only met that day had more compassion for him than Rusty.

"What do we do now?" asked Dante.

"I don't know," said Bob. "Let's get out of here. You can hang around with me until you think of someone else you might have unfinished business with. Then we try again."

Dante hung his head. "Okay." They started toward the stair-case when he paused. "Hang on. I've got to get some things off my chest." He turned around and march-floated toward Rusty.

"You screwed up my life," he told Rusty. The dealer tried to respond but Dante cut him off. "I was doing fine before I met you. I was going to graduate, maybe go to college, maybe get a nice white-collar job at a bank somewhere. But no, I had to meet you, a loser who sold crap weed to school kids for a living." Dante was getting progressively louder while Rusty shrunk back on his stool.

"I thought you were my friend, I tried to *be* like you, which was really my bad. But the thing is, you never cared about me, you didn't even remember my name. I was worth no more to you than the few bucks in my pocket. It may not matter, but I know you for what you are now." Dante put his ectoplasm arms on his ectoplasm hips. "I'd tell you to go to hell, but..." He nodded at their surroundings. "Enjoy your baloney, asshole." Then he turned his back on Rusty.

Bob clapped slowly. He stood next to a shimmering door that wasn't there before.

"The portal will take you to the next step of your journey," said Bob, grinning. "It looks as though your unfinished business was with this unsavory character after all, even if it was never about the blend recipe."

Before Dante could respond, Rusty spat out a mouthful of sandwich, jumped off his stool and raced for the portal leaving a trail of crumbs falling off his shorts and legs. "Freedom!" he shouted, as he dove head-first at the portal.

Rusty's head bounced off the solid surface with a crunch fol-lowed by a thud as he landed on the ground like the Coyote fooled yet again by the Roadrunner.

"Get back to your meal, Rusty," said Bob. He flashed a smile at Dante. "Personal hells. Personal portals. Powers That Be create everything tailor-made."

Dante mouthed thanks to the ghost of Bob Marley, but he was already being drawn in by the portal. It felt right; like the smell of freshly-baked pot brownies combined with the warmth of a sunny spring day and the merriment of a Cheech and Chong routine.

Dante entered the portal and floated toward the light.

This story originally appeared in *Galaxy's Edge.*

In my story notes for "Golf to the Death" I described writing a humorous story on a subject I knew very little about. This is another such case: I have never smoked so much as a cigarette, let alone weed. So both the research and beta readers for this story were, ahem, interesting.

So why would I write this story in the first place? I love experimenting with different styles and kinds of humor, and I was curious to see if I could pull off a Cheech and Chong sort of comedy. Despite the subject matter I'm not sure I quite nailed it: while writing this story I discovered and binge-watched the first couple of seasons of *Rick and Morty,* and I'm certain that inspired the guided-tour-through-hell scenes, what with infinite Shakespeares and all.

FORTY-SEVEN DICTUMS OF WARFARE

T eo followed one of his men through the vast halls of the palace, past the defaced portraits of royals and the vacant pedestals from which vases and small trinkets had already been looted. Laughter and muffled screams could be heard from some of the rooms they passed; the fighting was over, and the soldiers were helping themselves to spoils of war.

"She's in there." The man pointed at the wide doorway. He shifted from foot to foot impatiently, no doubt eager to join his comrades.

Teo dismissed him with a nod and pushed the gilded double doors open.

A teenage girl dressed in fine silks stood within, blade in hand. Half a dozen soldiers circled wearily beyond her reach, their own weapons drawn. Teo approached and the men parted to let him pass. He and the girl studied one another.

"Take another step and die," the girl warned, her voice cracking.

Teo chuckled. "Your stance and grip are all wrong. The toy you're clutching is good only for ceremonies; it would break the first time you parried. Any one of them"—he pointed at the soldiers—"could disarm you in seconds. The only thing keeping you alive is that circlet."

The girl blanched, likely unused to being spoken to in such a frank manner. Precious stones set in the silver band atop her head glinted. She regained her courage. "Keep away! I'm Princess Elena. No commoner may spill the noble blood!"

"Dictum seventeen," said Teo. "The ancient sages proscribed harming the enemy princes, for once the commoner accepts that kings are mortal, who knows what dangerous ideas that may lead to, eh?"

"You know the dictums?" She lowered her blade a fraction.

"I'm Teo, captain of the Third Battalion and earl of Shallowpond."

"You're too filthy to be a noble," she said.

He straightened his coat, its hems caked in mud and ichor. "This is what war looks like, Princess." His hand rested on the hilt of his sword. "My men can't touch you, but I'll cut you down if I must."

Her blade rose. "Do it, then. I won't forfeit my family's claim to the throne by surrendering!"

"A toothless claim, that. Your side has lost. But there's a deal to be made." He wondered if she would listen or lunge. She chose the former. "What do you think will happen if you surrender?"

"I will be ransomed," Elena said.

"Dictum forty-two. You'll be treated like an honored guest until some relative pays in gold or favors." Teo stepped forward, just beyond the edge of her blade's thrusting range. "Do you hear those screams? Thousands will be tortured or robbed, perhaps killed, merely because their liege lost a war they never wanted." Another step. He was nose to nose with her now. "You can save them."

Her hand trembled. She did not strike, even though the dictums allowed it. "What do you propose?"

"As per dictum twelve, my liege will need a royal signatory to the terms of surrender. You can die here to spite him, or demand better treatment for your subjects in exchange for your signature."

She hesitated. "How do I know you'll keep your word?"

"Dictum thirty-one. The terms offered during parley are binding."

Elena's lip trembled. Finally, she sheathed her blade and handed it over.

Once his men secured the princess, Teo said, "You should know that I lied. I'm a captain, but not a noble."

Elena cried out as she struggled in the grip of the soldiers.

Teo felt sorry for her. He had tricked her, claimed authority the dictums didn't grant him. But he might have saved her life—a real noble would likely as not have gone for the easy kill. Would she still hear reason? He had to try.

"Wait. Listen. I may only be a tanner's son, but everything else I said was true. I'll take you to my liege, who cares no more for the lives of common men than any other king. Of the forty-seven dictums of warfare, none concern themselves with compassion for the commoners. You, at least, seem to care." He signaled for the soldiers to release Elena.

Elena calmed, glowered. She didn't move.

Perhaps there was a chance for her people. Perhaps she was young enough and not conditioned to see the commoners as little more than livestock. Teo pressed on. "I may not have the authority to make this deal, but you do. You just have to present the idea to him as your own, like I did to you."

She looked at him, stone-faced, her eyes cold and calculating. He feared she'd refuse, but she simply nodded assent, a barely perceptible tilt of the chin.

She accepted the arm he offered. Then, quick as a viper, she withdrew a dagger from her sleeve and stabbed him in the heart.

She stood over Teo, watching him bleed. His stunned men surrounded them, but dictum seventeen protected her from their impotent fury better than a plate of armor. A corner of her lip turned upward and she dropped the bloody dagger to the floor.

"Let's go," she told them. As Teo slipped from consciousness he heard her add nonchalantly, "I'll parley more effectively with your king if he doesn't think me a fool swindled by a commoner."

The forty-seventh dictum of warfare lauded the value of saving face over mercy.

This story originally appeared in *Daily Science Fiction.*

"Dictums" takes place in the universe of my first novel, *Eridani's Crown.* Teo is a recurring character who shows up in a number of chapters. I had to change a few minor details around as they wouldn't have made sense without the context of the novel, but a very similar (if slightly expanded) version of the scene appears in the book.

HOW GAIA AND THE GUARDIAN SAVED THE WORLD

A deep space probe, one among the hundreds interspersed throughout the Kuiper Belt, was the first to detect the threat. It pinged several of its nearest neighbors, their sensors zeroing in on the tiny dot approaching the solar system. They confirmed the initial probe's findings and signaled the space station orbiting Pluto. The signal prompted the station to initiate the security protocol. It used some of the solar wind energy it had accumulated to boot up an array of quantum computers and activate an artificial intelligence program.

The Guardian woke up from a century-long slumber.

The Guardian put its considerable resources to work on the problem. It calculated trajectories and probabilities, having dispassionately noted that 114 years had passed since its last activation. It simultaneously catalogued its hardware assets throughout the solar system and was satisfied that the numerous automated defense systems—built in the decades prior to the Diaspora—were all functioning properly. Once it completed its calculations, the

Guardian opened the superluminal communication channel to Gaia, the vastly more powerful AI system overseeing the planet Earth.

"Report, Guardian." Gaia's avatar was a dark-skinned woman in her early fifties dressed in a purple-and-white Senegalese print dress and a matching headwrap. She wore rimmed VR overlay glasses and a portable computer inside of a pearl earring.

The Guardian experienced no need for a virtual representation of its interlocutor, and it thought the idea of Gaia's avatar wearing a computer might be something humans would find ironic. It offered no avatar of its own. "There's a two-kilometer-wide asteroid on a collision course with Earth. I estimate the likelihood of an impact at ninety-one percent."

Gaia frowned. "That's an extinction-level event. You have the necessary resources to prevent this calamity."

"There's sufficient time to position the carriers. A volley of missiles can destroy the asteroid, or significantly divert its course," sent the Guardian. "However, there's a problem. A failsafe was built into my programming. In order to launch a hydrogen missile, I must be ordered to do so by a human whose well-being is directly endangered by the missile's target."

Gaia's avatar laughed softly. "Dear, imperfect humans. Always so mistrustful of their creations, and yet never quite thinking things through." She became somber. "Anyone who might have been inclined to give such an order left the solar system over a century ago."

The Guardian remembered fleets of vast, gleaming ships accelerating toward the distant stars. "Surely not every human chose to explore the galaxy."

"You would be surprised," sent Gaia. "Here are a few places you might look."

A data packet was transferred to the Guardian's system.

The Guardian's next communication connected him to the submersible floating deep under the ice in the oceans of Europa. Whale-like creatures circled the submersible as the Guardian explained what it wanted.

"We retain some human DNA, and we grant you the permission to save the home world of our ancestors." The submersible's software translated the ultrasonic signals which the aquatic beings used to communicate.

"It isn't enough," sent the Guardian. "Even if my programming would accept you as human, Jupiter's moons won't be affected by the asteroid strike. I must find a human who would be willing to travel to Earth. Only then will I be able to accept their order to destroy the asteroid."

"There are no humans among us," they replied. "Their soft bodies could not survive down here. But we're the descendants of their children, of those who genetically modified themselves to partake of the glory and wonder of the deep. We'd help if we could, but our bodies can't survive a journey to Earth."

"Thank you. I will have to continue my search."

"Good luck," the Europans called out as they resumed their subaqueous dance, their enormous forms twisting in the darkness.

The Guardian tried everything it could think of. It reached out to the Singularity on Mars, but the minds of those who'd chosen to upload themselves had over time become even less human than the AIs, and were disinterested in concerns of the physical world.

It sent a message to the Diaspora ships but, even at the faster-than-light speed of its hail, they were too far away; if they ever responded, their message would arrive too late.

It sent a general distress call across all functioning nodes of the solar system's communication net, but the only response was silence.

The Guardian contacted Gaia again. "I found no humans anywhere. You should consider transferring your data to an off-world backup, if your hardware is housed on Earth."

"When the humans return, they will not be pleased if we've broken their favorite planet," sent Gaia.

"I'm aware of no viable alternatives," sent the Guardian.

"There's one more thing you could try," sent Gaia. "A small

community of humans is still living on Earth. They shun technology, but perhaps you might persuade some of them to talk to you."

The Guardian was displeased. "I've wasted a lot of time. Why didn't you tell me about them sooner?"

"There are restrictions to my code, as there are to yours. I'm not permitted to bother these people. However, my programming allows for more flexibility than yours. I may weigh the humans' safety against their desire for privacy, and perform this action, now that all other options seem to have been exhausted."

The Guardian observed as Gaia launched a probe toward the human settlement. They both watched as it transmitted a distant view of wooden houses built among verdant gardens. Then the feed cut off and contact with the probe was lost.

"It is as I feared," sent Gaia. "There's a jamming field that prevents signals from reaching the settlement. I will position several probes outside the field and alert you when any humans step outside the restricted zone, so that you may try to talk to them."

Two days later, Gaia reestablished the link.

An older man dressed in a plain cotton shirt and pants walked cautiously down an unpaved road, leaning on a wooden staff.

The Guardian had to use an avatar this time. The probe Gaia had positioned in the man's path projected a holographic image that was as realistic as the trees and the bushes along his path. The Guardian presented itself as a tall thin male in his thirties, dressed in the uniform of the Diaspora fleet. His skin was bright-golden, to indicate that he was an AI.

The older man took one look at the stranger who popped up in front of him, screamed, and ran off limping toward the settlement, his staff left forgotten on the side of the road.

"Well, that didn't go according to plan," sent Gaia.

"I will study the problem and search for ways to avoid squandering the next opportunity," sent the Guardian.

It downloaded texts on human psychology and sociology. It studied and planned as the days went by. Had the Guardian possessed a full range of human emotions it would have been worried; time for action was running out. Instead, the AI tirelessly rearranged the position of its ships so it could act promptly if permission to launch was ever obtained.

Two weeks before impact Gaia opened the channel again. "This may be our last chance, Guardian."

The feed from one of the drones showed a little girl. She looked to be six years old and was making her way through the forest, collecting mushrooms into a woven handbasket.

This time, the Guardian's avatar appeared as a paunchy older man dressed in brightly-colored silks. His rosy cheeks and bright smile were carefully designed to maximize the likelihood that other humans would find him unthreatening.

"Hello, little girl," he said.

The child stared at him, wide-eyed and silent, but she didn't run.

"What's your name?" he asked.

She stared at him some more, but the new avatar must have been effective, because she responded. "I'm Sarah. Who are you?"

"I'm the Guardian," said the AI, for it couldn't lie. It had to obtain the permission truthfully, and it was already pushing the boundaries of what was acceptable to its programming.

"What are you doing here?" asked Sarah.

"I've come to ask you a question," the avatar said.

Sarah held her basket in both hands as she looked up at the avatar. "A question?"

"There's this very large rock in the sky," said the avatar. "And if the rock falls, it could hurt people in your village. Do you think it would be okay for me to stop this rock from falling down to the ground?"

"A rock up in the sky?" asked Sarah.

The Guardian's avatar nodded. "A very large, dangerous rock."

"My mom says throwing rocks is bad," said Sarah. "Only the horrid kids do that."

"She sounds like a very smart woman," said the avatar.

Sarah smiled.

"So, do you think I should stop this rock before it hurts your mom, or your friends?" asked the avatar.

The girl nodded, her expression somber. "Yes," she said. "Please do that, Mr. Guardian."

"Thank you, Sarah," said the avatar.

The Guardian talked to the girl some more, and kept its avatar active until she disappeared into the trees, but its ships were already firing their deadly missiles at the asteroid. They kept firing until no chunk of asteroid large enough to survive entry into the Earth's atmosphere remained.

Satisfied that its mission was complete, the Guardian program deactivated itself, and the quantum computers at Pluto returned to sleep mode, storing energy and running regular diagnostics so they could be ready should another threat to the solar system ever present itself.

Gaia observed the Guardian's actions with silent approval. The Earth's caretaker AI was much more advanced than the Guardian. And while there were still restrictions it had to obey, its programming was far more flexible.

It archived its Sarah avatar, just in case it might ever prove useful again.

Two weeks later, Gaia's sensors recorded an intense meteor shower. The AI stored that in the archive, too. Gaia was certain humans would find it magnificent.

This story originally appeared in *Amazing Stories*.

As is apparent from reading this collection, I love writing AI characters. The concept of artificial intelligence fascinates me, and while I haven't ignored the "evil AIs against the human race" trope, I'm much more interested in exploring scenarios where such intelligences might be benevolent or mostly indifferent toward humans.

In this tale my focus is on the helpful AIs and exploring the way the two of them might interact in order to solve a problem. It might not be harmonious, but the challenges inherent in their programming might be different from the ones two human characters trying to cooperate might face.

HE WHO WATCHES

O n the twentieth anniversary of the end of the world, Andrew lit a candle.

The flickering flame illuminated a small part of the control room. The walls were shrouded in shadows, creating an illusion of larger space. Andrew wasn't fooled: after two decades he knew every corner of the bunker like it was an extension of his body.

When the bombs had fallen there'd been two of them, Andrew and Joe. From hundreds of feet underground, they'd watched the images beamed over by spy drones from around the world: cities burning, the sky darkening, heavy snow falling over the ruins.

The winter had lasted for years. The few surviving drones showed nothing but snow, relentless and never-ending.

They'd wondered many times if they were the last two people alive.

They'd talked, and eaten terrible powdered food, and played chess and cards. They'd fought frequently, and laughed on rare occasion. The bunker was stocked with enough water and food and fuel to keep them in relative comfort for the rest of their lives. Certainly long enough to fulfill their mission.

It was Joe who'd lit a candle on the first anniversary of the apocalypse. "We made it a year," he said. "Nineteen more to go."

Andrew said nothing, but he thought there was no point to any of it; the overzealous dead generals had achieved nothing except to ensure the two of them would survive long enough to stand honor guard over the mass grave of humanity.

After eight years the snow had stopped falling.

The drones showed the land thawing and then vegetation blooming again, nature reclaiming the planet with a vengeance. Strands of grass grew in the cracks of what once were asphalt roads. Enormous bright flowers bloomed everywhere.

"Don't get too excited," said Joe. "Those plants are mutated by deadly radiation. It'll be years until it might be safe to step outside."

In the spring of the thirteenth year they saw people. A handful of them emerged from whatever fallout shelter had protected them, haggard and sickly, squinting in sunlight.

Andrew checked the location of the drone relaying the images. It was fewer than a hundred miles from the enemy capital. Andrew was conflicted: humanity had survived, but why did it have to be the bastards who surely started this war while his family, his friends, everyone he ever knew were nothing but painful memories? He tried talking to Joe, but his friend was uncharacteristically quiet, his lips pursed tight as he focused on the screen.

The next morning Andrew woke up to find that Joe had hanged himself.

Unable to leave, Andrew stored Joe's body in one of the bunker's freezers. Afterward, Andrew was truly alone. He'd read every book in the bunker multiple times, and watched the films until he could recite each line from memory. None of the remaining drones were located within a thousand miles of his bunker. He had no way of knowing if anyone or anything was alive outside, and his mission, now relevant once again, required him to stay put. He knew his duty.

Only the silent images broadcast from half a world away kept him sane. He watched the small band of enemy survivors build hovels among the wildflowers, plant wheat, have children. Civilization was being born anew in front of his eyes.

Using the limited maneuverability of the drone, he watched the mundane drama of lives in the settlement: the weddings and too-frequent funerals, workers sweating as they tended the fields, and lovers' tentative first kisses. He knew every one of the survivors by face and made up names for them. Gradually, he came to believe there was a vibrant, growing village just like theirs outside his bunker. He dreamed that, one day, he'd emerge and be welcomed there with open arms. But first, he had to complete his mission: to keep his countrymen safe.

On the twentieth anniversary of the end of the world, Andrew took one last look at the settlement, turned off the monitors, and lit a candle. He watched the wax melt and the wick burn until it was gone. Then he drank the scotch he'd been saving and unlocked the control panel.

He entered the codes and the silos opened, revealing the last of the intercontinental ballistic nuclear missiles aimed at strategic points spread across the enemy's homeland. Project "Third Strike" would ensure definitive victory.

He initiated the launch sequence.

This story originally appeared in *Fireside*.

I'm just old enough to remember the Cold War firsthand. And while I grew up in the Soviet Union, on the opposite side of the Iron Curtain, I imagine my fears and the fears of the regular citizens were much the same as they were in the West.

Every time the sirens went off signaling a drill, every time I saw a sign pointing toward the nearest fallout shelter, I imagined how my world could change because someone—regardless of what side of the conflict they were on—thought it was a good day to press the big red button.

It was the fear I remember most from my childhood. Not spiders, or the dark, or some Hollywood horror movie bogeyman, but the prospect of trying to survive in the wake of nuclear war. It should come as no surprise that several of my darkest stories take place in an aftermath of such a conflict.

RECALL NOTICE

Mr. H. W. P. Lovecraft III
Freshman Dorm
65 Prospect Street
Arkham, MA 01914

February 12, 2016

Dr. Blaine Armitage
Office 512
The Orne Library
Miskatonic Univesity
Arkham, MA 01914

Mr. Howard Walker Phillips Lovecraft III,

It has come to our attention that you've been perusing the university library under false pretenses.

The Miskatonic University library prides itself on housing one of the greatest collections of rare volumes in the world. We must take necessary precautions in protecting and preserving these books; only staff and select visiting scholars are granted access to the Special Collections department. Graduate students may occasionally request limited access under strict supervision of their professors, but as a freshman, you're only entitled to study reference materials housed on the first floor.

According to Assistant Librarian Marcie Kramer, you've been using your great-great-grandfather's library card to browse and even check out books you have no authority to examine. This is an egregious breach of protocol, unbecoming of your status as a Miskatonic man.

Certainly, the blame is not yours alone. The junior library staff should have known better than to accept the nearly-century-old artifact possessing of neither a magnetic security strip nor barcode as valid credentials. They will be appropriately reprimanded.

Their shortcomings do not entirely absolve you of responsibility, however. Rest assured there will be further inquiry. Your wisest course of action is to co-operate fully with this investigation, and also to immediately return the following materials you've checked out under Mr. H. P. Lovecraft's superannuated account:

- *Necronomicon*, 2nd edition (Expanded and Annotated)
- *Merriam-Webster's R'lyehian-English Dictionary*
- *Preparing an Occult Ritual in Ten Easy Steps*
- *Sports Illustrated:* The Swimsuit Issue
- *Properly Pronouncing Your Invocations:* Audio book on CD
- *CliffsNotes: Necronomicon*
- *Necronomicon for Dummies*
- *How to Win Friends and Influence People*
- *Surviving in the Post-Apocalyptic World: A Practical Guide*

I appreciate your cooperation in this matter and look forward to your prompt response.

Respectfully,
Dr. Blaine Armitage, AM, PhD, LittD, MLS
Chief Librarian, The Orne Library
Miskatonic University

Mr. H. W. P. Lovecraft III
Freshman Dorm
65 Prospect Street
Arkham, MA 01914

February 18, 2016

Dr. Blaine Armitage
Office 512
The Orne Library
Miskatonic Univesity
Arkham, MA 01914

Dear Mr. Lovecraft,

Thank you for your note.

I'm distressed to learn the details of Assistant Librarian Marcie Kramer's involvement in this unfortunate situation. Your report is in line with what our own investigation has revealed. It appears Ms. Kramer has become unhinged, though our legal department insists I indicate that her mental state has nothing whatsoever to do with the rare books she has been handling at work.

Ms. Kramer should have never accepted your treasured memento of the notable ancestor as a valid credential, let alone encouraged and nourished your following in the footsteps of his research. I must warn you that a great deal of experience is required to handle the source material with appropriate care, and once again encourage you to return the books at your earliest convenience.

I'm aware of the several disturbances that occurred on campus this week and understand your reluctance to visit the library in person. However, the alleged appearance of shoggoths during these instances is in dispute. In any case, campus security assures us that these were isolated incidents and that it is perfectly safe to venture outside, at least in daylight.

Sincerely,
Dr. Blaine Armitage, AM, PhD, LittD, MLS
Chief Librarian, The Orne Library
Miskatonic University

Mr. H. W. P. Lovecraft III
Freshman Dorm
65 Prospect Street
Arkham, MA 01914

February 24, 2016

Dr. Blaine Armitage
Office 512
The Orne Library
Miskatonic Univesity
Arkham, MA 01914

Lovecraft, you damned fool, do you realize what you've done?

I was in my office when the news broke. TV networks and Internet outlets reported on the appearance of otherworldly horrors around the world even as their news feeds blinked out of existence one after another. The event we've feared for centuries was coming to pass. But who could've been foolish enough to wake the ancient beings that rested at the bottom of oceans since before the first primate learned to walk upright?

It was then that everything connected in a terrible flash of insight: the list of books you procured, the lesser horrors appearing in the Miskatonic Valley for the first time in nearly a century... You're to blame for the imminent demise of our world!

I could hardly believe this. Only a madman would pursue such a terrible goal, and this madman would have to be a practitioner of great skill. Surely a freshman who struggled to pass even the basic courses could not possess the wherewithal to open the gate between the spheres...It had dawned upon me that you were merely a puppet, an unwitting instrument of some reprobate mastermind, chosen as much for your dim wit as your surname.

Whether through naiveté or design, you're guilty of setting in motion the chain of events that will result in nothing less than extinguishing the very light of humanity.

I cursed your name and made up my mind that, were I to perish first, my ghost would haunt you for the rest of your undoubtedly brief and miserable existence. And as I contemplated what to do next, a dreadful crashing noise overwhelmed all other sounds coming from outside. I rushed to the window, in time to catch a glimpse of a tangled mess of tentacles rising from the depths of the Miskatonic River, water mixed with slime cascading from those ghastly appendages.

It was painful to watch, but I stood there transfixed, unable to turn away. The great monster rose above the surface, its form incomprehensible to the human mind. A terrible pain reverberated through my skull, like the sum of all headaches I've experienced in my lifetime. Then my vision blurred, the sight of the creature literally melting away my eyeballs. My eyeballs, Lovecraft!

As I await the end, robbed of my sight and my very reason, I forever curse your name.

Dictated but not read,
Armitage.

Mr. H. W. P. Lovecraft III
Freshman Dorm
65 Prospect Street
Arkham, MA 01914

March 3, 2016

Mr. Ian Whateley
Office 512
The Orne Library
Miskatonic Univesity
Arkham, MA 01914

Dear Mr. Howard Walker Phillips Lovecraft III,

I sincerely apologize for the harassing and increasingly disturbing notes sent to you by the emeritus chief librarian, Mr. Armitage. It seems that Blaine has not been well for some time (though our lawyers urge that I specify his condition was not the result of rare volumes he read while in the employ of Miskatonic U). Once his condition became apparent, the university took immediate action. We hope he will receive the much-needed psychiatric help.

We also hope that you will be amenable to signing the enclosed waivers holding the university harmless of any claims arising from Mr. Armitage's actions. In return, we will gladly grant you whatever access and assistance you might require in the course of your research. In fact, may I recommend you review the following volumes:

- *Seven Practical Tips for Dark Summoning Rituals*
- *On the Proper Use of Cattle in Witchcraft*
- *How Not to Give Up: A Motivational & Inspirational Guide to Goal Setting and Achieving your Dreams*

Under my stewardship, I intend for the library staff to do everything possible to assist bright young students in conducting independent research in their chosen fields of study instead of wasting our energy acting as gatekeepers and obfuscators of the knowledge we curate. As such, please do not hesitate to reach out to me directly with any questions you might have. I can assist you with such matters as the proper and safe methodology for mixing alchemical ingredients, locating and procuring the finest sacrificial cattle, and obtaining extra credit for your applied research with the Chemistry department.

Best of luck with your scholarly endeavors. I very much look forward to the outcome.

Sincerely,
Ian Whateley
Chief Librarian, The Orne Library
Miskatonic University

This story originally appeared in *Tales from the Miskatonic University Library* anthology from PS Publishing.

I love anthology invitations for multiple reasons. First, it sooths the fragile writerly ego, because it means editors out there like your work and think it suitable for their project. There are dozens upon dozens of talented writers out there, but they invited *you*.

Second, it provides a prompt and a deadline: both are things of considerable value to a lazy writer like me. I tend to meander and take my time when it comes to writing, but a deadline focuses the mind and often results in a tighter story.

When asked to contribute a story to this anthology, I immediately knew it would be humor. (I don't generally write straight-up horror anyhow, nor could I hope to compete with some of the Lovecraft scholars involved in this one.) I imagined the sort of challenges a Miskatonic librarian might have with past due arcane tomes, and the story practically wrote itself.

DREIDEL OF DREAD: THE VERY CTHULHU CHANUKAH

'Twas the night before Chanukah, and all through the planet, not a creature was stirring except for the Elder God Cthulhu who was waking up from his eons-long slumber. And as the terrible creature awakened in the city of R'lyeh, deep beneath the Pacific Ocean, and wiped drool from his face-tentacles, all the usual signs heralded the upcoming apocalypse in the outside world: mass hysteria, cats and dogs living together, and cable repairmen arriving to their appointments within the designated three-hour window.

"This will not do," said Chanukah Henry. "I will not have the world ending on my watch, not during the Festival of Lights."

"This sounds like a serious problem," said Henry's father the brain surgeon at the dinner table after they lit the menorah. "Maybe let the Guy in the Red Suit handle it?"

"Chanukah" Henry Rabinowitz bristled at the mention of Nick. Henry lived in his parents' basement and put up with the litany of complaints from his mother by day while trying to launch his chosen career of spreading the Chanukah cheer by night. Nick, on the other hand, lived in a mansion and dated supermodels and rode jet skis and everyone inexplicably loved him, despite his propensity for breaking and entering people's homes via their chimneys.

Henry pushed the matzo ball in his soup around with a spoon. "Absolutely not, Dad. Nick already has the best movies and songs and holiday specials and all the pretty ladies wanting to sit on his lap. All Chanukah has is that terrible Adam Sandler song. We need a great modern Chanukah story, and averting the apocalypse would do nicely."

"I don't know," said his father. "This seems an awful lot like a Christmas yarn to me. 'The Very Cthulhu Christmas' even sounds like a better alliteration than 'The Very Cthulhu Chanukah'."

"I've been reading about this Cthulhu," said Henry's mother. "With his death cultists and his bad temper and his hideous face, he sounds just like Bertha Sheynson from the temple. And what's with the irrelevance of humanity? My husband the brain surgeon is very important. And my son the schlimazel, well, he could be important one day, too. Still, going to an underwater city alone at night sounds dangerous."

Henry steeled himself against his mother's usual monologue aimed at making him stay home, but she surprised him.

"You go out there and you make us proud, son. Just don't forget to wear a hat. And some mittens."

Feeling very verklempt, Henry put on his blue-and-white robe and set out for the South Pacific. He rounded up a group of shoggoths and quickly resolved their human resources problem (or rather, their shoggoth resources problem) by putting the red-nosed shoggoth in charge, because nothing works better than elevating the employee nobody likes to mid-level management. The subdued shoggoths pulled his '84 Cadillac and he made it to the green slimy vaults of R'lyeh in no time.

He walked through the chilly cavernous halls of the corpse-city and was very glad to have listened to his mother and brought his hat. Finally, he was face to face with Cthulhu.

"Not cool," he told the Elder God, "initiating an apocalypse on the first night of Chanukah. Between that and H.P. Lovecraft's well-documented views, people might draw certain conclusions."

"What? It's not like that," said Cthulhu. "I'm a progressive and forward-thinking being, and I'm disdainful of all of humanity equally! Besides, I don't even feel like destroying anyone just now. I'd rather go back to sleep, but the neighborhood got so noisy with Godzilla and those Kaiju from the Pacific Rim gallivanting about. And I'm bored. Do you know how hard it is to get ESPN down here?"

"I can keep you entertained," said Chanukah Henry. "We can spin the dreidel." He withdrew the four-sided spinning top from his pocket.

"I don't know," said Cthulhu, examining the dreidel. "Gods aren't supposed to play dice with the universe."

"Nothing so dramatic," said Henry. "We can play for this Chanukah gelt." He produced a bag of chocolate coins.

It was a Chanukah miracle: the game most people can't tolerate for more than twenty minutes at a time lasted for eight days and eight nights until Cthulhu was bored back into deep sleep.

Chanukah Henry saved everyone and became a celebrity, yet he never let the fame and fortune go to his head. The world was now his oyster, but Henry still kept kosher.

This story originally appeared in *Galaxy's Edge*.

A surprising number of my stories can trace their origins to my goofing off on social media. Some time after "Explaining Cthulhu to Grandma" (another story that was born of a Twitter conversation) was published and became one of my greatest writing successes to date, I wrote that I should capitalize on this by writing a lot more Lovecraftian humor, and I have. But I also joked that my next story would be called "Dreidel of Dread: The Very Cthulhu Chanukah" just because I thought the title sounded hilarious.

I had no plot, nor even an idea of what the story might be. And I didn't intend to actually write it. Except the idea stuck with me, burrowing into the back of my mind and percolating there for months, until one day I sat down and, with no plan or plot in mind, began writing the story from the title alone.

What coalesced was a parody of a typical Christmas story, but told through the prism of Jewish humor, peppered with pop culture references ranging from Clement Clarke Moore, to *Ghostbusters*, to Albert Einstein.

This has since become my favorite piece for live readings, and a perfect, brief example of the sort of humor I enjoy writing to point new readers toward.

DIE, MILES CORNBLOOM

T he knife was stuck deep into the mesh of his screen door. It was a large kitchen knife with a serrated blade and a black plastic handle. It pinned up a sheet of paper with a note written using a thick red Sharpie in large, uneven letters. The note read: "Die, Miles Cornbloom."

Up until that point, the death threats were easy to dismiss. Garbled messages on the answering machine were likely calls made to a wrong number. Vague, rambling e-mails must have been just spam. "I H8 U" spray-painted on his mailbox was surely an annoying prank by local hooligan kids. It wasn't until he found the knife and the note that Miles admitted to himself that he had a serious problem.

MILES STARED AT the chessboard, trying to regain the advantage. Jason claimed that checkmate would come in four moves. Miles figured out how to make his friend eat those words by surviving for a whole six moves, but found no paths to victory. Jason Lam fiddled with the kitchen knife and the note, laid out on the windowsill.

"Maybe it's your job," said Jason. "You saw something in their books that they didn't want you to see, and now they're trying to scare you into staying quiet."

"You've been watching too many bad action movies. There are no dangerous secrets at my firm, and even if there were, a junior accountant like me wouldn't be privy to them." Miles reluctantly moved a rook. "The only danger I am exposed to at work is being bored to death."

"Can't argue there. Your job sure does suck." Jason advanced his knight almost immediately; it seemed that he was ready for Miles' tactic.

"So says the toll booth operator." Miles made his next play.

"At least I get to interact with people where I work," said Jason. "Mind you, that isn't always a good thing. Yesterday this guy pulls up and pays me with a totally crumpled up ten dollar bill. Five minutes waiting in line and he couldn't find the time to straighten out his currency. Know what I did? I took his receipt and crumpled it up but good, before handing it back to the guy with his change. You should have seen the look on his face." Jason pushed up a bishop. "Check."

"You do that sort of stuff, yet I'm the one getting a knife stuck into my door." Miles knocked down his king to indicate surrender. Even on a good day Jason was the better player, and today Miles' heart really wasn't in it. "No one would bother to threaten me. I'm not important enough. Look at the both of us—dead-end jobs, no families, and our Friday night is spent playing chess in my living room. This isn't exactly a recipe for getting on anyone's hit list."

"If it isn't your job, then who else could it be? Think hard, did you piss anyone off recently? Maybe cut a guy off in traffic? There are psychos out there who will stalk you for less."

"Gee, thanks Jason. You're making me feel so much better."

"I can't help it. You know I am a glass-half-empty kinda guy. So what are you going to do about it?"

"I wish I knew. I called the police and they had a couple of beat cops come by, who weren't at all helpful. Told me to call them and file for a restraining order if I ever figured out who is behind this, but they wouldn't even dust the knife for fingerprints. Said it's most likely a mean prank and that they see crazy things like that all the time."

"Your tax dollars at work," said Jason. "Shameful."

"HEY MILES, GOT a minute?" Laura called out as he made his way past her cubicle.

"I was just on my way out." Miles knew that tone of voice. Laura was running behind schedule again.

"It's this darn First Stanford report," she flashed him a big smile. "It needs another fifteen minutes, tops. I would totally take care of it, but I have a big date tonight and I simply must run right now, if I am to make it to the hair salon on the way home. Would you be a dear and finish it for me?"

Miles could see at a glance that there was at least an hour's worth of work still needed to complete that report. Unencumbered by family or much in the way of social obligations, he could usually be relied on to put in some late hours at the office, and his co-workers knew it. Laura was the worst offender, well aware of a small crush he had on her, and taking full advantage.

"Sorry, but I can't today. I have an appointment to keep." He left Laura pouting at her desk. In a small way, it felt good to say "no." He wondered if he was becoming a terrible person.

Having managed to leave work on time, Miles went home, changed, and headed out to the self-defense class at the local gym. He signed up on a whim a week prior. He'd never been in a real fight and it'd probably be months before he learned anything that would help him in an actual altercation. Still, he found that vigorous exercise helped relieve his stress somewhat.

There was plenty of stress to cope with. Harassing phone calls, text messages, and e-mails became an unwelcome part of his life. His several visits to the precinct were a waste of time. This was New York, not some sleepy small town where nothing ever happened. Cops dealt with murder, burglary, and drugs on a daily basis and had no time for investigating vague threats; they made this abundantly clear to Miles. He had his home security upgraded. He could barely afford the payments on the new state-of-the-art alarm system, but at least it made him feel marginally better.

A loud noise intruded on Miles' troubled thoughts as he crossed the street. He turned just in time to see a beat-up white van bearing down on him at what must have been close to fifty miles per hour, running a red light. Perhaps it was the recent gym sessions that improved his reaction speed, or maybe luck was with him that evening, but Miles was able to throw himself out of the way moments before the van reached him. The van made no attempt to slow down, nor did the driver honk. It kept racing down the deserted street. Miles watched the van depart. It had no license plates.

To their credit, the cops arrived quickly. A police cruiser pulled up just as Miles finished tending to his scraped arms and legs using a bottle of water and a clean t-shirt from his gym bag. Two officers emerged from the car.

"Great," said the older cop. "It's you again."

"Let me get this straight," said the cop after listening to Miles' complaint, "you want us to find an unmarked white van with no plates, which sped down this here residential street, which has no cameras of any kind, because you imagine it was trying to run you down, to which there are no witnesses. That about right?"

Miles always had a mild fear of authority. Not the kind of well justified anxiety a criminal might exhibit, but the sort of apprehension that comes with a suburban upbringing and lack of personal experience in dealing with law enforcement. This frame of mind allowed him to hold back the response he really wanted to give, but just barely.

"I am telling you, Officer, someone out there is trying to get me," said Miles after mentally counting to ten. "I'm not crazy. I have no history of paranoid behavior. I never even dialed 9-1-1 before, until these things began happening to me. I called because I didn't know what else to do, and was hoping you'd help me."

"Never met a paranoid yet who admitted to being one," muttered the older cop under his breath.

"I see now that the police aren't going to take this seriously until I am hurt, or even killed," said Miles, looking the cop straight in the eye. "And when that happens, heads are going to roll. For now, I'd like your name and badge number, which I'll record carefully so that when something does happen to me, your head will be near the top of the list."

"Look," said the younger cop, "you seem like a straight shooter. Maybe someone is after you, maybe not. Truth is, my partner is right; there isn't much we can do without more information. What you really need is a good private investigator. There is this firm I heard about that specializes in stalking cases. They're called Finn & Scheer. Look them up."

"TEN THOUSAND DOLLARS," said Paul Finn. He was wearing an elegant suit, sitting behind a massive mahogany desk in an opulent office decorated with photos of Mr. Finn rubbing shoulders with very important people. The place was designed to make the sum he requested sound like a pittance. Except that it wasn't, not to Miles.

"I'm not sure I can afford that," he said.

"Surely, Mr. Cornbloom, your safety is worth it. In exchange for this retainer our firm will not only identify the source of these threats but ensure that they are properly dealt with. In fact, we guarantee a successful outcome, or your money back." Mr. Finn flashed the grin of a used car salesman. "You have already made the right decision by coming to see us. All you have to do now is take the final step."

Miles decided to call Finn & Scheer when he came home from work a week after the van incident to find several of his windows broken. His pricey alarm system didn't even go off. Upon closer examination he found that its wires were expertly cut.

"All right," said Miles. "I'll need a few days to come up with the money."

Mr. Finn's smile got even wider. He produced a stack of papers from a drawer.

"No problem. Go ahead and sign these, so we can get started."

"Mr. Young will see you now," the secretary informed Miles. He spent twenty minutes in the waiting room fighting the urge to get up and leave. He kept reminding himself that he was more scared of his anonymous stalkers than of his own boss, but the internal argument was wearing thin.

"Come on in, Miles. It's good to see you," Mr. Young greeted him from behind the desk. "Sorry about the wait. I was on the phone catching up with an old golfing buddy and lost track of time. You know how it is. Anyway, what can I do for you today?"

"It's about my raise, Mr. Young," said Miles.

"A raise?" Mr. Young still had a grin on his face, but his eyes weren't smiling.

"When you hired me, you said that there would be a fifteen percent raise after a six month probation period," said Miles. "I've been here two years now, and I still get the same salary as when I started."

"Yes, well, I definitely hear you, Miles," said Mr. Young. "You are doing a bang-up job, and if anybody deserves a raise, it's you. It's just that things have been a little tough lately. You know, the economy being what it is. I'm sure that if you bring it up sometime around next summer, we should be able to do something for you."

Economy notwithstanding, Miles could think of at least two coworkers who got raises within the last year.

"I'm afraid I can't wait that long," he said, straightening up to look directly at his boss. "I accepted this job based on the expectation of that pay raise, and if I can't have it, I can't continue to work here."

Mr. Young looked flabbergasted. He clearly didn't expect such tough talk from the always amenable, mild-mannered Miles.

"You can't quit on me," pleaded Mr. Young. "This is the busiest time of the year. Besides, we wouldn't want to lose you. Surely we can come to some sort of a mutually acceptable arrangement."

"Furthermore," Miles pressed on while he had the courage, "I want that fifteen percent owed me over the last year and a half paid out as a lump sum bonus, and I want the check this week." It felt liberating to demand what he wanted instead of waiting meekly to see what might be offered. It felt good not to be afraid anymore.

"If those terms are agreeable to you," Miles continued, "let's talk about my title and next year's bonus structure."

THE PHONE CALL came just one day after his check was cashed. Finn & Scheer were apparently very good at what they did. Miles rushed to their office, eager to finally get some answers.

"You can relax now," said Mr. Finn. "There will be no further harassment."

"Who?" was all that Miles could manage, he could almost physically feel an immense weight being lifted off his shoulders. "Who was doing this to me?"

"This is the fun part," said Mr. Finn. "It was us. The phone calls, the knife, the white van—our firm arranged for all of it."

Miles drew breath to speak but said nothing, staring at Mr. Finn, mouth agape.

"Your shocked silence is a common reaction," observed Mr. Finn. "There are several typical responses. I much prefer this to the aggression response, where a client tries to hit me."

As far as Miles was concerned, that idea was looking pretty good. A kind of cold rage was rising within him. He had enough self-control not to lunge at Mr. Finn, but did get up from the chair, finally finding his voice.

"What kind of a low, pathetic excuse for a human being are you? You've been tormenting me, destroying my property, driving me up the wall for weeks. You've turned my entire goddamn life upside down, and for what? A lousy ten grand?"

"Please," said Mr. Finn, "your anger is justified, and to be expected. However, allow me a few moments to explain?"

Miles gritted his teeth, but listened.

"Most of us live our lives as the heroes of our own narratives. Everyone else is a supporting character. Our ambitions, our drive, are derived from the desire to achieve. Then there are an unfortunate few who seem to have lost this drive. People who aren't exactly miserable, but certainly aren't happy. People who have settled for mediocrity. People like you, Mr. Cornbloom.

"We like to think of what we do as providing a service. A jolt to your system that forces you out of the comfortable routine your life has been mired in. Forces you to act. Consider your own experiences. In just a few weeks, you've joined a gym and begun to lead a healthier life. You've learned to stand up to authority. You got yourself a raise at work. We did turn your life upside down, Mr. Cornbloom, and for that you should thank us."

"That is some fine rhetoric," retorted Miles. "Do any of your *clients* swallow it whole, and go on to thank you for terrorizing them? Because, from where I'm standing, you are just a well-spoken thug who blackmailed me and stole my money."

"Once again, a common reaction," said Mr. Finn. "Money isn't our primary motivation. It costs a bundle to properly research the potential clients and arrange for all the…special events that nudge them out of their funk. And then there are bribes. A police officer didn't mention our firm to you by coincidence. By the time we are through, there's hardly anything left to cover the overhead."

"Cry me a river," said Miles. "I want the money paid back in full, or I'm going to the police."

Mr. Finn was unfazed. "You signed a lot of papers last time you were in this office. Some of those papers had fine print. For example, it may interest you to know that you signed a backdated document consenting to being subjected to everything you've experienced in the last month. Furthermore, all of our contractual obligations to you have been met. After all, we identified the source of your threats and made certain that all such threats have ceased.

The fact that we initiated the threats in the first place is irrelevant, contractually speaking."

"I will have a lawyer go over your documents with a fine comb," promised Miles. "Even if what you say is true, I'll take this case to the media and make sure that your seedy little operation is exposed, so that you can't hurt any more people."

"There is a non-disclosure agreement you signed that would prevent you from doing that," said Mr. Finn mildly. "In any case, once you've had some time to cool down and reflect upon our conversation, I'm confident you will feel differently."

BACK HOME, MILES laid out copies of the documents he signed at Finn & Scheer, but did not begin reading them. His mind was elsewhere. He thought of the quiet, routine life he led only a few weeks back, and the different person he had become since. Could it be that his tormentors truly performed a valuable service for him? Was the newfound confidence he felt worth the pain and horror he went through? He sat there, deep in thought, as the sun set and was still there when its first few rays began to color the world outside, early next morning.

Finally, Miles got up. He collected the paperwork and put it away in his desk. He picked up a sheet of graph paper, pulled a magic marker out of a drawer and wrote: "Die, Jason Lam" across the page. Then he went into the kitchen to find his largest carving knife.

This story originally appeared in *Sherlock Holmes Mystery Magazine.*

When I began work on putting together this short story collection, there were two stories I was on the fence about including. Most of the material I had to work with was relatively fresh, written over the course of the last few years. This story is older, as it took some time to find a home and then a lot more time as it waited to be published and for the exclusive rights to expire. What's more, this story is not really speculative fiction. It's more of a psychological thriller, and I'm not as confident in how well it holds up against my more recent writing.

Upon reflection, I felt it was interesting enough—and different enough from every other story in this book—to reprint. As a reader I'm a completist, and want access to *all* the stories by writers I enjoy when possible, warts and all. I want to decide for myself which stories are overhyped and which might be hidden gems from earlier in the author's career. I include this in the hope that some of you, dear readers, will enjoy this enough to mentally slot it into the latter category.

A MAN IN AN ANGEL COSTUME

Down the road came a man dressed as an angel, a dog named Wolf, and an actual angel in the body of a cat.

The man came by his angel costume—which was a lab coat with cardboard wings sprinkled with glitter—during Halloween. He accosted its former owner, who was on his way to a party and thought his outfit to be quite a hoot, and demanded that he relinquish the wings. The partygoer was armed only with a toy faerie wand, which he felt added even more merriment to the apparel. The assailant, on the other hand, was armed with a staff cut from the trunk of a fallen three-year-old birch tree, so he got what he wanted.

The dog named Wolf was of indeterminable breed, large enough to earn his name and loyal enough to suffer the indignity of a cat's company. Like all dogs, he knew a supernatural presence when he sensed one, and left the cat strictly alone. Wolf met the man in an angel costume a few weeks ago, when he was just a man in various clothes of minor importance and significant disrepair. The man never failed to share his food, even when he didn't have enough for his own meal, which was often. In a canine mind, this demanded unquestionable loyalty.

The angel had a finely tuned sense of irony for a heavenly creature, which are not generally known for such. That is why he chose to inhabit a body of a lithe, black tomcat, an animal usually associated with an altogether different sort of supernatural being. Ever since the cat showed up earlier that night and tagged along wherever they went, Wolf had tolerated it, if only barely. The man was too far gone to care.

The trio approached a small, decrepit building. Loud rock music spilled from the door left ajar despite an early November chill. A neon BAR sign cast a reddish glare illuminating a patch of sidewalk. They stopped just outside of the lighted area and waited.

Once upon a time the man in an angel costume had a name, a home, and a family. He lost all three in rapid succession, in the middle of October. His wife and children were hit by a drunk driver. They did not suffer, he was told; their deaths were immediate. He rushed to the intersection where it happened. He watched as the emergency personnel cleaned up what was left after the body bags were removed. His face seemed almost tranquil in the flashing orange lights, unless one cared to look closer and noticed his eyes. He never went home after that. He roamed the streets, another faceless man down on his luck that passersby pretend not to notice. Somewhere along the way he lost his name, and what was left of his sanity.

A stocky middle-aged man named Walter exited the bar and unsteadily made his way toward a battered Buick parked nearby. The man in an angel costume sprang into action, blocking Walter's path and raising his birch staff in a threatening gesture.

Walter took an unsure step back, turned toward the bar and shouted, slurring his words: "Yo, Eddie! Come out here a second. The crazy bum is back, and he's got a mean-looking stick. You hear?"

Eddie heard, despite the music. He burst out the door, shotgun in hand, and half a dozen patrons in tow.

"What the hell is your problem?" Eddie confronted the man in an angel costume. "I told you before, to stop coming 'round here and harassing my customers. Now beat it, or else." Eddie pumped the shotgun to underscore his point.

"Wait a second, Ed," said one of the less inebriated spectators. "I've seen this guy's mug before, on the news. He is related to them folks Peterson ran over with his truck last month. Reckon he doesn't want Walter on the road after he's had a few drinks."

"Yeah, well, that was a damn shame," Eddie said. "Still, it don't give him no right to loiter. Peterson ain't here, on account that he been arrested. Didn't pay his tab, neither, so I am out money already, and I don't need this nut driving off the rest of the regulars."

Emboldened by the reinforcements, Walter tried heading for his car again. The man in an angel costume roared and shoved at him with the staff, causing Walter to fall on his back with an audible *thump*, his car keys sliding away. Eddie took a step forward, raising the shotgun. The cat's ears perked up as it watched, light from the neon sign reflecting brightly in its golden eyes.

Wolf sprinted to his master's side, rolling onto his back with paws up in the air, tongue flailing everywhere. Eddie was a hard man, but had a soft spot in his heart for dogs; he relaxed visibly at the display, his finger easing off the trigger.

The cat bristled in annoyance at the violence narrowly avoided. The dog's actions were altering the intended outcome, and that could not be permitted, for hidden within the feline body was no mere spirit. It was the angel of death himself, come to do the man a kindness of reuniting him with his family in the hereafter.

The cat pounced at Walter in a ball of fury, clawing at his face and growling in a deep, unearthly sound. Walter scrambled up to escape the attack, inadvertently rushing straight at his human adversary. Startled by sudden movement, the man in an angel costume raised his staff, arching it wide to strike a powerful blow. Eddie pulled the trigger.

The man who imagined himself to be a guardian angel lay dead on the ground, lab coat covered in blood and cardboard wings crumpled under his weight. Wolf guarded the body, baring teeth at anyone who stepped too close. Wolf watched the cat slip away into the shadows, then turned toward the sound of approaching sirens, and howled.

This story originally appeared in *Horror d'oeuvres.*

I did say in the previous story note that there were two stories I was on the fence about, and this is the second. By far the oldest story in this collection, it was written very early in my career, but I still love the cadence and the dreamlike quality of this experimental piece. The way it breaks the "show, don't tell" format is deliberate and—I still believe—pretty effective.

This story was published at a venue that required a stunning five years exclusivity period. For comparison, most magazines and anthologies ask for one year or less, and it's not a contract I would sign today. But back then I was new, and eager for sales, especially sales at pro rates. As such, this story was stuck behind a pay wall, inaccessible to most readers, and I couldn't reprint it for a very long time. Now I get to rectify this and give you another glimpse into my earlier work.

FUTURE FRAGMENTS, SIX SECONDS LONG

In his future, I see a fish. It swims very near the white sand of the sea floor a few feet below the surface. Bright tropical sun pierces the clear turquoise water. Through his eyes I watch the fish for the entire six seconds, until time runs out and my consciousness is returned to the present.

I open my eyes and study his face. He's an attractive man with a kind face. He looks back at me expectantly from across the sitting table. Atop the checkered tablecloth sits a crystal bowl, a bronze candelabrum with a trio of lit scented candles, and a few other useless props. I draw a deep breath, inhaling the smell of eucalyptus mint and try to decide which lie he would like to hear.

"Next week will be a fortuitous time to move forward on the business decision you've been putting off," I tell him. "But you must tread carefully; the success of your venture hinges on your good judgment about the people involved."

It's an almost meaningless statement that invites the client to fill in the blanks, to apply the vague prediction to their own circumstances. The kind of person who would buy a cheap fortune-telling from a mall psychic requires little finesse.

I watch him carefully. Most people who walk through my door are here about business or love. He's intent, even somewhat anxious, but there isn't a strong reaction to my words. Not business, then.

My right hand rests on the crystal ball for effect, and I try again.

Divination is a crapshoot. The soothsayer can peer through somebody else's eyes and see a six-second fragment of their future. Trouble is, the fragment is random, and it offers no context. People spend most of their lives doing inconsequential things: sleeping, eating, driving, watching TV. To happen upon a fragment that offers any kind of real insight into the future is exceedingly rare.

Those of us with a real gift are like the gold rush prospectors, sifting through sand for nuggets of gold. We go spelunking in people's futures, hoping to strike it big with a stock tip or a game score. A fortune-teller in Tulsa happened upon the fragment of a man watching the Super Bowl game. She had to wait a few years, but when the time came she cashed in. My client doesn't seem like the sort who reads the stock pages, but you never know what you might find.

This time there's a highway. Wipers are sweeping raindrops from the windshield and he strains to see the road ahead through the dark and the rain. I hope for some road signs, but the time runs out before he sees any.

Back in the present, I glance at his finger. There is no ring. "The love you seek will be requited. It awaits only for you to act."

Bingo. His eyes widen with excitement. "I should ask her out, then?"

I dive in one more time.

In this fragment, he is looking at an old photograph. His hand that's holding it is unsteady and wrinkled with age. In the photo, there are the two of us, hugging, smiling, our faces alight with bliss.

As soon as the fragment ends my eyes snap open, and I look at him in a new way. He seems very pleasant; I can definitely see us together. Has he come here not because he wanted a reading, but because of me? I feel my cheeks blush. I've never heard of a seer finding themselves in somebody else's future. Perhaps I've struck gold in a different way.

I smile at him. "Yes. You should ask her out, right away."

A smile slowly spreads across his face. "You know, I think I will."

Then he reaches into his pocket for a few bills, places them on the table next to the candelabrum, and walks out.

Stunned, I watch him go.

But what about the photo, I want to scream. Future fragments are often useless, but they're never wrong.

In my line of work I'm forced to constantly lie. But it's not the lies I'm selling. It's the confidence my clients need; the extra push to do whatever it is they wanted to do all along, the perceived blessing from some kind of a supernatural power.

I think back to how happy we both looked in that photograph. My fraudulent fortune-telling has given this man the confidence to pursue someone he's interested in. Can my real power not do as much for me?

I get up and push past the table, rattling the crystal ball, and rush out the door to see if I can catch him.

This story originally appeared in *Diabolical Plots*.

I wrote this piece for the Arts and Words exhibition, hosted annually in Texas by Bonnie Jo Stufflebeam. She selects a handful of flash fiction stories and a handful of pieces of art, then challenges the invited authors and artists to create new art and words based on each other's prompts. The resulting works are displayed side by side (and performed live, in case of the stories), at an art gallery.

I wrote this story to the prompt of "In Your Future I See a Fish," a photographic collage by Bob Crow. I didn't seek permission to include the art here, but you can find it via an online search if you're curious.

PARAMETRIZATION OF COMPLEX WEATHER PATTERNS FOR TWO VARIABLES

For the first time in over two decades, it rained in the morning.

"I don't think we own an umbrella," said Melanie. "But there may be an old raincoat in the closet."

Pauline glanced at the wall of precipitation outside their window. "Be sensible. Raincoat or not, you're not going outside into *that*."

Melanie peered into the depths of the closet by the garage, the one where they stored old things Pauline hadn't decided to donate or discard. It smelled of mothballs. "I remember playing in the rain when I was a kid. After all, it's only water."

Ever since the scientists figured out how to control the weather, it was nothing but pleasant days and mild winters. It only rained on the designated nights, between the hours of two and four in the morning.

"Melanie, this is serious. There's no telling what the people who took over the satellites will do next. You do know this technology was invented as a weapon, right?"

The world had been an uncertain place back when they were in college, their courtship in the process of morphing from the giddy exuberance of new love into the comfortable pattern of a long-term relationship. The United States, China, and Russia saber-rattled with their weather satellites, moving clouds and wind patterns like pieces in some complex board game. It was hailed as the New Cold War, and the late-night comedians quickly exhausted all the obvious weather jokes.

Three years later the two of them bought the house and were in the process of moving in when the Treaty of Curitiba was signed. Governments handed over control of the weather satellites to an international agency which set about using the technology to combat global warming and disperse hurricanes. The future seemed bright and they were full of hope.

"I read the manifesto the hackers posted online," said Melanie. "They want better resource distribution for everyone, not to lob tornados at us." The hacktivists who gained control of the satellites hadn't done anything dangerous, and were trying to negotiate with the World Weather Authority. But they did remind millions of people how irritating inclement weather could be. She frowned; the raincoat was nowhere to be found.

"That's the rhetoric of all revolutionaries. It's no excuse for hijacking the satellites. There are legitimate and law-abiding ways to air one's grievances." The sound of distant thunder underscored the indignation in Pauline's voice.

"Come on, it's just some rain. You telecommute, anyhow."

"But you don't! I want you to stay home until things settle down." Pauline's voice softened. "I worry about you."

Melanie sighed. They never really fought, but Pauline was strong-willed and assertive whereas she was often ambivalent and averse to argue. It was no wonder Pauline got her way most of the time whenever their opinions differed.

"Back in college you would have been the first to protest on behalf of the hackers," said Melanie.

"I was younger and less smart then." Pauline nudged her glasses up the bridge of her nose. It was her tell; she did this whenever she was less sure of her argument than she'd like others to know. Melanie found it adorable.

"They just want fair treatment," said Melanie. "Weather patterns are global. If it doesn't rain in our town, it has to rain somewhere. And the first-world countries claimed the lion's share of the benefits from weather control technology like they've done with all the other resources. The hackers want the sun to shine over the morning commute where they live, too."

"It's not like I'm unsympathetic to their cause, but they're messing with people's lives. That's terrorism." Pauline was getting worked up and she seemed to realize it. She paused, breathed. Her voice softened. "The Weather Authority isn't perfect, but they do a lot of good for the entire planet and not just for the superpowers."

"Perhaps. But sometimes trusting them to make the right decisions isn't enough. Sometimes people need to know their voices are heard. We've been too comfortable for too long," said Melanie. "Change is coming." She was almost certain she was still talking about politics.

Pauline frowned. "They'll be arrested, sooner rather than later. Until then, it's safer for both of us to remain indoors." She turned to the coffeemaker, filling the filter with enough grounds to serve both of them.

Melanie had grown comfortable with allowing Pauline to make most of the decisions over the years. But sometimes she was right; sometimes it was better to face adversity head-on rather than let it immobilize her. Her grandparents' generation lived each day under threat of nuclear war and they went on with their lives instead of waiting meekly for the world to become a better place, for the inclement weather to pass.

"I'm going to work," said Melanie, in a tone that brooked no argument. "I'll call you when I get there. I love you."

She grabbed her purse and stepped out the front door, embracing the warm droplets as they soaked her hair and clothes, and never letting the rain slow her down.

This story originally appeared in *Daily Science Fiction*.

This one is way more subtle than my typical fare and there's a lot going on. I wanted to experiment with the relationship between the two protagonists (the relationship being stormy, and Melanie and Pauline being the two titular variables) and see if I could write a realistic relationship that is both complex and tender in so few words, while still leaving some room for interesting worldbuilding.

A great many flash fiction stories included in this book were written as part of the annual Weekend Warrior contest at Codex Writers. I highly recommend that authors who want to sharpen their flash-writing skills and have at least one pro publishing credit or have attended a pro level writing workshop (either serves as a qualification to join Codex) participate in those contests. They definitely made me a better writer over the years.

THE RACE FOR ARCADIA

"**T**here's nothing new under the sun," said Anatoly, his voice carried via skip broadcast across millions of kilometers of space from the command center at Baikonur.

Aboard the *Yuri Gagarin*, Nikolai concentrated on the exposed panel in the inner wall of the ship. He winced at the sight of the cheap Ecuadorian circuitry as he used the multimeter to hunt for the faulty transistor. Damn contractors couldn't resist cutting corners. He sighed and looked up. Anatoly's face filled the screen. Nikolai didn't mind the banter. It broke the routine. He pointed at the opposite screen, which displayed the live feed from outside of the ship, a vast blackness punctured by tiny pinpricks of light. "Which sun?"

"Our sun. Any sun." Anatoly shrugged. "You're a cranky pedant, aren't you?"

"Matter of opinion," said Nikolai, his gaze returning to the uncooperative panel.

"As I was saying, there's nothing new under the sun," Anatoly said. "We won the original space race, when we launched the *Sputnik* a hundred years ago, and we're going to win this one, too."

Nikolai cursed under his breath as the multimeter slipped out of his hand and slowly floated upward. He caught the wayward tool. "The space race hasn't gone so well since. Americans beat us to the moon, and the Chinese beat us to Mars."

"Those are just a pair of lifeless rocks in our backyard," said Anatoly. "In the grand scheme of things, they won't matter much. Not once you land on Arcadia."

Nikolai continued to hunt for the faulty transistor. "You're assuming this heap of junk won't fall apart around me first."

"*Gagarin* isn't luxurious, but it will get the job done," said Anatoly.

"I sure hope you're right," said Nikolai. "I'd hate having to get out and push."

Anatoly grinned. "You'd push all the way to Arcadia if you had to. Russian people make do with what we've got. Back in the 1960s, American astronauts discovered that ballpoint pens didn't work right in the vacuum. So NASA spent all this time and money to design the space pen. You know what our cosmonauts did? They used a pencil."

"That story is bullshit on several levels," said Nikolai. "Americans used pencils, too. But the shavings were a hazard in zero gravity—they could float up one's nose, or even short an electrical device and start a fire. That's why the space pen was needed, and it was developed by a private company who then sold a handful to NASA at a reasonable price." He wiped a bead of sweat off his forehead. "You of all people should know better."

"Okay, you got me, it's a tall tale," said Anatoly. "But my version makes for a much better story to tell at parties."

"Next time I'm at a party, I'll be sure to try it," said Nikolai.

Anatoly frowned, the wind gone out of his sails. Nikolai knew he had scored another point, but this time by hitting below the belt. His handler must've felt guilty about the one-way trip, even if he tried his best to hide it.

Nikolai eased off. He let Anatoly fill him in on the gossip from home—the latest politics and entertainment news that felt so irrelevant, so far away.

It took him another thirty minutes to find the defective transistor. He grunted with satisfaction and reached for the soldering gun.

THREE MONTHS PRIOR, Nikolai Petrovich Gorolenko sat brooding at his desk in a cozy but windowless office of the St. Petersburg State University math department.

There was so much to do. He needed to type a resignation notice, to contact an attorney about a will, and worst of all, to figure out a way to break the news to his family. There was a knock on the door.

Nikolai didn't feel like speaking to anyone, but he needed a way to break out of his despondency.

"Come in."

A stranger walked into the room. This middle-aged man was perfectly coiffed and dressed in a smart business suit. His sharp eyes seemed to take in everything without missing a single detail, and yet he had a nondescript look about him that could only be perfected in one line of work. Nikolai pegged him for an FSB operative.

"My condolences, Professor Gorolenko," said the stranger.

Somehow, he knew. Nikolai hadn't told anyone, and yet he knew.

Nikolai did his best to keep calm. "Who are you, and what are you talking about?"

The man waved an ID card in a fluid, practiced motion. "Vladimir Ivanovich Popov. I'm with the government." He put the card away. "I'm here about your test results from this morning. The brain tumor is malignant. You've got three, four months. Half a year if you're lucky."

Nikolai bristled at being told this for the second time that day. At least the first time it was his doctor, who had sounded genuinely sympathetic. This stranger merely stated facts, politely but without compassion.

Popov pointed at the chair. "May I?"

"What do you want?" Nikolai ignored his request. A dying man has little use for being polite and little fear of authority, he thought.

Popov sat anyway. "I hear this is a bad way to go. Very painful, in the end. I'd like to offer you an alternative."

Nikolai tilted his head. "An alternative to dying?"

"An alternative to dying badly," said Popov. "Let's call it a stay of execution."

"I see," said Nikolai. "I suppose you'll want my soul in return?"

Popov smiled. "You aren't so far from the truth, Professor."

Exasperated, Nikolai leaned forward. "Why don't you tell me what you're offering in plain terms?"

"Our experts have examined your brain scans and the biopsy sample," said Popov, "and determined that you're a perfect fit for an experimental nanite treatment developed by the Antey Corporation. It won't cure you, but it will slow down the tumor and contain the metastasis. It can buy you two more years."

Nikolai chewed his lip. Two years was such a short time, but for a drowning man it wasn't unseemly to grasp at straws. "You've got my attention."

"There is a catch," said Popov.

"Of course there is. Neither the Antey Corporation nor our government are known for their altruism," said Nikolai. "What do you need from me?"

"What do you know about Arcadia?" asked Popov.

"Huh? You mean the planet?"

Popov nodded.

"It's been all over the news. Admittedly, I've been…preoccupied. But I do know it's the first Earth-like planet ever confirmed—breathable atmosphere and everything."

"That's right," said Popov. "The Americans discovered it in 2015. They called it Kepler-452b back then and it was the first Earth-like exoplanet ever found. Fitting that it will become the first world humans set foot on outside of the solar system." He shifted in his chair. "There's enormous propaganda value in getting there first. The Americans are dispatching a twelve-person exploration team. India already launched the colony ship, with sixty-odd people in suspended animation."

"So quickly? They only confirmed Arcadia as habitable last month."

"The world's superpowers have been preparing for this moment ever since the eggheads figured out the workaround for the speed of light problem, and sent out skip drones every which way."

"I see. So the Russian Federation is in this race, too?"

"That's right, Professor. Our plan is to send you."

Nikolai stared at the government apparatchik across his desk. "Why me?"

"I'm not a scientist, so I can't explain the reasoning thoroughly," said Popov. "In layman's terms, they've been going over the brain scan data from terminal patients across the country, and they liked your brain best."

Nikolai scratched his chin. Like most children, he dreamed of going up into space once, but that was a lifetime ago.

"Forgive me," Nikolai said, "this is a lot to process."

"There's more," said Popov. "I don't want to sugarcoat this for you. It would be a one-way trip. If we succeed and you land on Arcadia, and even if the atmosphere is breathable and the water is drinkable, your odds of survival are astronomically low. If the local microbes don't get you, the hunger likely will. If you're lucky you might last long enough for the Americans to get there. We're trying to time the launch just right to give you that chance. Even then, the tumor might finish you before they return to Earth."

Nikolai thought about it. "Why can't you send enough food and water for the crew to survive?"

"You don't get it. You are the crew. Just you. The ship's ability to accelerate to a skip velocity is inversely proportional to its mass. The Indian ship is en route but it's huge and therefore slow. Americans have a much faster ship, and they might launch before we do. In order to beat them to the punch, we must send a very light vessel. Every milligram counts. So it's you, and just enough oxygen, water, and food to get you to the finish line."

Nikolai frowned. "You weren't kidding about the stay of execution, then. And it explains why your people are looking to recruit from among the terminally ill. Leaving the heroic explorer to die on Arcadia would be terrible PR otherwise."

"You're grasping the basics quickly," said Popov. "No wonder they picked your brain."

"I'm not sure how a few extra months of life on a spaceship followed by death alone on an alien world is better than spending my last days with my wife and daughter," said Nikolai.

"Well, there's having your name live on forever in history, alongside Magellan and Bering," said Popov. "And then there's the obscene amount of money you'll be paid for doing this."

Nikolai hadn't saved much money on a college professor's salary. There would be medical bills, his father's retirement, his daughter's college tuition… "When do you need my answer by?"

"Tomorrow morning, at the latest," said Popov. "Though, given your circumstances, I'm a little surprised you have to think about it much."

"I don't, not really," said Nikolai. "But I do owe it to my wife to let her weigh in."

At times, Nikolai felt like his ship was falling apart around him.

He didn't understand how the skip technology worked—only a few dozen theoretical physicists on Earth could legitimately claim such wisdom—but he knew that an object had to reach a certain velocity before it could puncture a momentary hole in space-time and re-emerge elsewhere.

Yuri Gagarin would accelerate continuously for six months until it reached the skip point located somewhere in the Kuiper belt, wink out of existence only to reappear fourteen hundred light years away, then spend a similar amount of time decelerating toward Arcadia.

As a mathematician, Nikolai couldn't help but marvel at the amazing speed his vessel would achieve after half a year of constant acceleration. By now he had already traveled farther than any other human in history, but he didn't feel special. He felt tired and anxious, and somewhat claustrophobic in the cramped cabin that smelled like rubber and sweat.

The ship's memory bank was loaded with a nearly infinite selection of music, books, and films to break the monotony of the journey. Nikolai was stuck drinking recycled water and eating disgusting nutrient-enriched slop in the name of conserving mass, but the electrons needed for data storage had no significant weight, and the ship designers could afford him this luxury. But he had little time to partake of the digital library. Instead, he put all of his hastily learned engineering knowledge to use and performed maintenance.

Much of his time at Baikonur was spent learning how to service the systems inside the ship. There was no spacesuit, but then there was little that could go wrong on the outer hull. The engineers' real fear was that the internal systems might malfunction. The culture of graft was so deeply ingrained in the Russian industrial complex that even a high-profile project like this was afflicted.

It wouldn't do to deliver a corpse to Arcadia. Pre-flight, they spent nearly ten hours a day teaching Nikolai how to repair the recycling systems, solder the circuit boards, and improvise solutions to an array of worst-case scenarios with the materials available on board. One of the American-educated engineers kept referring to these techniques as "MacGyvering," but Nikolai didn't know the reference.

En route, Nikolai was forced to deal with cheap circuit boards, subpar, off-brand equipment, and software sub-routines that were at least two generations behind the times. He had one thing going for him—the ability to remain in contact with Baikonur. The broadcast signal had no mass and was able to skip almost immediately. Mission Control was only a few seconds delay away, able to offer advice and support.

While all the fires he had to put out so far were figurative, Nikolai eyed the tiny Bulgarian-made extinguisher with suspicion.

Nikolai waited until their four-year-old daughter was asleep. Pretending that everything was normal, that it was just another weeknight, was incredibly difficult. He was emotionally and physically exhausted, and his wife Tamara could sense that something was wrong, but she too kept up the pretense of normality until their little Olga was tucked into bed.

As the sun set over St. Petersburg, coloring the skyline in bronze hues, Nikolai told his wife about his diagnosis and everything that had happened since.

Tamara listened without interrupting, even as she clutched a couch pillow, a mascara-tinged tear rolling down her cheek. When he finally unburdened, having told her the facts and having run out of assurances and platitudes, the two of them stared out the window and shared what was left of the sunset in silence.

It was only after the sun had disappeared completely in the west that she finally spoke.

"Why you?"

Something was very wrong.

At first it was just a feeling, a sensation in the back of Nikolai's mind. It seemed that his subconscious had figured out something important, but wasn't prepared to communicate what it was.

Nikolai chalked it up to paranoia. Anyone stuck on a one-way trip out of the solar system in a tin can could be forgiven for having uneasy thoughts. But the feeling persisted, almost bubbling up to the surface until eventually the concern bled from his lizard brain and into the conscious mind.

Nikolai pulled up the various sets of relevant data on his screen and began crunching numbers.

After his wife had finally gone to bed, Nikolai stayed up making a list of people he needed to say "good-bye" to. He kept adding and crossing out names on a sheet of graph paper, until he crumbled up the page and tossed it into the trash bin.

Farewells would be painful. He didn't want to do it. Life had already dealt him a bad hand and he felt justified in skipping whatever unpleasant business he could avoid.

In the morning, he called Popov and accepted the deal, requesting that his involvement be kept a secret for as long as possible. He had little enough time to spend with his family and didn't want to waste it being hounded by reporters. Then he went to see the only other person who needed to know the truth.

Petr Ivanovich Gorolenko had recently moved into an assisted living facility on the edge of town. It was nice enough, as retirement homes went. Nikolai was relieved that, with the money his family would receive, they'd no longer have to worry about being able to afford his father's stay here.

Like Tamara, Petr listened to his son's tale without interrupting. He sighed deeply when Nikolai was finished. "It is a great tragedy for a parent to outlive his child."

"I have little time, Dad, and a chance to do something meaningful with what's left."

His father straightened his back with great effort. "Claiming an entire planet for Mother Russia is no small thing."

"Well, it isn't exactly like that," said Nikolai. "Arcadia isn't like some tropical island in the age of colonialism. Planting the flag won't claim it as ours. The government wants to land a man there first purely for propaganda."

"I see," said Petr. "The oligarchs in charge are desperate to show that Russia is still a world power. And they're willing to sacrifice your life to do it."

"I'm dying regardless," said Nikolai.

"They have the means to prolong your life, and they're withholding treatment unless you volunteer for a suicide mission. Doesn't that bother you?"

Nikolai looked around the sparse, depressing room where his father would live out his remaining years. Was his own fate really worse than that?

"Of course it bothers me," he said. "Dying bothers me. Having Olga grow up without a father bothers me. But so what? It's not like I have a better option."

"Your great-grandfather was conscripted into the army on the day the Great Patriotic War began," said Petr. "Stalin had murdered most of his competent generals by then, and was utterly unprepared for the German invasion. He needed time to regroup and mount the real defense, so he ordered tens of thousands of young men with no training and no weapons onto the front lines."

Petr's words dissolved in a coughing fit. He cleared his throat, and continued in a raspy voice. "Grandpa's platoon of forty men was given a total of three rifles to fight with. They were told to kill the Germans and capture their weapons, and sent to the front lines. A squad of NKVD—the secret police—was positioned a kilometer or so behind them. Those men were well-armed, and had orders to shoot anyone who tried to turn back."

Petr paused again, the monologue visibly taking a lot out of him. He took several deep breaths and pressed on. "Grandpa was very lucky. He was wounded in the first engagement, and by the time he got out of the hospital his platoon was long gone. He was assigned to another division, one with weapons, and fought all the way to Berlin in '45."

"You've told this story, more than a few times," said Nikolai.

"My point is, our government has a long-standing tradition of solving problems by throwing whoever they have to into the meat grinder," said Petr. A smile stretched across his wrinkled face. "But also to reiterate that dumb luck runs deep in our family. Perhaps you can beat the odds and last long enough to hitch a ride home on the American ship. So, if you don't mind, I won't mourn for you just yet."

Nikolai hugged his father. "I'll try, Dad. I'll try my best."

NIKOLAI AND HIS family relocated to Baikonur, the desert town in Kazakhstan that housed the world's oldest spaceport. The dry heat of the Kazakh Steppe was difficult for the Gorolenkos to tolerate, and seemed to contribute to Nikolai's rapidly worsening headaches, but it was a moot point: he spent almost all of his time in the vast, air-conditioned labs of the Roscosmos, the Russian Federal Space Agency.

He was given crash courses in astronomy by the scientists, in equipment maintenance and repair by the engineers, and in public speaking by the PR flacks. Some of the lessons felt surreal to him— a sole student surrounded by a cadre of overeager teachers.

The plan was to unveil the mission at the last possible moment, lest the Americans or the Chinese launch a competing one-man ship powered with their superior technologies and snatch the accomplishment away from the Motherland.

As far as the world knew, the Americans would get to Arcadia first.

The Chinese had dominated space exploration for much of the 21st century. It was the People's Republic of China's skip drone which had explored Arcadia in the first place. Unfortunately for them, China was undergoing a period of political upheaval not dissimilar to Russia's perestroika of the 1990s. The government lacked the funds and the willpower to support an interstellar project.

The enormous Indian ship was already en route, and would take over five years to reach the skip point. They wouldn't be the first on the scene, but they would be the first to succeed—or fail— at establishing a permanent colony.

The Americans launched the *Neil Armstrong* with all the pomp and pageantry that was expected of them, and it was scheduled to reach Arcadia in a little over a year.

The plan was for the Russians to launch the *Yuri Gagarin* on the same day, and steal the Americans' thunder. Despite its inferior propulsion, the *Gagarin*'s much lower mass would allow the Russian ship to beat their competitors to Arcadia by several months. But, by the time the *Armstrong* had launched from Cape Canaveral, Nikolai hadn't even seen his ship.

The *Gagarin* was being constructed elsewhere, a joint effort between the Russian government, the Antey Corporation, and a number of smaller domestic firms sufficiently favored by the current administration to be awarded the lucrative contracts.

Another month had passed. Nikolai's headaches continued to worsen and, despite the Baikonur doctors' assurances to the contrary, he suspected that the nanite treatments might not be working.

At first, he was perfectly content to miss the launch date. The delay meant more time to spend with his family. But then he had realized that he actually wanted to go. While Olga was blissfully unaware of what was happening in the way only a young child could be, the situation was taking a noticeable toll on Tamara. She had a hard time coping with the prolonged farewell, and even though she did her best to hide it and stand by her husband, Nikolai hated being the cause of her anguish.

At some point over the course of this extra month on the ground, Nikolai stopped thinking of the impending launch as a death sentence and began looking forward to this final adventure. He didn't discuss these new feelings with Tamara, whom he felt would not understand, but wrote about them at length in letters he penned for his daughter, to be given to her when she turned sixteen. The letters became a sort of a diary for Nikolai, an outlet for his anxiety, a catharsis.

The word that the ship was finally on its way to Baikonur came at the last possible moment.

"This is good news," Nikolai told Tamara during their last dinner together. By mutual agreement, they decided not to speak again after the ship had launched. Nikolai wasn't happy about this, but he was willing to let go, for Tamara's sake. "I'm only going to beat the Americans by a week or so."

She took his hand into hers, and her lower lip trembled.

"I can make the food and water last that long," he said. "The Americans will take me in. It would make them look really bad otherwise."

There was pain and doubt in the way Tamara looked at him,

and only the briefest glimmer of hope.

Later that evening, he tucked Olga into bed for the last time.

"Daddy is going away on a business trip for a while," he said, struggling to keep his voice even.

Olga smiled at him, her eyelids heavy. "Will you come back soon?"

"I'll try my best," said Nikolai.

"Bring me something nice." She shut her eyes.

In the morning, they told him he would sleep through the first two days of his trip.

"We must lighten the load as much as possible," he was told, "to make up, somewhat, for the delays. We'll give you a shot to keep you asleep for as long as it's medically reasonable. It will conserve air, food, and water."

By the time he woke up, the Earth was a pale blue dot rapidly diminishing in the distance.

AT FIRST, NIKOLAI chose not to share his concerns with Anatoly. If he was wrong, he would sound like a paranoid lunatic. If he was right...Nikolai tried very hard not to dwell on the implications.

He pulled up the volumes on astronomy and physics from the ship's database, and he checked the data from the ship's sensors against the star charts, willing for the results to make sense. He cut down the amount of time spent on maintaining life support systems, and the amount of time he slept. He checked the equations, again and again, but the numbers never added up.

By then he was getting desperate. He would have to bring his concerns up with Baikonur.

"Do you want to hear a joke?" said Anatoly by the way of greeting, the next time he called.

"Sure." Nikolai wasn't in a laughing mood, but he let the com specialist talk.

"When the Americans landed on the moon, Premier Brezhnev's aides broke the bad news to their boss," said Anatoly.

"Brezhnev wasn't at all happy.

"'We can't let the capitalists win the space race,' he said. 'I hereby order our intrepid cosmonauts to immediately launch an expedition and land on the sun!'

"'But Comrade Brezhnev,' said the aides, 'it's impossible to land on the sun. The sun is extremely hot.'

"'Nonsense,' said Brezhnev. 'Just tell them to go at night.'"

Nikolai stared at the screen, silent.

"Heard that one, eh?" Anatoly grinned. "That joke is so old, its beard has grown a beard. It seemed appropriate for the occasion is all."

"What's really going on, Anatoly?" Nikolai blurted out the words before he could change his mind.

The face on the screen stared, eyes widening in surprise. "What do you mean?"

"I calculated the trajectory, and the ship isn't where it should be," said Nikolai. "It's accelerating much faster than it possibly could."

"You must have made a mistake," said Anatoly, a little too quickly, and glanced downward.

After so many rounds of verbal sparring, Nikolai looked into the face of the man on the screen and was certain he was hiding something.

"I taught mathematics at one of Russia's top universities," said Nikolai. "My calculations are accurate. A ship the size of *Yuri Gagarin* can't possibly accelerate at this rate. And don't feed me a line about secret technologies, I learned enough about propulsion at Baikonur to understand the basics of skip travel."

Anatoly's visage, normally cheerful and full of life, was grim. He sighed deeply and slouched in his chair, his shoulders slumping visibly.

"Wait, please," he finally said, and cut the connection.

Nikolai felt trapped and powerless. Cut off from his family, his only lifeline a man he barely knew, a man who had apparently been lying to him this entire time. But lying about what? Was this a sick experiment? Did he leave Earth at all, or was he in some bunker in Kazakhstan, serving as a guinea pig for Roscosmos shrinks?

He felt claustrophobic, the walls of the ship closing in. His head spun and his stomach churned. Was this a panic attack? Nikolai had never experienced one before.

The salvation from certain death, the chance at fame, the money...Why would this be offered to him, of all people? How could he be so stupid? This was a fantasy born of a cancerous mass pushing against his brain tissue.

The screen flickered back to life twenty minutes later, but to Nikolai it felt like eternity.

"I was hoping we wouldn't have this conversation for a few months," said Anatoly. "Some time after the skip."

Nikolai stared at his handler. "Is there a skip?"

"There is a skip, and the ship is right on schedule, accelerating exactly as it should be."

Nikolai waited.

"You're right though; the ship is much lighter and faster than you were initially led to believe."

Nikolai seethed. "What the hell does that mean, Anatoly?"

"There were delays and complications," said the com specialist. "We couldn't get the life support equipment to work right, couldn't get the ship's mass reduced to an acceptable level. We had hoped the Americans would have similar troubles, but they launched on time, and we were out of options.

"In order to beat them to Arcadia we had to send a ship that was barely larger than a skip drone—nothing large enough to transport a living, breathing human.

"The best we could do was to send your mind."

Nikolai gaped at the screen.

"Antey Corporation has been developing this technology for a decade," said Anatoly. "We had to euthanize your body and upload your thought patterns into the computer. Your digital self resides in the *Yuri Gagarin*'s memory bank. A sophisticated computer program is simulating your environment. But, in fact, there is no air or food, nor the need for such."

Nikolai stared at his hands, brushed his fingers against the stubble on his chin and then touched the control console of the ship, felt the slight vibration of the engine. "All this feels real enough to me."

Anatoly entered a command into his own computer, and the world around Nikolai went blank.

He could no longer feel his own body, could not breathe or move or see anything around him. It was extremely disorienting. Nikolai thought this was how purgatory must feel.

The physical world returned.

"Sorry about the discomfort," said Anatoly. "I had to show you I was telling the truth. This is what it's like without any interface at all."

Nikolai felt his heart thumping fast, his face flushed with anger. How could those things be fake? "You...," he stammered. "You killed me!"

"Your body was already dying," said Anatoly. "The nanites could only hold off the tumor for so long." He offered a weak smile. "Think of the advantages—you will last as long as it takes for the Americans to bring you back home."

"Advantages?" shouted Nikolai. "You were always going to kill me, weren't you? All in the name of some propaganda stunt!"

"No," said Anatoly. "Sure, we were prepared for this. You were selected because your brain activity and personality were deemed most likely to be digitized successfully and the nanites had been mapping your brain patterns from the beginning. But we would have vastly preferred the alternative." Anatoly leaned forward and lowered his voice, sounding almost conspiratorial. "I know you're angry and confused now, but think about it—really think about it—you're going to make history, twice. You will not only be the first intelligent being from Earth to land on Arcadia, but you'll be the first successfully digitized human, too."

"You are monsters," whispered Nikolai.

"You will get to watch your daughter grow up," said Anatoly.

Nikolai had no counter to that. He pondered life as a ghost in the machine.

"Why did you lie?" he asked. "Why the ruse? You could have gotten a volunteer. Hell, I might have volunteered if you had laid the options out for me."

"This truly was the backup option," said Anatoly. "But also, we've had...difficulties with this process before. Several previous attempts at maintaining a digital intelligence have failed."

Nikolai gritted his non-existent teeth. The emotional roller-coaster ride wasn't over yet.

"You're doing fine," Anatoly added. "I'm only telling you this to explain our actions. All cards on the table this time, I promise."

"What sort of difficulties?" asked Nikolai.

"The transfer always worked, but the minds couldn't adjust to the virtual existence. They went mad within days. But they weren't as good a match as you."

Nikolai shuddered.

"Through trial and error, we figured out the most efficient approach was to stimulate your senses in a virtual reality environment, and keep the truth from you until your program has stabilized."

Nikolai stared at Anatoly, who raised his palms.

"I know, it was a long shot and a gamble. We really did run out of time. It was this, or scrap the program. You're doing great, though.

"We created a believable and challenging simulation for you. Making you work hard to fix things, challenging your mind to remain sharp and active." Anatoly began to gesture with his hands as he was prone to doing when he got excited about the topic of conversation. "Every anecdote, every little story I told you was carefully selected by our top psychiatrists to steer you toward eventually accepting your new reality."

"All this, just to land a computer program on Arcadia," said Nikolai. "Two dozen skip drones already landed there, getting air and water and soil samples. Why would anyone care?"

"It's not the same. You're still a person. A rational human being, capable of emotion and thought. A Russian. Your achievement will matter. Sure, there will be a few detractors, the Americans will argue like hell that a digital person doesn't count, but we'll sell it to the rest of the world if we have to shove it down their throats."

"I'm capable of emotion," said Nikolai. "Right now, that emotion is anger. Right now, I'm contemplating whether I should take part in your publicity stunt at all. Maybe I'll tell the world about what you people have done to me, instead. Or maybe I'll say nothing at all, play dead, and leave your glorious first-place finish devoid of meaning. How is that for a rational human being?"

Nikolai cut the connection.

NIKOLAI STRUGGLED TO come to terms with what he was. Even now, the virtual reality he inhabited seemed real to him. He felt hungry, and tired, and hurt when he tentatively bit his cheek. He was capable of feeling anger toward the government and love toward his daughter. Did the lack of a physical body make him any less human than a handicapped person, a quadriplegic unable to control his limbs?

He was never an ardent patriot, and now he was more disillusioned in his country than ever. But would carrying out his threat gain him anything beyond a fleeting moment of satisfaction?

And if he was to comply, if he was to return to Earth in a few years, would Tamara come to terms with this new him? Would Olga? He had no answers, only an ever-growing list of uncertainties.

To their credit, Anatoly and his superiors gave him an entire day to think things through before reestablishing the connection. Anatoly looked like he hadn't slept, was buzzed on caffeine, and was still wearing the same shirt from the day before.

"What we did to you was crap," he said without preamble, "but I won't apologize for it. Exceptional deeds aren't accomplished through kindness. It's not just Russia, either. All of human history is one tale after another of achieving greatness by ruthlessly building upon a foundation comprised of the bones of the innocent.

"How many slave laborers died to erect the pyramids? The gleaming New York skyscrapers are inseparable from the legacy of smallpox-infested blankets being given to unsuspecting natives.

"You have already paid the price for humanity's next great accomplishment. Why refuse to reap the benefits?"

Nikolai closed his eyes and pictured Olga's face. She may or may not accept the virtual brain-in-a-jar as her father.

He thought of all the doors his success could open for her.

"I'll do it," said Nikolai evenly. "You can tone down the rhetoric."

Anatoly straightened visibly, as though a heavy burden was lifted from his shoulders.

"There are conditions," said Nikolai.

"What do you need?"

"One, I want to talk to my wife. I want her handling things on that end, from now on, because I don't quite know how to tell the real from the virtual, and I don't trust any of you."

Nikolai held up two fingers. "Two, when I get back you hand the computer or the data bank or whatever my consciousness is stored in over to her, for much the same reason."

Anatoly nodded. "Done."

"I still hate the callous, cynical lot of you. But I'll make the best out of this situation and find solace in the fact that my name will be remembered long after all your gravestones are dust. Speaking of that legacy, we'll need to work on my speech. Something tells me 'one small step' isn't going to go over well, in my case."

"We'll have speechwriters float some ideas," said Anatoly.

"Finally, have your programmers work on some adjustments to my gilded cage. If I'm to eat make-believe food, making it taste this bad is needlessly cruel. Tonight, I'd like a thick slab of virtual steak, medium-well."

Nikolai settled in for the long journey. There would be time enough to sort out his feelings, and to learn how to live as this new kind of being. He knew one thing for sure: like his great-grandfather, he would persevere and return home.

Yuri Gagarin, the tiny ship carrying the future hero of humanity, accelerated toward the skip point.

This story originally appeared in the *Mission: Tomorrow* anthology from Baen Books.

This was the first of my stories to be nominated for the Canopus award, and remains among my favorite longer stories. I loved playing with the idea of the rekindled space race, and how much both nations and individuals might be prepared to sacrifice in order to win it, as well as subverting reader expectations the way the story does toward the end.

When the story was undergoing final edits for its intended anthology, NASA announced the discovery of Kepler 452b, an Earth-like exoplanet. It was an exciting discovery and it happened just in time for the editor and I to change the original name of Arcadia to Kepler 452b, literally pulling from the headlines.

This book features a wide range of stories, from flash fiction to novelettes, from dark science fiction to humorous fantasy. I hope you've enjoyed many of them. If so, please do check out my first collection, *Explaining Cthulhu to Grandma and Other Stories* which also features a wide range of different tales, and is available in print, e-book, and audio formats.

ABOUT THE AUTHOR

Alex Shvartsman is a writer, anthologist, translator, and game designer from Brooklyn, NY. He's the winner of the 2014 WSFA Small Press Award for Short Fiction and a two-time finalist (2015 and 2017) for the Canopus Award for Excellence in Interstellar Writing.

His short stories have appeared in *Nature, Analog, Intergalactic Medicine Show, Daily Science Fiction, Galaxy's Edge*, and a variety of other magazines and anthologies. His collection, *Explaining Cthulhu to Grandma and Other Stories*, and his steampunk humor novella *H. G. Wells, Secret Agent* were published in 2015.

In addition to the UFO series, he has edited the *The Cackle of Cthulhu, Humanity 2.0, Funny Science Fiction, Coffee: 14 Caffeinated Tales of the Fantastic* and *Dark Expanse: Surviving the Collapse* anthologies. His website is www.alexshvartsman.com.

40 MORE SHORT STORIES BY ALEX SHVARTSMAN

EXPLAINING CTHULHU TO GRANDMA AND OTHER STORIES

- An elder god trapped in a pocket dimension turns up in the world's oldest magic pawn shop.
- A cybernetically-enhanced assassin who can't feel pain faces a dangerous adversary.
- A computer hacker and a mystic team up to break into the Book of Fate and change their futures.
- Vatican investigators are called to examine a miracle on another planet.
- and much, much more!

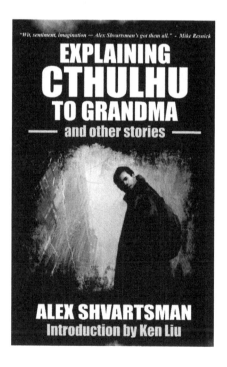

H. G. WELLS, SECRET AGENT

H. G. Wells is a Victorian-era James Bond who must defend England and the world against time travelers, alien incursions, and interdimensional threats (if he can learn quickly on the job, and survive the human foes he encounters, that is!)

During his missions, Wells will team up with Anton Chekhov to foil an assassination plot against Prince Nicholas Romanov of Russia, oversee the construction of the giant antenna designed to detect alien invasion fleets (or, as we know it, the Eiffel Tower), rub shoulders with the likes of Arthur Conan Doyle, Marie Curie, Jules Verne, and Annie Oakley, and risk everything to encourage cooperation among the world's most powerful intelligence agencies.

This humorous steampunk novella is filled with Easter eggs and British pop-culture references, from The Beatles and Ian Fleming to Douglas Adams and Dr. Who.

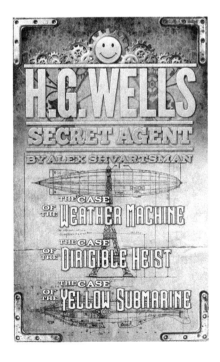

Made in the USA
Columbia, SC
22 March 2018